A Sticky End

by

Joanna Sheen & Julia Wherrell

Victoria Farm Press Ltd.

This edition published 2013 by Victoria Farm Press Ltd,
Stokeinteignhead, Devon TQ12 4QH
www.victoriafarmpress.co.uk
ISBN 978-0-9926844-0-2

Printed and bound in Great Britain by:
Maslands Printers Ltd of Tiverton, Devon.
Set in Minion Pro.

For my girls Pippa and Emily
Joanna

For mum and dad
Julia

Acknowledgements

Joanna and Julia would like to thank their 'other halves' Richard and Neil for their support, patience and cups of coffee. Thanks also to Rod, Pippa, Judy and Jo for their input and suggestions and Andy Jackson for his help and advice.

Special thanks to Sue Viccars our editor.

Chapter 1

Victoria slammed the car door and swore under her breath. She walked round and stared at the flat tyre, frustrated by her inability to change it: so much for being a twenty-first-century female! Ah well, she'd just have to ring someone and wait in the car. Digging in her handbag, she fished out her mobile and found the number for the breakdown service. She pressed the buttons… nothing. She peered at the screen: 'No service'. How could this be? She looked around, scanning treetops and the cloud-filled sky, half expecting to see some kind of obvious obstruction. There was none. It was simply called 'being in deepest, darkest Devon'.

Taking a deep breath of soft country air, Victoria felt the weight of her four-hour car journey lift slightly. She was only some 200 miles from London and yet already she felt she had crossed a border into a new land, a new adventure, a new life. But really! No mobile signal? She frowned and checked the screen again. Nothing.

She sighed and looked along the beautiful Devon lane. Tomorrow was the first day of May and the high banks were studded with primroses, bluebells and masses of other wildflowers she couldn't name. The hedgerow was alive with twittering birds and – despite her current predicament – for the first time in ages she felt a small flutter of happiness as she stood surrounded by such energy, life and beauty. The lane was barely wider than her car but she had steered into one of the few passing places to try and avoid completely blocking it. Unfortunately, she had managed to park the front wheel neatly between two large boulders in the bank and the offending tyre was close to inaccessible.

But which way to walk? She thought her aunt's cottage wasn't far, but how far was 'not far'? She really didn't relish the idea of walking miles and miles and abandoning her car. Looking up again, she was not surprised to see it was threatening to rain. Typical.

She opened the car door and reached inside. Did she need to trail her suitcase, take her handbag, or was it safe to leave things in the car? She heard a loud engine noise, and cursed that someone would be hassling her to move out of the way, but then it stopped. She turned and stretched over to the parcel shelf and felt her back twinge at the unusual contortion as her bottom wedged between the two front seats.

"There's a fine sight if ever I saw one – but you can't park there my lover – you're blocking the lane!"

Victoria thought her heart would leap out of her chest. She pushed herself back into the driver's seat, catching her hip as she did so, and peered out of the door. A tall, tanned man with thick dark hair, greying at the temples, stood in front of her. It was hard to tell how old he was – maybe in his fifties, but still very attractive in an 'outdoorsy' sort of way.

"You're going to have to move out the way you know, can't stay there!" he said with a grin.

She gathered every shred of dignity she could find and replied, "Excuse me, but I am not parked, I have a flat tyre and there appears to be no mobile network service here, so I was about to set off to find help."

"Ah, now that mobile thing's a bugger, I'd try mine but I left it at home. It's a damn nuisance, always ringing. I'll change the wheel if you've got some tools in your boot?"

"Umm, how embarrassing… I moved all the tools out to make more room for my stuff and seem to have left them behind in London." Victoria knew she must appear a complete idiot.

He gazed at the car for a while longer. Victoria wondered whether he was waiting for her to say something. Then he looked up at her. "You'll be wanting a lift somewhere then…?"

Victoria pondered the safety aspect and the whole 'Don't get into a stranger's car' thing, felt the first few drops of rain and didn't hesitate. "That would be very kind of you – just to the nearest phone box so I can call the AA?"

"Naw, take hours that will. I'll fetch Tufty, genius with cars he is, he'll get you sorted."

"Well I'm very grateful, thank you."

Victoria grabbed her handbag and stepped out of the car. The rain was getting heavier and she tried to look on the bright side: there had at least been an, almost, knight in shining armour on the scene to help her, and this Tufty (she couldn't help but visualise a cross between a hobbit and a red squirrel) was apparently going to solve all her problems.

She turned towards the man and then, to her horror, spotted his vehicle. The rain became heavier and she realised there was no way out of the situation: there, taking up almost the full width of the lane, was a very old tractor. It had clearly seen better days and she wondered if it had just been driven straight out of an agricultural museum. True to its age, it had no cab, just a metal bucket seat – open to the elements, of course.

"Is that…?" she began to say.

"She's called Carol – after the first girlfriend."

Victoria frowned and then shook her head. Fine, in Devon tractors obviously had names. This was getting more surreal by the moment.

3

He ambled off towards the tractor. Reviewing her options, she decided that she was just going to have to make the best of a bad job. She had to get used to living a real country life, so why not start now?

He climbed onto the seat of the tractor with an economy of movement that suggested he had been doing just that his whole life. She looked nervously at him and wondered where his passenger was supposed to sit.

"Get on up then, you'll have to hang on. Just pretend it's some flashy Harley and I'm one of those rockers, won't take us more than ten minutes."

There are times when wearing comfy jeans was the best decision you'd made all day. Today was not such a day and she had decided to wear leggings and a long tunic; this was not going to be a good look. Clambering on, Victoria put her bag strap diagonally across her chest and wondered where to put her arms.

"You're going to want to hold on, she's built for work, not for comfort!"

"Thank you. My name is Victoria West – and yours?" It seemed only right that she knew his name before she clasped her arms around his waist.

"Albert, Albert Moreton."

"Oh that's..." Victoria trailed off as the tractor started up with a roar and leapt forward, her mind suddenly focussed solely on staying alive and clinging on with grim determination. By driving half up the bank – the tractor tipping at an alarming angle – Albert squeezed past her car with what looked like millimetres to spare, and they were off.

She had never really enjoyed fairground rides, and what with the potholes in the road and the tractor's enormous tyres this ride was more extreme than any big dipper or waltzer she had ever endured in her youth. The tractor bounced and bucked along as she clung on, uncomfortably aware of the way everything about her person was jiggling around. There was no sign of another vehicle until they emerged at a junction with a reasonably sized road where they turned left and gathered speed, a queue of cars building up in their wake.

The increased airflow made her tunic flap and Victoria reflected on the fact that her leggings were not as thick as she would have liked; Marks & Spencer's Basic Essential leggings were probably not designed with a view to being worn astride a tractor. As they progressed it seemed as if every car or van hooted or waved, and her embarrassment mounted. She could feel Albert chuckling as he raised his hand in friendly acknowledgement to other drivers and generally seemed to be having a whale of a time.

They pulled into a ramshackle garage with an AA sign outside that must have dated back to the 1940s, and a rusted, disused petrol pump from a similar era. Not so predictably, a smart BMW sat outside with a pair of denim-clad legs sticking out from underneath.

"Hey Tuft," Albert moved gracefully off the tractor and kicked one of the denim legs. Victoria stood, shaking slightly, leaning on the bucket seat.

"Young lady needs service here!" Albert turned and winked at her and Victoria smiled ruefully; at forty-three she had little chance of passing for a young lady! She clambered, very cautiously and somewhat gracelessly, off the tractor.

"Well that'd be more up your street matey, the missus would have me guts for garters!" The denim legs slid out and the rest of Tufty's not very substantial body and shock of red hair appeared. Her original thoughts of hobbits returned and she tried not to smile.

Tufty proffered an extremely oily hand. Victoria hesitated and then just nodded. "Thank you Mr Tufty, this gentleman tells me you might be able to sort out my car. I left it a few miles back with a puncture."

Albert rolled his eyes at Tufty and said, "Might have to be a tow job Tufty. Lady here's parked it neatly between two gurt rocks at the side of the road and had no tools anyway to change the wheel. Better sooner than later as it's up at Hammerdown, not a lot of space there for abandoned cars!"

Victoria opened her mouth to speak but thought better of it and just looked at the two men. They were obviously both enjoying a laugh at her expense but, as she needed help, it seemed smart to stay quiet.

"Right oh, on my way, Eddy's here an' he'll gimme a'hand." Tufty turned and yelled something towards the back of the garage and a small replica Tufty came out and, having been filled in as to his part in the mission, rolled his eyes at Victoria with the manner of a nine-year-old going on fifty!

"It'll take Tufty a while to sort it out – is there somewhere you were going?" Albert said as the red-headed pair walked towards an antique tow truck.

"Well, actually I'm just moving down to Devon," Victoria hesitated. "Speaking of which, are there many Albert Moretons around here? It's just that's the name of my new neighbour and I have to collect the keys from him."

"I should have guessed you were Edith's girl!" Albert grinned. "She was hopeless with cars too, always rescuing her from some scrape or another!" He laughed and shook his head, and a faraway look came into his eyes. "Ah yes, Edy and her cars... ah well."

Victoria thought she saw sadness and perhaps even tenderness in his eyes which, she also noticed, were a very nice blue.

He straightened up. "Funny old way for us to meet up again,

but I'm your man, keys all neatly labelled ready for you. You lift yer leg over again Miss Victoria and we'll get off!" Victoria duly lifted her leg and found her leggings had now split in the worst possible place, and she prayed it was a short journey to her aunt's cottage.

Aunt Edith. Her mind was suddenly filled with images and memories of her childhood visits. She'd always seemed old, even though she must only have been in her forties when Victoria was born. Those school-holiday visits to the country and the nearby coast had always been a mix of excitement and fear, a pretty potent combination for a small girl who loved reading The Famous Five, was a bit of a tomboy, but who got incredibly homesick. She had been twelve the last time she saw Aunt Edith and the farm and she had often conjured up pictures of the cottage, the hens and wildflowers, always wildflowers.

The tractor bounced and Victoria jiggled. Albert Moreton. Did she remember him from her childhood, this well-built, dependable-looking man she was now embracing rather too closely? Yes, she did have a dim memory, a tall, dark-haired young man, dashing and, if she was honest, a little bit exciting! He must have easily been ten years older than her which had seemed very old at the time, him being all of twenty-two or thereabouts!

Turning down a rough track, Victoria yelped as they hit a particularly massive pothole and Albert laughed. "Hang on – we're nearly there!" – and shortly after he swung left into a farmyard. Two barking and yelping collies raced towards the tractor.

"That's enough Nell, Nancy," Albert bellowed. Victoria raised an eyebrow and he grinned. "Yup, previous girlfriends" – and disappeared into the barn.

Victoria managed to get off the tractor, thinking how a helping hand would have been nice, straightened her clothes and pushed back her hair. Thankfully the rain had stopped. She looked around the farmyard and tried to get her bearings but couldn't see her aunt's pretty thatched cottage anywhere.

"You coming then or just staying stood there?" Albert looked at her for a moment and then retreated into the barn.

Victoria followed, wondering where he was leading her. The barn was huge, with a gaping entrance that had lost its doors along the way. Once inside in the gloom she noticed a matching doorway at the far end. Albert was striding on ahead so she followed, the dogs prancing around them both. As they emerged at the far end of the barn, she realised that her aunt's house was barely 100 yards away from the farm building. Far from being the chocolate-box cottage that she remembered, it looked rather forlorn, not rundown exactly, but somewhat unloved. The rambling pink rose around the front door was gone; only ivy clung to the wall now and there were no chintz curtains behind sparkling window panes.

"Oh! I didn't remember it like this at all." She stood and stared, unable to believe her happy summer holiday recollections had been so wrong. "We used to drive down a narrow little track and park in front of the cottage."

She turned a full 360 degrees, looking puzzled. "Oh, I see," she said, eventually spotting an overgrown thicket at the side of the barn, into which the faint tracks of an old drive could be seen disappearing. "It's all overgrown. There was a pretty garden full of lupins and hollyhocks, a rose round the door," she pointed at the cottage, "and I don't remember the barn at all!"

Rubbing his chin, Albert said, "That depends how long ago you last came here, barn's been here some 25 years maybe."

"So why did Aunt Edith want a great big barn next to her house?"

"Well, I don't rightly know. Convenience I suppose. Meant our vehicles were right on hand, stored her horse hay here," he waved at a corner of the barn now standing empty. "She could get to feed the chickens in the yard easier and, as she got on a bit, it was all just, you know... near."

Victoria was acutely aware that no, she didn't know, and hadn't seen her aunt in too many years, and certainly not since her health had started to fail. Despite their regular exchange of letters, she'd never questioned the accuracy of her aunt's upbeat accounts of her life and well-being. She had been a proud woman who didn't like to admit weakness – and especially not her own failing health.

"But how on earth did you get planning permission?"

"Ah, countryside doesn't need planners, this isn't London you know," Albert smiled. "We were both happy, so built it was. Sheep could all come in if the snow was bad, just a quick step for us to borrow her Rayburn to warm the orphaned lambs. At one point she had thirty-odd chickens she kept in the yard but it all got too much for her. We were friends for many a year."

There was a silence. Albert walked back into the barn and returned with a bunch of keys. Victoria had barely moved. She thought she ought to say something; she wanted to ask lots of things but could say nothing, feeling a lump in her throat.

"So you been over with your parents in America all this time then?" Albert said, looking at her intently.

"Oh not entirely," Victoria hoped he wouldn't want a blow-by-blow account of her life. "My parents and I moved out to Boston, as you know, about thirty years ago, but sadly they died ten years later, so I've been on my own since then." Even after all this time Victoria still felt their loss keenly and felt the familiar drag in the pit of her stomach as so often happened when painful memories came to the front of her mind.

"I moved over to London a few years ago but I've been too busy to come down, I needed some medical treatment at the time."

Victoria didn't want to mention her breast cancer to a virtual stranger and just wanted to get all this 'Hello nice to see you again' stuff over with.

Albert smiled gently at her and said, "Don't worry maid, your aunt told me all about the last few years, she was very worried about you. We always shared our troubles over a cup of tea you know. I hadn't realised the treatments were in London though, just assumed you were still over there."

Now Victoria felt irritated that he knew all her medical details. Blast Aunt Edith for discussing it with all and sundry! Then she took a deep breath and realised she was being unkind; Edith had only chatted to a close friend as she probably would have done herself. Come to that, she had mentioned the 'nice young man' who lived next door in her letters. "Oh, I see," she said. There was a long pause.

"So anyways, I expect you'll be wanting to settle yourself in and have a good look round. Be seeing you later I expect," said Albert and, with a cheery wave, disappeared with the dogs close on his heels.

Victoria looked up at the cottage. It was smaller than she remembered, but wasn't that always the way when you came back to a childhood haunt as an adult? The earlier rain dripping gently off the eaves gave it a sad look and its windows, peeking out from beneath the 'eyebrows' of the thatch, looked empty and far away. I'll bring you back to life, she thought.

Unlocking the back door, she stepped inside and found she was holding her breath. She wasn't sure if she was listening for something, or hoping for the smell of freshly baked bread, but there was nothing. She laid her bag on the kitchen table and flopped into a chair, an old-fashioned kitchen chair that she did remember from Aunt Edith's time. Sitting back, she massaged the pressure points on either side of her head.

Well, it had certainly been an adventure so far!

"Please tell me I am doing the right thing," she said talking in the direction of a particularly loud tea towel that suggested 'Your Country Needs You', hanging over the rail on the Rayburn.

Now the rain had passed and the late afternoon sun streamed in through the open back door, she noticed that all the surfaces actually looked quite clean, no layers of dust, no spiders' webs or other nasties – and, surprisingly, the Rayburn was warm. Someone must have been looking after the place and keeping it tidy even after Edith had died, and that was a comforting thought.

As she sat and gathered her wits, she realised there was one familiar sound that did bring the memories flooding back: the slow and rhythmical ticking of Aunt Edith's grandfather clock. Victoria smiled and walked into the hallway. Yes, there it was, standing in the corner, just as she remembered.

"Hello old chap," she said and ran her hand across its face, something she'd never been tall enough to do before. The regular deep tick-tock was like a soothing heartbeat. The hallway was cool and dark, yet somehow cosy. The flagstones beneath her feet were worn smooth by the passage of hundreds of feet over several centuries. It felt like the centre of the cottage, the heart of the place. Victoria breathed deeply and thought, I'll put a chair or a bench out here as it feels like a good space, a space to sit and think.

She walked back into the kitchen, took down a mug that hung from a shelf on the dresser, and poured herself some water.

She'd been so sad to hear Aunt Edith had died, and then guiltily excited when the solicitor had passed on the news that everything – cottage, contents and a little nest egg – had been left to her. It was like a dream come true. Having fought breast cancer for the past three years – and despite the tentative 'all clear' – on bad days she still felt as though an evil mutant cell was waiting to return and deal a final fatal blow.

She deeply regretted that she hadn't come down earlier to see Aunt Edith, but the trips and time spent in hospitals seemed to dominate her life. The disease had consumed her and sadly her job, her home and her friends had all been neglected as she'd fought her private battle. All through her treatment, the weekly letters had been a lifeline, almost like having Edith with her, but her aunt had said she felt too old to travel up to London in person.

No, this would be a new start, a new beginning. Edith had given her this wonderful opportunity and she wasn't going to waste it. She smiled and sat back down in the chair, enjoying the comforting warmth of the Rayburn, and closed her eyes. This was the start of her new, relaxed life, without pressure or stress...

"Coo-ee! Anyone home?"

Victoria's eyes flew open as a shadow fell across the open doorway and a well-groomed woman peered round the door and smiled at her. A good hairdresser had added blonde streaks to a perfectly smooth bob, the clothes shouted designer casual and there were definite signs of the smoothing away of unwanted wrinkles in her face.

"Hello you must be Victoria! Welcome to Swaddlecombe, I do hope you'll be very happy here, I'm an old friend of Edith's – Grace Simmons."

"Oh, yes, hello." Victoria pulled herself to her feet to greet her first guest, feeling somehow guilty, as if she'd been caught slacking by the headmistress, although she wasn't sure why. "I am still a bit disorientated, do come in and oh, thank you so much!"

Grace proffered a magnificent chocolate cake and a tin marked 'Grace S's shortbread'. "Edith and I were friends for many years, my dear. We met first at the WI farmers' market, she took her eggs and

I used to sell our jams and marmalades, oh, simply aeons ago."

Victoria opened her mouth to reply at the same time as a very loud revving accompanied by the squeal of tyres announced the arrival of a car. There followed a far more fearsome noise as another vehicle, even more rackety, juddered squeakily to a halt.

Victoria and Grace both went to the door and saw Victoria's car in the middle of the yard, a dust cloud settling around it, with Tufty at the wheel. Behind was Albert, this time in an old white van, except the driver's door was blue and one of the back doors appeared to be multi-coloured.

"Just taking Tufty back to his garage," said Albert, beaming.

"But wait! How much do I owe you? You have been so kind."

"Go on, made my day rescuing a damsel in distress," Tufty grinned. "I'm not as used to damsels as young Albert here, you want to watch him! Just come in and sort it out next time you're passing, no rush!"

With this warning, and much guffawing, the two men upped and left in the white van, gravel flying as they disappeared from view, Albert's hand waving languidly from the driver's window.

"It seems as though you've met a few of the local characters already Victoria?" said Grace. "Let's put the kettle on and you can try some of my chocolate cake while we get to know each other a little."

Not entirely sure if she enjoyed being manipulated in this way, Victoria smiled. "Happily, although I have absolutely no idea where anything is at the moment, I haven't even brought in my suitcase."

As she talked she opened cupboards and drawers and peered into a cavernous larder. "I had a puncture up near somewhere called Hammerdown, I think, and then Mr Moreton came along in his tractor and – oh!" She stopped as she heard a tap turned on and off and the sound of a kettle being placed on the Rayburn.

Emerging from a cupboard after a fruitless search, she saw that Grace had laid the table, put the kettle on the Rayburn and the teapot stood ready to be filled.

"Why don't you just sit down and rest dear, it sounds like you've had a rather trying time. I know where everything is, Edith and I have spent many, many hours in this kitchen. I know it almost as well as my own!"

"Thank you, right." Victoria returned to her chair and looked at the woman bustling around the kitchen table.

Her memory of Aunt Edith was of a serious-looking woman, tall and angular, either wearing a tweed skirt and sensible shoes (for going out) or corduroy trousers, a holey sweater and wellingtons for all the other times. She found it hard to see her aunt and this Martha Stewart lookalike ever having very much in common.

Underneath a rather severe exterior, Aunt Edith had possessed a wicked sense of humour, a spectacularly dry wit and a very ripe vocabulary, when required. Her own mother, Edith's younger sister, specialised in sounding shocked when Edith let rip and would always cry 'Edith! The child!', a sure way of making Victoria remember exactly what the naughty words were. Edith had been a warm, no-nonsense woman and Victoria again found herself regretting she hadn't visited more.

"Milk, sugar?" asked Grace, playing hostess as if it were her own home.

"Let me, please, this is my home now after all," said Victoria firmly, feeling she needed to assert herself before she found herself sent to bed early with a milky drink. She poured the tea and they both tucked into the chocolate cake. It was, unsurprisingly, delicious. "My goodness, that's wonderful," said Victoria, rolling her eyes in ecstasy. "I'd love to have the recipe!"

"Ah, bit of a trade secret, I'm afraid," laughed Grace. "Always wins me a prize at the annual fête you see."

"A fête – that sounds great fun. I'm looking forward to getting involved in village life. I rather fancy growing enormous vegetables and baking sponges."

"That's splendid to hear, you'll be welcomed with open arms! So many people move down here and want to change everything to be like London or the Home Counties, or they decide the countryside is terribly scary and smelly and run away again. Of course, I expect you take after Edith in some ways. She was your mother's sister I believe?"

"Yes, she was a bit older than Mother and although they got on very well, they were chalk and cheese really. Sadly, my mother died twenty years ago when she was only forty-nine."

"Cancer?"

Victoria felt herself tense at the way the woman casually said the dreaded 'C' word. "No, actually, she and my father were killed in a car accident in America."

"Of course!" Grace clutched her forehead. "I am sorry, of course, I knew that, I had forgotten. Edith was distraught at the time. Terrible. No age at all. Are you alright dear, you've gone rather pale?"

Victoria smiled in what she hoped was a convincing manner. "Yes, fine, I'm just a little tired."

"I'm not surprised after all that drama with Moreton and his cronies! He's a dear, dear man, utterly trustworthy, but he can be a bit of an old goat sometimes!" Grace laughed and, for the first time, Victoria thought she could see why Aunt Edith may have got on with her. They were both strong women who spoke their minds.

"Look, I'll buzz off and let you settle in. If you need anything just ring me on 443210 – easy to remember! You'll find the fridge has all the basics in it. I've left you a list of what's where and who's who that you might find useful." She pushed a neat typewritten sheet of paper across the kitchen table.

"That's terribly kind, thank you," said Victoria, feeling guilty again, this time for thinking Grace was bossy and interfering when she'd been so kind. "And everywhere is spotless too, you really shouldn't have."

"Oh good Lord, that's not me! That's Jean Burnicombe, salt of the earth. Worked for Edith for donkey's years. Me, I don't know one end of a broom from the other!"

Victoria wondered how long it would take her to stop putting her foot in it. Years, probably. "Thank you so much for calling in, it was lovely."

"No trouble! You must pop in and see our little enterprise some time. I seem to recall Edith saying you were a journalist?"

"Yes, I was, up in London."

"Was? Have you given it up?" Grace looked perplexed.

Victoria made a face. "Well, not exactly. Well no, but I'll be working freelance for my old magazine. I plan to mix writing with photography and also taking things a little more easily."

"Oh that won't last!" Grace laughed. "You'll soon be wanting to work full time. I've never been able to slow down. My sons would like me to 'bugger off', as they put it, but I keep plugging away!"

"What is your 'little enterprise'?" asked Victoria, feeling now that she had no choice but to ask.

"Oh, we are Primrose Cottage Preserves. You may have seen our jars here and there." Grace positively purred and waited expectantly for Victoria to say the right thing. Being a sensible girl, Victoria did. "Of course! I've seen your lovely jams in some of the delis in London, and don't Harrods stock your marmalade?"

"Yes, they do, I'm very proud to say! My husband Henry and I founded the company years ago, and we've gone on to do rather well. Perhaps you could write an article about us, thriving business out in the wilds, bringing wealth and jobs to the rural community etcetera."

"That's very interesting, thank you. I had been thinking about local food producers as an angle for my work. Perhaps I should start with Primrose Cottage Preserves?"

Grace looked like a cat that had got the cream. She clasped her hands together. "Would you? Oh, that would be wonderful! Now look, I really mustn't keep you!"

She was gliding towards the front door with the air of a woman who has achieved what she set out to do but no, Victoria chastised herself: that was mean. She needn't have gone to so much trouble just to get herself a write up.

As Grace walked to her car a bicycle wobbled slowly into view, its rider seeming to stay upright in defiance of the laws of gravity. Victoria expected that at any moment she would grind to a halt and topple sideways into the hedge.

"Ah," said Grace in a not-very-warm tone. "Here's Jean now. I'll leave you to it." And with that she got smartly into her car, rammed it into gear and careened out of the yard just as the cyclist arrived, agonisingly slowly, at the front gate.

My God, it's as bad as Piccadilly Circus, thought Victoria as she braced herself for yet another visitor. She smiled warmly at the cyclist, a woman in her late fifties with extraordinarily bucked teeth. Her greying hair was scraped back in a bun and she wore large-framed pebble glasses on the end of a long thin nose.

'First a hobbit-cum-squirrel, now a mole,' thought Victoria and upbraided herself for such uncharitable thoughts. What was wrong with her today? "Hello, you must be Jean!" she said, extending her hand.

"That I am," said the new arrival.

Although a painfully slow bike rider, once released from the contraption Jean's movements were quick and darting. No, definitely more squirrel than mole, thought Victoria as a small dry paw quickly grasped her hand and then withdrew.

"Please come in."

"I'm not stopping, m'dear. I just wanted to check everything was OK for when you arrived," said Jean. "I popped in real early and did you today so you can settle in in peace tomorrow." She had trotted into the cottage and was now surveying the kitchen, hands on hips, frowning at the remains of the chocolate cake on the table. "Ah," she said, and then turned round to face Victoria.

"Won't you even stop for a cup of tea?" Victoria smiled encouragingly.

"No, no, I'm sure you've got plenty you want to get on with, what with all that bother about your car. And Albert Moreton making you travel on the back of his tractor, he's a lad!"

She gave a short snorting laugh and rolled her eyes, made huge by the glasses. Victoria had a terrible urge to laugh, while also wondering how this curious little woman already seemed to know so much about her.

"And then you've had her in here holding you up. I dunno." She shook her head. "Anyway, 'tis like this. I did for your aunt every Tuesday morning from nine sharp 'til noon. Now I been doing it for thirty year or more so, if it's alright with you, I'd like things to stay as they are. I could change me days, but t'would cause trouble at the factory."

"Factory?" said Victoria.

"Jam place. Lady Muck's place, Grace Simmons. I works there part-time, well almost full-time really and I'd have to swap things around, and they don't like change, that they don't. So if it's alright with you, we'll stay as we are."

"Oh absolutely," Victoria found herself saying. "Um, what is it you do, I mean did, for my aunt?"

Jean looked at her closely through her thick lenses, her expression implying she was questioning Victoria's wits. Victoria felt she was about to start questioning them herself if this kept up much longer.

"Why, I done for her. I polished, I vacuumed, I did the ironing. All that stuff. I done for her." After a pause she said defensively, "She were always satisfied. She always said to me 'Jean, you are a treasure'."

There was another silence as Victoria wondered if the quick-fire delivery was actually at an end. Then, just as she felt it was safe to speak, Jean added, "I miss her, your aunt. She were good to me. She could be a right old bag, mind. But she were good. Really."

After another pause, Victoria felt the speech had finally stuttered to a stop and that it was her turn. "That all sounds fine Jean, I'm sure we can carry on just as before. Thank you for getting the house ready for me." Jean nodded curtly. "It was lovely to arrive to such a... such a warm welcome." Jean's head bobbed up and down again.

"That's fine. I'll be off then." She turned on her heel and Victoria followed her to the door. Then Jean stopped so abruptly that Victoria almost blundered into her. "The clock. You remember? When you was a little 'un?"

Victoria frowned. Remember? She hadn't a clue what the woman was talking about.

"You always used to wind it when you were a little girl, you forgotten? Your aunt told me. He's never allowed to stop. I've never let 'e stop after your aunt died four month ago you know, wouldn't be right."

"The key!" said Victoria suddenly. "It's on the top of the

bookcase, behind Three Men in a Boat!"

Jean beamed. "Course it is!"

"Oh my goodness, I'd forgotten all about that! We used to wind him, I mean, 'it', every Sunday morning and you had to go slowly at the end so as not to overwind it."

Jean gave her curious snorting laugh again. "That's it! That's right! You've got it! Right, I'm off now then, see you soon!"

She gave a quick wave and climbed back on her bike. Victoria watched, fascinated as she wobbled, slowly, very slowly, out of the yard and down the lane.

Chapter 2

Bright sunlight streamed through the gaps in the curtains, making Victoria blink and retreat back under the covers. She snuggled into the warm, if slightly lumpy, pillow and easily resisted the urge to jump out of bed and explore some more. That quiet thinking time just before going to sleep or after waking was when she dreamt up so many of her best ideas.

Her arrival at April Cottage yesterday had been somewhat eventful. She smiled at the memory of Albert turning up on that decrepit old tractor and, oh! those leggings... what had she been thinking? To her surprise – and slight irritation – she found she was rather attracted to him, even though he was at least ten years older than her. What is it they say about older men?

She shook off her daydreaming and pondered weightier things, like money. She really needed to think about earning some before long. Her aunt's nest egg was very useful, but sadly not nearly enough to retire on. Her flat in London must be kept on and let. It would have to be her pension. Still, as Aunt Edith had said often enough in her letters 'Something will turn up dear' – and so Victoria believed it would. But nothing was going to do anything unless she got out of bed and got moving.

She flung back the covers and leapt upright and was instantly reminded of her uncomfortable twist in the car yesterday. Her back really ached; it was obviously going to take a day or two for the muscles to forgive her. She stretched gently and, humming under her breath, moved across to the window and flung open the curtains.

She screamed as a grinning male face loomed large on the other side of the central pane, shouting a cheery "Morning!"

She automatically whipped the curtains shut again and breathed deeply. It wasn't some deranged Peeping Tom: it was Albert. (She hoped they didn't turn out to be one and the same thing.) Opening the curtains again in a calm and, she hoped, more dignified manner, Victoria put her hands on her hips and said, "Albert, what on earth do you think you are doing outside my window?"

Albert looked surprised, and then almost offended. "Well how was I supposed to know which bedroom you were sleeping in? And anyway, who sleeps at this time of the day?"

Feeling guilty about her short lie-in (heavens! it was only eight-thirty), Victoria glared back. "Well, I'm not sure what business it is of yours which bedroom I sleep in."

"I was just coming up to finish cutting off this ivy," he gestured at the mass of dark green leaves. "Edith always asked me to keep an eye out, or before you know it, it's grown into the thatch. Not up to climbing ladders she wasn't, so I just assumed you'd want me to do the same."

"Oh. Well thank you very much but I'm sorry, you did give me a fright." She paused. "Would you like to come in for a coffee in a minute?"

"Proper job my beauty," Albert smiled. "Tea, two sugars, but you might want to put a few more clothes on, can't have the neighbours talking about us!" Victoria looked down at the very small T-shirt she had pulled on last night; she'd been too tired to unpack properly. She could feel the colour flooding into her face.

Oh my God, she was almost naked!

She couldn't look Albert in the eye, so mumbled, "Downstairs, five minutes" and angrily yanked the curtains closed again. She sat on the bed, trying to calm down. Outside the window Albert was laughing. "It's alright – I didn't look... honest!"

She searched through her suitcase for a sweatshirt and a proper pair of jeans. Then, for good measure, she pulled out a cardigan as well. Suddenly she stopped and tried to laugh at herself. Since her mastectomy she had become such a prude when it came to undressing. She'd had a full breast reconstruction and – even in a tiny T-shirt – nobody would know, but she still struggled madly with insecurities about her body.

She skipped a few stages of her morning routine, just scrubbed at her teeth and ran down to get the kettle on. Glancing over at her mobile, left on the kitchen table, she noticed two missed calls: damn! (though she realised, with some relief, that there was a signal at April Cottage). Checking who'd rung, she was surprised to see it was her erstwhile employer, Country Days magazine. She'd ring them back shortly.

There was a loud knocking on the back door. "Hello! Is it safe to come in now?" came an amused voice. "Are you decent?" She sighed and pulled back the bolt. Albert stood there smiling at her and she smiled back, despite herself. "Sorry I'm being slow, kettle doesn't seem to have boiled yet."

"Ah, you've got the hang of the Rayburn then?"

"Oh yes, I think so." Victoria felt a lot less sure than she sounded.

"You stoked it up already then?"

"Ah no."

"So, it's not hot then?" asked Albert. Victoria rested her hand on the cold metal, and grinned foolishly. "I'm sorry, I hate being so clueless, it's not how I usually am. Honestly, I just didn't know."

"Well, no surprise really, why should you? It's wood-fired, you've got to light it about half an hour before you need hot water, see?" He opened a door on the front of the Rayburn and gestured into its blackened depths. "Jean lit it for you yesterday, I expect." She nodded and he added, "Anyway, there's an electric kettle in the larder. Edith used it sometimes in the summer, we could use that."

The phone rang and, unable to ignore a call, Victoria answered.

"Georgie hi, how are you? Yes I noticed a couple of missed calls from you, sorry I'm up a bit late today, knackered after yesterday. Yes I know it seems ages." Victoria paused for a moment as she noticed Albert looking at her, a puzzled expression on his face. He shrugged, gave a wave that said 'later' and left the kitchen quietly.

"Sorry Georgie, slight hiatus here, the Rayburn's not hot yet. This country living's no walk in the park you know! Now tell me, how are the rest of the gang? Right now I could do with an emergency girls' coffee morning to get me grounded and sane enough to sort out this new life!" Victoria pulled out a chair and sat at the table, hoping for a long natter. But it was not to be.

"Oh, right. An urgent call... well I did think it was strange you'd rung earlier... a deadline?"

"Well, of course I need to earn money, I wasn't joking when I said I hadn't won the lottery!"

"An article for the mag? I'd love to."

She sat forward. "A slight drawback... what's that then?"

"In a week? You're kidding! I haven't even got broadband sorted here..."

"Well, ten days then, that's great, I have heard of internet cafés, but I'm not sure Devon has!"

Victoria gazed out of the window and saw Albert kick the tyre of an old Range Rover which was parked outside, and wondered why he seemed so disconsolate. She turned her concentration back to the call.

"OK, let's give it a go, rural living…"

"Can I be your local correspondent from darkest Devon?" Victoria smiled. It was fun to be in work mode again.

"Successful local companies, creating employment, exporting across the country etcetera, yes, that all sounds great." She laughed. "Actually, I might even have our first victim, sorry, I mean subject! There's a jam-making enterprise round here called Primrose Cottage Preserves, yes twee, but no, good company, sells to Harrods and Harvey Nicks, great profile."

"Two thousand words plus photos? OK, but you're killing me with the ten-day deadline, but I'll do it and yes, we must meet up soon."

Clicking off the phone Victoria looked out of the window again and saw no sign of Albert. Strange behaviour, but then he was proving an unusual sort.

She sat back and drew a deep breath. So, she'd got a commission. That would certainly get her moving and concentrate her mind. But she couldn't neglect her new and interesting surroundings either. It had been getting dark by the time yesterday's dramas were resolved and all her visitors gone, so she still hadn't properly explored the cottage in daylight.

Arming herself with a large notepad and a pen, Victoria decided to start efficiently at the top of the building and work down. She climbed the stairs, feeling several treads creak and give a little under her weight, and jotted down her first note: 'Have staircase checked and repaired'.

Turning left at the top of the stairs she went into the bedroom that had obviously been her aunt's, and marvelled at how little it had altered in the last thirty years or so. Pretty flowered curtains hung at the window with, bizarrely, a row of wooden clothes pegs along one edge. Then she remembered Edith's need for complete darkness to get a good night's sleep: she must have used the pegs to hold the curtains tight together. The basic decorative state of the room was fine. It needed brightening up a little but, as she didn't plan to use it herself, a complete makeover was not a priority. The old bedstead was metal and, once painted, would look pretty good, she thought.

The same couldn't be said for the bathroom. Victoria looked round with a sigh and wondered just how much a complete refurbishment would cost, bearing in mind her funds were definitely limited. It was clean (thank you Jean!) but the deep enamel bath was stained at the taps, there was no shower and a rickety set of shelves seemed to be the only storage. The lino on the floor was patched with tape... the list of jobs on her pad got longer and longer. It was easy enough to 'tart up' a bedroom with nice linens and accessories, but a bathroom was a far more major undertaking.

As she wandered through the other two bedrooms and down through the 'parlour' (yes, she promised Aunt Edith, I'll try and still call it the parlour) and the dining room, she realised that she might well need a rather bigger fund than she could manage at the moment. But she guessed all could be accomplished in small stages – maybe Albert could help her locate trustworthy local builders? She wasn't so naïve as not to realise it was easy to be taken in and ripped off as 'the new kid on the block', especially if you were female – and from London.

Arriving back in the kitchen, she decided not to depress herself any further by assessing the exterior as well. The list was already far more than she could afford, so why add to it? Not for the first time, she wondered if she might end up having to sell her London flat. "Push that thought away Victoria, it's your pension," she said aloud. She could see the cottage had huge potential, and if she was thrifty and creative knew she could make it into a lovely warm and welcoming home.

Victoria saw Albert's mug, complete with unused teabag, sitting on the kitchen table. Funny man. He'd said there was an electric kettle. She ought to dig that out and make a pot of coffee – she desperately needed a caffeine hit!

The Rayburn sat smug and shining, its exterior face bland and impenetrable, challenging her to coax it into life. Victoria opened one of the two doors and found an oven. She closed that and opened the other (the one where you put the wood, or coal, or something). Was there an instruction book? She'd like to master it herself rather than ask Albert for help.

Admitting defeat – for the time being, at least – she looked along the rows of shelves in the pantry and spotted a surprisingly shiny chrome kettle with, yes, oh joy! a lead and plug that looked safe and usable.

Once she had brewed the coffee and was sitting back at the table, notebook in front of her, her thoughts turned to the article. It was an interesting subject and she certainly needed to earn some money. And, if she was honest, she wanted to 'do something' constructive. She flicked back a couple of pages, found the number Grace had given her yesterday, picked up her phone and dialled.

"Oh hello, could I speak to Grace Simmons please. Yes, yes I'll hold. My name? It's Victoria West, she'll know why I'm calling."

"Hello Grace, thank you for taking the call… Yes it was nice meeting yesterday. It's about the article. The magazine thinks it's a wonderful idea."

"Heard of you? Of course, and they were thrilled you might want to be featured. Now, when would be a good time? I am on rather a tight deadline but I have all my things arriving in a van tomorrow.

"Next Tuesday? Well, no, I'd really need to see you sooner than that. Is that possible? Ah, I see. Well… if you could."

There was a long pause. Victoria was put on hold as Grace apparently went to check her busy schedule.

"This Friday? Yes that would be wonderful, thank you, mid-morning, eleven o'clock, yes that would be fine and it's OK if I bring my camera? Yes, yes me too, bye for now then."

Sighing, she leaned back in her chair and thought again how hard it was not to be steamrollered by that woman. She was no doubt one of the pillars of the community, but that didn't make her any easier to deal with! Victoria felt sure Aunt Edith would have coped with her far more effectively. Taking a long sip of her now tepid coffee, she decided today was a serious coffee day and got up to pour another cup.

The back door opened tentatively and Albert peered at her. "You finished yapping to your young man then?"

Victoria paused and then laughed. "Who, Georgie? Oh dear, no George, or Georgie, is the editor from Country Days magazine where I used to work. She and I used to go to school together, we're good friends."

"Georgie? Why do people want to go around using boys' names for girls?" Albert frowned. "Seems proper contrary to me."

"George is short for Georgina. So would you like that cup of tea now?"

"That I would. What kinda cake you got? Can't have elevenses without cake."

Victoria looked at her watch and was about to point out it was nowhere near eleven o'clock (and in fact wasn't even ten yet), but decided that was just being picky and she'd like some of Grace's chocolate cake too, only in her case it could be her breakfast!

"So, tell me a bit about you, Albert," Victoria said, as she licked her finger and dabbed it into the last few cake crumbs on her plate.

"Me?" He looked wary. "Well I dunno. What do you want to know? My name's Albert Wyndham Moreton and I was born in 1960, I think, and I left school at…"

Victoria interrupted. "It's OK, I don't mean to interrogate you, I just wondered how long you've lived here, what you farm and a bit about the village, you know, that sort of thing."

"Ah," he said, reaching forward to carve off another slab of chocolate cake without so much as a by-your-leave. "Alright this cake. You make it?"

"No! I'm hopeless at baking! At school, my scones were used as ammunition to throw at the boys from the grammar school next door!" He stopped chewing and looked shocked. "You don't bake?" he said through a mouthful of sponge.

"No. I don't." Victoria felt nettled. "But I do cook plenty of other things rather well actually. I make my own pasta and I cook a mean risotto."

Albert wrinkled his nose. "I'm not sure I like the sound of that. Sounds foreign to me."

"It is, it's Italian."

Now he looked positively uncomfortable. "You mean, stuff with herbs in it and," he shuddered, "garlic?"

She couldn't help but laugh. "Yes, and it's delicious!"

"I like good food, good plain English food."

"Ah, well we'll have to agree to differ on that score then." How strange: she thought everyone ate garlic these days.

"Grace Simmons baked this cake, didn't she?" he said suddenly, prodding the remains of the cake with the knife.

"Yes, she did. How did you know?"

"You'd be surprised what I know about baking cakes Miss Victoria West," he smiled. "You'd probably be surprised what I know about Grace Simmons too!"

Victoria sat up and paid more attention. "Really? Tell me more, please!"

"Oh you don't want to be bothered about Grace, she's a funny old bird." He laughed. "She and I were at school together, bit like you and your friend George, but without such a daft name."

"I'm going to see her on Friday, I'm writing an article about Primrose Cottage Preserves. I'm possibly going to write a whole series on local food producers."

"Oh, right." Albert didn't seem too impressed and Victoria felt quite put out. "There's all sorts making things round here these days. It's 'trendy', all this stuff, bleddy llama burgers, artisan cheese makers, if you've ever heard of such a thing and everything got to be organic of course!" He shook his head. "I dunno what's wrong with a few home-made pasties and some farm cider. Now my brother Oggy, he brews his own cider," he chuckled, "that'd make your toes curl! Maybe you should interview him?"

Victoria smiled sweetly. "Well, that's all very interesting, I'm sure. Perhaps you can introduce me to Oggy at some point."

"I can, but you'd probably regret it."

"Oh, really?"

"Never mind, you don't want to know!" Albert smirked at her.

"Well, I'm starting with Primrose Cottage Preserves, they're well known and seem to produce a top-quality product. I'm going to interview Grace and the other directors and write a company profile."

He nodded and smiled ruefully. "Oh right, that'll be interesting then! You'll meet those daft bleddy sons of hers."

"They run the business now, don't they?"

"Supposed to, so I hear. But Grace is a tough nut – and then there's Henry," he chuckled. "I can't see either of them handing over the reins just yet a while."

"Do you know Henry well?"

"Pretty well."

"Did you go to school with him too?" Victoria was getting the impression everyone knew everyone around Swaddlecombe.

"He was a bit ahead of me. He's done well for himself, but then he's always had Grace driving him on, quite a team those two."

She sat back and looked at him through narrowed eyes. "You don't like him much, do you?"

"Nope. Bit of a plonker."

She laughed. "Well, that's honest!"

"Old Henry, he spends too much time wondering what other people think of him, what impression he's making. Daft beggar. Takes after our Aunt Fanny, she was always like that."

"Aunt Fanny?" Victoria tried to keep a straight face. "Your Aunt Fanny?"

"His and mine, we're cousins, Henry and me. Still a plonker. Course, you'll find a lot of that round here, you might want to be careful."

She frowned, confused. "Sorry? What do you mean?"

"You incomers often come a cropper early on. Most of Swaddlecombe's related, see, cousins, half-brothers, all that caper. Me, I'm only related on one side, my mother was a blow-in, so I'm reasonably normal!" He laughed and shook his head. "Your face, maid, it's a picture! But don't worry – I'll give you the low-down on who's who and what's what." He laughed again, and Victoria thought how his face lit up when he smiled and how you couldn't help but smile back.

"Never mind about me, you tell me what you're up to and what you'll be doing round these parts. This to be a holiday home, or what? I expect you'll be back up to London once the novelty's worn off?"

Charming, Victoria thought. "No. April Cottage is going to be my home. All my furniture is arriving tomorrow. Once I've sorted things out in London, I will be a full-time Swaddlecombe resident."

"Why's that then? Your aunt always said how much you loved your city life and how well you were doing, always so busy."

Shifting uncomfortably in her chair Victoria looked away. "Well yes, that's true, but times change, people change. I'd been thinking about a less stress-filled life and then this," she waved her hand at the kitchen, "happened and I've been incredibly lucky to be left this place."

"Won't you get bored? No bright lights, no parties, no eligible bachelors to sweep you off your feet?"

"Albert, take it from me, some of us city girls are happy on our own, we don't all need a man around. I am a very self-contained person." She realised she sounded a little shrill and saw he looked suitably taken aback. "Anyway, I shall be kept quite busy enough trying to sort this house out."

"Sort it out? Why, what's wrong with it?"

"Well, it could do with a bit of a spruce up you must admit."

"Oh right. I thought Jean had done alright cleaning, you not satisfied?" He frowned.

"No, she's done an excellent job. I meant the décor and the facilities. The bedrooms just need redecorating, but the bathroom is grim."

Albert seemed to grow taller in his chair. Victoria explained: "Well, there's no shower for a start and the bath is all stained."

"Shower? What do you want one of those things for? You want to relax in a nice hot bath at the end of the day, relax your muscles.

That bath's quality, it weighs a bleddy ton, it took Oggy and me half a day to get it upstairs. Hell of a great tub that is, cracking bit of traditional cast iron, proper job! We got it at the auctions for Edith about, ooh, thirty years ago. She thought it was the business!"

Victoria felt flustered; she hadn't expected such a robust defence of an antiquated bit of sanitary ware. Hoping to calm him slightly, she switched her focus. "Well, I may end up just adding a separate shower unit, there's plenty of room. I could whip out that shelving unit and put one in there."

"Whip it out? That took me a week to build that did!"

"Oh dear, really? Well, it looks a bit, well, a bit rickety?"

"Rickety?" Albert was starting to turn rather red. "It's a bit widdy-waddy that's all, but that's on account of the floor!"

"I'm sorry?" She seemed to be having trouble understanding him – maybe he was getting incoherent with rage. He certainly seemed to be getting rather cross.

"Widdy... what did you say?"

"Widdy-waddy. On the gimp."

"Gimp?" Victoria couldn't understand.

"Gimp, lean, skewiff, widdy-waddy. Don't they speak English up in London? The floor isn't flat, 'tis at an angle. Bleddy hard to build something on a base like that you know." He folded his arms and scowled at her.

"I see, well, I'll have a think about it. I'm not rushing to make any changes yet, but I will be looking to modernise here and there, and update the kitchen." She realised she had said the wrong thing again.

"Update this kitchen? But what's wrong with it?"

"Well, the Rayburn for a start. It's not exactly convenient, is it?"

"Well that's because you don't understand it yet."

"I might go for something oil-fired or electric, and I certainly need to add some more cupboards and worktops."

"Well, there's no accounting for taste. Your aunt never complained. She produced wonderful meals in here. Always a roast cooking in the Rayburn, a ham boiling in a pot, fresh bread just out the oven, always a warm welcome and some ham and eggs if you wanted it at breakfast, bread and dripping at elevenses, bit of brisket for lunch." He seemed to run out of steam, his eyes were slightly misty. "Well, I'd better get on. Need to go and check the sheep in the flat field."

"Oh, but you didn't tell me about the farm…"

"Maybe another time."

He got up, and with a curt nod was gone before she could think of anything else to say to delay him.

The use of the word 'maybe' made her feel suddenly depressed. Had she just totally offended him with her clumsy suggestions about the cottage? He obviously cared a lot about the place and Aunt Edith. She felt she has made rather a fool of herself.

Just then her eye was caught by a bird performing a curious bobbing dance on the stone step outside the kitchen door, left open as Albert beat his hasty retreat. She walked slowly towards it and noticed its markings – black and white and grey – a sweet little thing, its tail bobbing up and down. Now where had she seen a bird book? She went into the hall and studied the bookcase next to the grandfather clock. An old and much-thumbed Guide to the Birds of the United Kingdom was indeed there. She must have noticed it subconsciously yesterday.

Back in the kitchen, Victoria flicked through the entries until she found a picture to match her small bobbing friend. She laughed – of course, a wagtail. 'There's a clue in the name' as her father would have said. She watched the delicate creature a little longer and then went in search of her camera, placed safely under her bed. A relatively new hobby, she hoped to make photography an integral part of her new life. Wildlife photography was high on her list of 'things to pursue' and she trotted back down the stairs to the kitchen.

The wagtail was still wagging and Victoria realised it was probably waiting to be fed. She was sure Aunt Edith would have been an enthusiastic bird feeder. A crusty loaf, wrapped in tissue paper, was sitting on the side by the Rayburn; Grace had clearly thought of everything. Victoria tore off a small piece, broke it into crumbs and tossed them to the bird. After an initial flutter of caution, it quickly settled and began pecking them up.

Victoria knelt down and fired off some photos just for fun, experimenting with depth of field and exposure. It was fascinating to watch the wagtail – its constant movement, its bright black eye ever watchful for predators or competition for food – but this bird had clearly got its own patch and happily cleared up the bread as she took picture after picture.

Eventually, realising her legs had all but gone to sleep, Victoria clambered stiffly to her feet and put her camera on the table. It was almost lunchtime, so she cut a slice of the loaf, topped it with butter and sat at the table to study the bird book further. As she leafed through the pages she became aware of the stillness. Outside, through the open door, she could hear a wonderful mix of birdsong and distant bleats and the odd lowing cow. Inside all was still, apart from the grandfather clock's rhythmical 'tick-tock', like a slow and reassuring heartbeat.

She was feeling sleepy. No one would know if she took a quick nap, would they? And whose business was it anyway? She was a free agent now and her time was her own.

She sat up, preparing to rise from the chair, when a peculiar feeling came over her. Her back stiffened and she suddenly knew what people meant when they talked about icy fingers crawling up your spine: she was being watched. She was sure of it. Someone was standing behind her in the doorway.

Victoria felt paralysed with fear. It wasn't Albert, she was sure of that. She'd heard no one approach and yet she knew, 100 per cent, that a pair of eyes was boring into her back. Trying to control her breathing she got carefully to her feet, turned slowly... and then screamed!

The sheep looked a little surprised and let out a loud bleat as if to reinforce its presence. In the confines of the kitchen it was extremely loud. Victoria screamed again and backed around the table.

The sheep advanced, a friendly light in its eyes, head slightly on one side, its jaw working furiously, chewing away at goodness knows what. It was huge – surely a mutant – and it was gazing at her with those weird eyes, yellowish green and with a vertical slit iris like some hideous alien being.

"Get out!" cried Victoria. "Go away!" She flapped at the sheep and it trotted towards her, a look of delight on its face. She screamed again but, even in fright, registered that the sheep had facial expressions. She stared at it in renewed horror. My God, she really had entered a weird world – was this sheep an intelligent being with thoughts and feelings? Was it about to speak? Was she going mad?

A puffing sound and heavy footfalls alerted Victoria to the fact that help was at hand. The sheep bleated again, its jaw still gyrating crazily.

"It's alright, I'm here!" Albert skidded into the doorway and stopped dead. "You alright?" he said breathing heavily. "Was that you screaming? What the hell's going on?"

"That!" She flapped at the sheep, now rapidly approaching her outstretched hand. "No!" she shrieked and leapt back. "Get away from me! Albert, DO something!" The sheep bleated again, its eyes fixed on her. At the sound of laughter, she tore her gaze away from the animal and saw that Albert was shaking with mirth, leaning against the doorframe for support.

"Why are you laughing?' she yelled. "There's an enormous sheep attacking me in my own kitchen and you think it's funny?"

He was bent over now, hands on knees, regaining his breath while still laughing. "Bleddy hell," he puffed, "I thought something awful'd happened, not just Betty come to say 'hello'."

"Are you mad? What are you talking about? Get this animal out of the house! I could be in danger!"

"Betty'd be as likely to harm you as I am." He stood upright and wiped his brow with the back of his hand. "Blimey, that's the fastest I've moved since the last girlfriend threw me dinner at me. Albert Moreton, you're unfit."

He looked at Victoria, now braced against the worktop. "For God's sake woman, it's a sheep. It's Betty. Your aunt hand-reared that ewe when we brought her into the warming oven a year back. Feeble little scrap of a lamb and Edith, she bottle-fed her and made her into the strapping beast you see before you. Daft as a brush. Totally harmless."

The sheep was still chewing furiously while she gazed adoringly at Victoria.

Albert smiled ruefully. "Bottle-fed sheep are always a problem as they think they're part human. She knows this kitchen and silly beggar, she thinks you're maybe Edith come back to make a fuss of her. You can stroke her if you like."

"What?" Victoria crossed her arms. "It's all mucky!"

"It's a sheep."

At that moment, the ewe's jaw was momentarily stilled. It

screwed up its face, paused, then coughed and farted, at the same time.

Victoria didn't know whether to laugh or cry. She felt herself start to shake and realised that Albert was having the same problem... and suddenly both burst into helpless laughter. The sheep bleated again and twitched its head from side to side, looking at them both in turn out of the corner of its strange eyes, unsure what it had done to release the tension in the air.

Chapter 3

Thursday dawned dry and bright but the furniture van arrived late and dirty. The crew had got hopelessly lost and had spent hours meandering down ever-narrowing lanes resulting in much reversing, getting stuck in farmyard muck and a general loss of humour.

Albert, arms folded and leaning casually against the garden gate, shook his head as he watched the removals team lumbering back and forth with bits of Victoria's belongings. "Should've got a Devon firm in. They'd have known the way no problem. Probably cost a lot less too."

The leader of the crew looked at him through narrowed eyes as he lugged a chest of drawers past.

"Yes, but they might very well have got lost in London!" said Victoria, anxious to stay on the right side of the men to ensure the safe handling of her belongings, if nothing else.

"Doubt it. I'm sure they could read a map," Albert snorted.

Victoria realised he was far from oblivious to the offence he was causing and was actually enjoying playing the 'daft' local and making his unsubtle points with seeming innocence.

"So, lady, where do you want this lot? It says 'loft' on the boxes, but as far as I can see you haven't got one down in Devon, although I'm sure you must have had one up in London," said the crew leader, his voice heavy with sarcasm.

Before Victoria could begin to think of an answer (and realising suddenly that he was quite right) Albert slipped in. "Oh, you can store it all in my barn if you like," he said casually, and waved his hand towards the far corner of the barn.

"Are you sure? That would be marvellous!" What a relief; she had been secretly worried about where all her stuff would go, since Edith's cottage – correction, her cottage – was already full of furniture.

The crew leader sighed heavily and picked up the box. "So, you want all the 'loft' stuff over there then?"

"If you wouldn't mind," she said meekly, as he signalled to the other two men and they set off to cover the eighty yards or so to deposit the boxes.

By five o'clock the removals men had gone, leaving Victoria bereft of tea, sugar and digestive biscuits. Having stirred everyone up nicely, Albert had disappeared to do something 'farmery' about three hours ago, and she hadn't seen him since.

Victoria looked at the boxes in the barn. They'd stay nice and dry in there and were easy to access, so that was really handy. She couldn't believe there were quite so many. Had they multiplied on the journey down? She realised she had no idea what was in most of them and regretted not having written more information on them as she'd packed, but it had all been a bit of a rush at the end. She wandered back into the cottage and went into the parlour, and then came straight back out again as yet more boxes were too depressing to contemplate.

Victoria sat at the kitchen table realising that, just like her aunt, this was going to be where she spent most of her time. She thought she'd be pleased to have all her own homely clutter around her but, now it was here she almost felt like she didn't want it. It was her old life and she wasn't sure it should be part of the new one. Boxes were piled up in front of the dresser, but at least they were suitably labelled. Taking a deep breath, she started to unpack her crockery and cutlery.

By nine o'clock her back ached, her knees were sore and she felt grubby from handling all the newspaper wrapped around her precious goods. Precious goods! She felt most of her retro fifties crockery and cutlery with the brightly coloured handles looked ridiculous next to Edith's old-fashioned blue and white china and silver knives and forks.

She had remembered to switch on the immersion heater an hour earlier, so was grateful to slip into a nice hot bath to relieve her aches and pains. The stains on the enamel seemed less offensive next to the impressively grubby ring she created. With her own sheets on the bed, her favourite pillow and her old quilt, it took her about five seconds to fall into a deep sleep.

* * * * *

Victoria could hear the distant trilling of her mobile and cursed the fact she had left it downstairs; she must sort out a landline.

"Hello?" she was out of breath; those stairs were steeper than they looked.

"Victoria, it's Grace, sorry to ring you early but I expect you were up and about?"

Victoria looked down at her pyjamas and smiled ruefully, then replied, "Oh absolutely, not a problem at all Grace. What can I do for you?"

"It's about the interview today, I'm afraid I simply have to cancel. My hair stylist can't even begin to fit me in and I need all the help I can get for photos these days – don't we all?"

Victoria decided to ignore the not-too-subtle put-down, but the thought of losing the interview panicked her. "But Grace, I simply can't delay this if I'm to make the magazine's deadline." Thinking on her feet, she said, "Tell you what, how about if I split the interview in two. I'll pop down today and talk to your husband and sons and key staff and take some general shots. Then we can plan another day for your interview and a relaxed personal photo session!" Victoria hoped that if she said it brightly and in a sufficiently matter-of-fact manner Grace would be unable to refuse.

"Oh but... well it really isn't, I mean I'm not..."

"It'll be fine Grace, I promise," Victoria cut in. "Let's face it – it's a fabulous piece of free publicity for you, it would be a tragedy to miss it!" On the other end of the line Grace sighed and agreed, obviously miffed at being outmanoeuvred.

Victoria crossed the kitchen and switched on the kettle to make her first brew of coffee. She sat at the kitchen table and tried to rough out a list of questions she might ask and possible shots she might need. This wouldn't be easy as she hadn't done any initial research apart from a hurried look at their website via her mobile phone. Damn, she must get some internet sorted out as a priority!

Just then Albert breezed cheerily through the back door. So glad we have obviously got past the having to knock stage, thought Victoria, as he plonked himself down at the table.

"Not having a proper breakfast then? Sets you up for the day does that."

"No Albert, I never have much for breakfast, coffee and maybe some toast is fine for me."

"You need fresh eggs, bacon, decent sausage and Grace's marmalade for your toast. That's a proper breakfast."

"Well, I'm not going to argue the point but, talking of Grace, I assume you mean Grace Simmons? I just had her on the phone about my interview with them today. Could you go over the directions again with me? I need to leave in half an hour or so."

"What's Grace want then, checking you've got a soft-focus filter before you take her picture no doubt? Vain bleddy woman she is. There's nothing wrong with being her age and no need to pretend you're twenty-nine when you're not. But there's no telling her! Pen and paper then?"

Victoria paused as she sorted the non sequitur out in her mind and realised he meant the pen and paper for the instructions. "I've got satnav, but I know it can be unreliable in out-of-the-way spots and I didn't want to end up late and at the wrong end of the county. If you could just help me with the last bit once I get near Hill Farm?"

"Tell you what, I haven't got a lot on today, well not a lot I fancy doing anyway, so how about if I drive you – free chauffeur service? I can see a couple of my mates that work there while you're busy? Maybe make a day of it and have a spot of lunch, you'll be starving what with skipping breakfast an' all."

Victoria smiled and realised her non-breakfast was going to be a recurring topic, but it was actually quite sweet to find that someone noticed if she ate sensibly or not. "Thank you so much, it's a really kind offer, but I don't think my car is insured for anyone except me to drive."

Albert rolled his eyes. "We'll go in my car!"

"No Albert, I'm sorry, not the white van or the tractor, this is an important business meeting and I, well, I don't mean to be rude, but I have to look businesslike."

"I do have other vehicles you know," Albert said, looking wounded. "I just choose different ones for different jobs."

Making a snap decision that she hoped she wouldn't regret, Victoria replied, "OK, let's leave here in say, twenty minutes – I just need to make myself look a bit presentable and finish these notes." She would like to have added "and have a quick shower".

Redoing that bathroom had to be first on her renovation list – she was missing her showers really badly.

A little later there was a loud 'toot-toot' outside the door. Victoria put her phone and notepad into her bag. She checked through all the bits and pieces in her camera bag and hoped everything was present and correct; she had a dread of arriving minus some crucial bit of kit. Inefficiency was something she hated, but as she got older she was annoyed to find she was becoming increasingly 'dizzy' and forgetting things.

Looking over her shoulder as she locked the front door she saw a distinctly aged Range Rover with a beaming Albert at the wheel. She walked over and peered inside. The back seats had been folded down to give more room for carrying 'stuff' and, judging by the debris, the previous loads had included straw, feedstuff and possibly, by the mud and other evidence, a sheep. A vision of Betty's adoring alien eyes and quivering lip made her shudder, and she turned back to see Albert had pushed the passenger door open.

"See, proper job," he said beaming proudly, "decent vehicle to give a bit of class to your visit!"

"But can't we…?" Victoria was going to go say can't we clean the back out a bit, but then shrugged and resigned herself to being practical; time was getting on. "I need to get the camera gear in the back." She hefted the tripod bag and moved towards the boot.

"'Save time, shove it through here and we'll be off."

Victoria passed the bags over to Albert and winced as he lobbed them carelessly into the back of the vehicle. Thank goodness the camera bag was well padded. They would slide around a bit, but she still reckoned this was a better option than trying to find the place on her own this first time.

They trundled through narrow Devon lanes with tight bends, crossed larger roads and negotiated small ones – all, it seemed, with a complete lack of signposts. Albert identified distant hills and breeds of cattle and told her who lived in farms and houses as they shot past tracks and driveways, and generally kept up a stream of information like a city tour guide. Victoria felt increasingly disorientated and, at the same time, more and more grateful for his help.

"It is a good thing you offered to drive me Albert, I'm not sure I would ever remember this route again. I had no idea it was so far!"

"Nearly there now. I took you the scenic route, thought you'd like to see the pretty lanes and that, since you're new. We could have been here ten minutes ago but it always takes that bit longer round the back roads."

She closed her eyes and massaged her temples in the hope she could avert a stress headache. What part of being on time did he not understand? Oh well, maybe she was just being a total townie!

They drove up to what might have been a farm gate in years gone by, only indicated now by the remains of two sturdy posts each side of the driveway. There was an incongruously smart sign saying 'Primrose Cottage Preserves' in burgundy and gold with a twee depiction of a clump of primroses enclosed in an oval. Under the smart signboard hung a tatty unpainted piece of wood into which was burnt 'Hill Farm'.

"So this is Hill Farm, but the business is Primrose Cottage?" Victoria's brow was furrowed as she tried to remember the company's details.

"That's right," replied Albert. "Grace and Henry bought up old Jonesy's farm many moons ago, mainly for the outbuildings I reckon, and they converted the old milking parlour into the jam place. The house is up there, behind that hedge. Keeps it all in the one place I suppose. Grace thought that Primrose Cottage sounded suitably posh for her jams and such."

They drove slowly along the track, the potholes recently filled with gravel to reduce the bumps. A strip of concrete driveway took over, which was far more comfortable, if somewhat narrow. Finally they drove into a large area of rough ground that seemed to serve as a car-parking area.

"It's just upalong," said Albert waving his hand vaguely. "I'll take the car right up outside so you can get your camera gear out and then come back and park here."

Victoria was looking round madly, trying to take everything in. There was a large, very tidy farmhouse behind a hedge about fifty yards further up the hill, but far more imposing was the big concrete and steel building off to the left. There were windows in the far quarter, a couple of large ones on ground level and smaller ones on the next floor. The rest was clean but distinctly utilitarian.

They parked immediately outside what appeared to be a general staff room, judging by the number of bodies moving around inside. Several faces stared at them, some wearing factory-style hats and overalls, others in more imposing white laboratory coats.

"Let's get the camera bits out and I'll go and introduce myself," said Victoria.

She got out of the Range Rover and went round to the back. Pressing hard on the button to open the boot she frowned when nothing happened. Yanking a little as she pressed the second time, still nothing moved. "Albert!" she called, "is there a secret knack to getting this open?" She could see several faces smirking through the window at her as she struggled.

"It's a bugger, often plays up. Here let me." Albert tugged on the back door and then shrugged fatalistically. "Nope, doesn't want to work today. No matter – we'll get them through the front."

Victoria could see the smirks had turned to laughter and she felt very uncomfortable. "Oh Albert, this is awful."

"Oh don't you fuss so, you're giving them something to smile about today, no more than that!"

Victoria walked round to one of the rear doors and tried to open it, but it didn't budge. She took a deep breath and said, as calmly as she could, "Albert, it seems the rear passenger door is also not co-operating."

"Nah, it's those child locks, they work but like back to front, opens OK from the inside but not from the outside, never did get that sorted. Engine runs like a dream mind, nothing wrong with that!"

Victoria gazed at the sky, wishing the ground would open up.

Albert climbed back in the driver's seat and then emerged, shaking his head. "Nope, it'll have to be you, I can't get through the two front seats to reach them."

The bends and tight turns on the journey over had resulted in the camera equipment lodging itself in the far corner of the boot, close to the rear tailgate, which would have been so convenient had they been retrieving it in the normal manner.

By now any attempt at keeping up appearances had to be abandoned and Victoria gave Albert one of her 'looks' (which, as he would soon find out, was never going to be a good thing). She thanked her lucky stars that she had decided to wear a trouser suit for today's interview, removed her jacket and laid it carefully on the driver's seat, then clambered between the front seats and retrieved the camera bags. As she put her jacket back on and shook out her hair she heard a loud cheer coming through the factory window and noticed several grinning young men giving her the 'thumbs up' sign.

Victoria smiled serenely at them. Then, determined to maintain her last few shreds of dignity and with head held high, she turned and opened the door of the building and followed the signs to reception. She seemed to have lost Albert but she felt that might have been a deliberate act on his part as he had no doubt correctly interpreted her glare and decided to make himself scarce. Setting down the camera equipment by the reception desk she looked around for a receptionist; maybe that was hoping for too much? While she waited she got the camera out of its bag. She stopped and listened and heard shouting coming from upstairs. An open-tread staircase led up to something – offices, maybe?

"Try bloody stopping me!" a distant voice yelled from above.

"I will!"

"God Almighty, you're just a stupid old man who wouldn't know a marketing plan if it hit him in the face." Definitely a young man's voice.

"Just shut up the lot of you, I'm on my way to sign right now, it's too late for talking." An older male voice. "I'm leaving now and we'll discuss this when I get back, bloody solicitors charge enough already without paying for waiting time!"

"Henry I'm coming with you, it's my company as well!" This time it was a woman's voice.

"No. Your presence is definitely not required."

With that a large, well-groomed man in an expensive suit thundered down the wooden staircase and stopped abruptly when he saw Victoria. The furious expression disappeared as if by magic, to be replaced by a charming smile. He glanced at the pile of camera equipment.

"Papped in my own office, eh!" He laughed as if highly amused by his own joke. "You press people do get about don't you! Well, always happy to have a few journos here! I usually get my wife to deal with it. Grace!"

He called up the stairs and a very smartly dressed Grace began her descent, faltered and looked startled when she saw Victoria.

"But I rang, Victoria, to say not today!"

"Yes, and I said it would be fine! Please don't worry Grace – as I said on the phone I am just doing background interviews and photography today..." she trailed off as she saw Grace and Henry's fixed smiles. Things were far from 'fine'.

"Well," said Henry with far more enthusiasm than was necessary. "The camera never could resist me, just a few, eh dear, then I must be off."

"And Henry – I am coming with you," Grace added.

Henry posed, with all the confidence of a man who believes himself still handsome (although he was ten years too late). Victoria hastily adjusted her camera and started firing off shots. His suit just reeked of Savile Row, and the outdated striped-tie-and-handkerchief look seemed just right for his 'old school' attitude.

"I love your eagerness, young reporter cub!" Henry said in an extremely patronising tone. She took another shot of him, now clad in an equally expensive camel coat, and snapped continuously to dissipate her anger. "And young reporter cubs deserve a break don't you think? So, if you pop back early next week I might just have the scoop of your career!" Henry tapped the side of his nose and looked down at her. "Exciting plans afoot my dear!"

Grace went to walk past him and then turned. "Henry, we need to leave." She gave Victoria a strange glance, an odd mix of regret that she'd been a less-than-perfect hostess and irritation that Victoria was there at all.

"No Grace. I need to leave. You need to stay." He leaned forward, saying the words carefully and with great force, very close to his wife's face. She didn't flinch, but kept perfectly still.

Henry strode out of the door. Grace hesitated and then followed. Victoria watched as Henry opened the boot of his Jaguar and slung his briefcase in the back. Typical, no problem with his boot opening, she thought. He climbed into the driver's seat, gave his wife a cocky half salute and roared out of the car park. Grace stood, her hands clenched at her sides, until the car had disappeared from view.

Slowly, Grace turned, her face drawn. She pushed open the door, but without coming in said, "I'm sorry, I have a frightful migraine coming on. I'm going to go to the house and take one of my tablets. I'll need to lie in the dark for a few hours. So sorry." She turned stiffly and walked away before Victoria could say anything.

Victoria didn't like conflict. She seemed to be slap bang in the middle of some considerable battle and she felt very uncomfortable. Maybe she should go and find Albert and just sneak off quietly... but she couldn't, she had this ridiculously short deadline. She sighed, and as she considered her current predicament a thought struck her: Grace had looked her usual immaculate self, so what was all that fuss about the hairdresser? Some people were very odd about having their photo taken.

Left alone at the reception desk, Victoria started to feel that the whole exercise might have been a bit of a mistake. She took some photographs of the awards hanging on the wall and waited patiently. Tentatively, she pressed a bell on the desk again in the hope of attracting attention. She heard it ring in the distance, but nothing happened.

After about thirty seconds a well-spoken and slightly testy voice said, "Can I help you?" Victoria looked around, unable to see a body to accompany it. "Hello? Can I help?" it said again, with even less patience.

Victoria looked around wildly and eventually realised the speaker was leaning over the balustrade at the top of the stairs. Peering upwards, Victoria said, "Oh, hello! Well, I'm here to write an article on the company, but I'm not quite sure what's happened.

My name's..."

"I don't know anything about this! Who did you speak to?"

Well really, you might come down and speak to me face to face, Victoria thought, crossly. "Grace Simmons."

"Don't worry, it's fine!" said an altogether different voice, smoother, almost drawling. She watched as a long pair of masculine legs came into view as their owner descended the stairs in a languid fashion. She found herself facing a tall man in his thirties. He wasn't exactly good looking – his lips were too thick and his eyes slightly too far apart – but she could see he thought himself irresistible.

"John Simmons, financial director, and you are…?"

"Victoria West," she said and shook his extended hand. A very firm alpha-male grip was applied and she did her best not to wince. "Sorry about this, obviously some sort of misunderstanding. You spoke to Grace, you say?"

"Yes, I've just moved into April Cottage." His grey eyes looked puzzled and so she added, "The house at Upper Swaddle Farm? Do you know it?"

"Hmmm, rings a vague bell," he drawled.

"Anyway, Grace was kind enough to call in and introduce herself as she had been a good friend of my late aunt, I believe." Victoria knew she was talking too fast.

"Really?" A sardonic smile and a little twitch of the eyebrows. He was enjoying making her squirm. Damn you, she thought, and decided to build up her own role in this affair. "I explained to her that I write for a leading country lifestyle magazine and I'd like to feature her company, so here I am."

"Oh, I see, how charming." His smile was distinctly reptilian. "Please, do come on up and I'm sure I can fill you in on everything you need to know." His hand steered her elbow towards the stairs.

"My camera!" Victoria half turned towards the pile of

equipment.

"Leave it to me." Catlike, he turned and gathered up the bags in one movement and followed her up the stairs.

At the top of the stairs she was met by a heavy-set man with enough of a resemblance to John to make Victoria sure they were brothers, but where John was long and lean, this one was shorter and dumpy. She couldn't help thinking he looked as if someone had put a large weight on his head as a child so he'd grown outwards instead of upwards. The weight of responsibility, perhaps? Concentrate Victoria, she told herself. "Hello, I'm Victoria West," she said with false cheerfulness.

"Oh," he said, unenthusiastically. "I'm William Simmons."

Victoria identified him as the unwelcoming disembodied voice of earlier and gave him her most winning smile, just to annoy him even more. In contrast to his brother's, William's handshake was slightly moist and half-hearted in delivery. "Pleased to meet you," she said, and waited.

John stepped into the void and said, "Victoria has spoken to Mother and is here to write about our burgeoning empire." He gave his brother a meaningful look that Victoria couldn't quite fathom.

"I see," said William, "right."

This was like pulling teeth. Time to take the initiative.

"If I could just have a chat with you both about the company, how it started, what your products are, where you source your ingredients, what your future plans are?" At this, John snorted and William glared at him.

"And if I could take a few photos of you both and go down onto the factory floor?"

William seemed to pull himself together at last. "Of course, let's go through to the office."

He held out his arm stiffly to indicate the way and Victoria crossed the small reception area and entered the office. The upper half of the end wall was glass, giving a view down over the factory floor. She stopped, surprised to see huge cauldrons full of bubbling goo with giant wooden spoons – more like paddles – propped up against the rim of each. The white-coated workers milling about looked like children. I feel too big, like Alice in Wonderland, thought Victoria.

"Gosh, that's interesting. I had no idea you actually made the jams in big saucepans like that – I thought it would all be done in huge sterile vats untouched by human hand."

"Ah yes, that's one of our big selling points," said William earnestly. "Our preserves are hand-made in the traditional way, gives a much more authentic flavour you know."

Just as Victoria turned to follow him into the office, she caught sight of Albert next to one of the over-large pans, waving at her, with a big grin on his face. She scowled and turned away. Honestly, looking at all professional with Albert around was an uphill struggle!

"John, could you ask Marilyn to make us some coffee – or would you prefer tea?" asked William, who now seemed to have thoroughly regained his composure.

"Coffee would be good," said Victoria.

"Yes of course," John's tone verged on the sarcastic, "and then when you've finished with Miss West, I'll give her all the important facts and figures she'll need." Ah, thought Victoria, message received and understood. With that, he left the office, shutting the door a little too firmly.

"Well now, where shall I start?" William sat back in his chair and studied the ceiling. After a moment he said, "Actually, why not take a look at our brochure, that's got all the history and that sort of thing in it. Probably tells you all you want to know." He delved in the desk drawers until he found a colour brochure, and handed it to her.

"Thank you." She flicked through it. "I'm sure this is all online on your website too but I'm afraid I haven't had a chance to get broadband installed yet. I only moved down a few days ago."

"Really?" he said, smoothing the desk blotter. "How interesting."

It occurred to Victoria that there wasn't a computer in the office, which seemed strange. "You do have a website, I assume?"

"Oh yes, of course. I think it's all up to date. We have a," he waved his hand vaguely, "a marketing person to do that sort of thing."

"I see. Well, this brochure will give me all the background I need, I'm sure. What are your main products? I know your marmalade is very popular."

"Yes, it is. Wins awards. We won something just the other day actually. I expect there's something in here about it." He opened and shut drawers again and seemed relieved when there was a knock at the door and a timid woman entered carrying a tray with a cafetière of coffee on it. Thank goodness for that, thought Victoria. At least it's proper coffee; might keep me awake.

"Marilyn, could you dig out that press release on the award we won last week please?" he asked, looking hopeful.

"Right Mr William, I think it's on your desk, I'll go and see…"

She scuttled out of the door like a nervous rodent. Mousy hair, small features, figure like a rail; never had a woman looked less like a 'Marilyn', thought Victoria rather unkindly. She had also explained why William couldn't find anything; this wasn't his office. Victoria looked a little more closely and saw photos of Henry receiving awards, or handing them out and, like Miss Marple, deduced to whom the office really belonged.

"Marilyn's a treasure, worked here for aeons," said William.

"Lost without her. Milk?" Victoria nodded, and he poured the coffee. "Of course we were robbed of several awards we should easily have won, the whole honey section really. Janners you know, another local lot, won them all, obviously better calibre bees there! Ha!" he laughed cynically.

The treasure trotted back in and handed William some paper. "Ah yes, gold award for the marmalade from the Food Council, jolly good." He handed the information to Victoria and sat back, seemingly exhausted with the effort. Victoria glanced through the press release, and waited for some more pearls of wisdom.

"Do you fish?" he said suddenly, sitting forward.

Victoria looked at him, a little startled. Well! she thought, sipping her coffee while contemplating her reply. People really are very strange in this part of the world, it seems – so it's not just Albert.

"No," she said eventually, replacing her cup in its saucer, "I can't say that I do. But I'm told it's a fascinating sport."

"Absolutely! A day's fly-fishing is as good as a week lying on a beach, I can tell you!" He had become animated, his heavy face almost attractive. "I'm experimenting with some of my grandfather's secrets – trout you know! I'd be out there now in my waders if I could. Marvellous. And the wildlife, birds in particular."

"So running the family preserves business isn't exactly your idea of heaven then?" Victoria said, smiling.

"Well no, not really, but there we are. Give me fishing any day. Tell me, did you realise trout would be tempted by bees?" Victoria tried to look half interested and smiled. He spread his hands in a hopeless gesture. "Thought not, not many know, grandfather used bee lures you know, complete replicas." Finally he seemed to register Victoria's silence. "Guess I am luckier than most with my job. Now John, he loves it." He sighed. "John could talk to you all day about margins on jam as opposed to chutney, each to their own I suppose. It's a good business, I'm not denying it, and we employ a lot of people locally, but it's all pretty cut-throat these days, what with supermarkets and all that malarkey."

Victoria had a sinking feeling. She wasn't going to learn anything from this man. She wasn't even sure he knew anything and, if he did, whether he was capable of articulating it.

As if reading her thoughts he said, "Look here, you'd be better off talking to John you know. He's got all sorts of facts and figures, draw you a pie chart as soon as look at you. Hang on," he stood up, "I'll see if he's free," and with that strode out of the room.

Curiouser and curiouser, thought Victoria. She went and looked down at the factory floor again. The whole effect was indeed very 'Alice in Wonderland'. She caught sight of Albert chatting to a woman with a clipboard, who was taking readings from a thermometer in one of the pans. They laughed at some joke, but to Victoria it was like watching a silent film as virtually no sound came through the glass, just the distant hum of machinery and the odd clunk.

"Ah, there you are," said William. Victoria wondered where he thought she might have gone.

"Yes, here I am!" She smiled warmly at him. Poor chap, she felt quite sorry for him. Eldest son leading a life he didn't want, still working with his domineering parents and pushy younger brother. Ah well, as he'd said, luckier than most.

"Our, I mean, John's office is down there, he'll take you through everything." He almost shoved her back across the reception area in his enthusiasm to get rid of her.

"Thank you. But I'd like to take some photos of you."

"Really? Oh I'm sure you don't need any of me! Probably break the lens!" Having got her into the other office he was already shutting the door behind her.

"Have a seat," said John smoothly. Victoria spun round to find him standing very close to her and gesturing her into a chair. "Oh, thank you." She sat down hastily.

"I took the liberty of moving your cameras in here, so don't worry, all safe and sound." He patted her camera bag in a way that made Victoria feel quite uncomfortable and almost concerned for her equipment.

"Thank you."

"Did my elder brother furnish you with any useful information about the company?" he said, sitting back in his chair and fixing her with a look. Victoria waved the brochure at him. "Oh yes, I'm sure all the background material is in here."

He grimaced. "Hmm, you'll find the website more up to date. It's got quite a lot of useful stuff on it, including details about our current full product range, which I'm sure you'll want. When you leave I'll send you home with a good selection so you can taste them for yourself." He smiled as if to emphasise the extent of his generosity.

"That would be great, thank you. If you could send me product shots of your most popular items, that would be useful too. What about seasonal items?"

"Oh yes, one of my mother's favourite things, the seasonals!" he sighed. "Hopeless from a financial point of view, but she insists it's vital to show our commitment to the traditional ways."

"I would think she's right – people are very keen on products reflecting the seasons and not being mass-produced."

"Yes, yes, so she always tells me, but they're all loss leaders and if we're to compete we have to keep our prices keen you know."

"Let me just get my notebook out," said Victoria. She took notes furiously for the next half an hour, learning more than she ever wanted to know about the unreliability of fruit crops, the inconvenience of health and safety regulations, the horror of sourcing jam jars and finally, and most vexing of all, employing staff.

Nearing the point of exhaustion, she sighed, sat upright and stretched. "Well, that's all been very interesting. I wonder, could we have a break and I'll go and take some shots down on the shop floor?"

John looked affronted. "But I've lots more to tell you – we haven't even touched on gross margins."

"I'd love to hear about gross margins, but I think I'd like to take some shots now and come back to them in half an hour or so, would that be OK?"

He still looked perplexed. "You want to go down there?" he nodded towards the factory floor. "Absolutely! I'd like to chat to your staff and take some photos of the jam-making process, if I may?"

"Well...," he paused, and said sulkily, "I suppose so."

"Excellent!" Victoria rose to her feet; her legs had almost gone to sleep after sitting still for so long. She took her camera out of the bag and picked up the flash unit. A phone rang in another room and she heard Marilyn's timid tones. Victoria glanced down at the factory floor, hoping not to see Albert looking back at her, but there he was, in the thick of it. He waved at her again. She ignored him.

"Do you know that person?" asked John in a puzzled tone as he moved to stand next to her, more closely than was strictly necessary.

"Sort of, yes."

Just then, Marilyn scuttled back into the room. "Mr John? Your mother's on the phone and she said could you and Mr William go and see her up at the house immediately?"

"What, now?" He glowered at the poor woman, as if it was her fault.

"Yes, she said it was proper urgent."

"Oh really!" He strode off towards the phone and Victoria heard a muffled, curt exchange. He reappeared and said loudly "Damn!" just as William emerged from his father's office.

"What is it?" barked the older brother.

"Mother. We've been summoned."

"Oh dear," said William, looking as if he was about to go before the headmaster.

"Well, I'm afraid that's probably it for today," said John, looking at his watch. "Once Mother's dealt with us, I'm afraid I have a full afternoon of meetings."

William nodded. "Ditto."

"No reason why we can't resume tomorrow though," said John. "The dust should have settled by then." He ushered Victoria down the stairs. "But couldn't I do the factory shots now?" she bleated as she was all but manhandled out of the main door.

"They'll all be stopping for lunch in a minute. We can organise the photos for tomorrow, along with the product samples. Don't worry, we won't let your deadline pass!" He smiled ingratiatingly and then disappeared back inside.

Victoria stood in the car park with her photography gear at her feet, wondering what on earth had just happened.

"Something wrong?" Albert made her jump – and for the second time that morning.

"Oh it's you! Yes, something is wrong! That family are wrong, I mean is wrong, oh I don't know what I mean! How very odd."

"Could have told you that. Anyway, let's get home then."

The farce with the boot was avoided as Victoria sat with all the equipment crammed on the front seat. "Are we going the scenic route again?"

"Maybe, I'll see how the mood takes me." He beamed at her as the Range Rover lurched out of the car park.

They'd been driving for about five minutes and had already swerved around a rabbit, then a cat, and backed up for a horse and rider, when Albert executed an emergency stop. Fortunately, the seat belts worked and Victoria disentangled herself from the tripod and looked up to see they were bonnet to bonnet with a bright red convertible BMW.

"Good grief, that was close!" she said.

"Aye. It's that bleddy woman from the Jams place," said Albert staring straight ahead.

"What, Primrose Cottage?"

"Nope, t'other one."

"There's another one?" Victoria felt confused. Life seemed so much simpler back in London.

"Janner's Jams. Mile or two down the road in Pinchleigh."

"Are you going to reverse then?"

"Nope." He got out his mobile phone and deftly sent a text.

Victoria was surprised and impressed by this action. She hadn't thought he would have a mobile, let alone be capable of rapid texting. And how come he had a signal when she didn't? She'd have to ask him which service provider he was with. She sat there, too embarrassed to look at the woman, but a furtive glance revealed what her mother would have called 'a flashy piece': a lot of brunette hair, an admirable cleavage and big sunglasses.

Victoria felt she was in a scene in a western where the two lead characters face each other in the main street ready to draw their guns. She wouldn't be surprised if Albert had a gun: in fact she was sure he would! As a farmer he probably took pot-shots at all sorts of defenceless wildlife. But not people, not brassy women in

BMWs, surely?

The sound of a roaring engine, growing louder by the second, dragged her back to the present. Victoria looked around in panic. It sounded like an aeroplane was about to land on the roof of the Range Rover.

"What on earth is that?"

"The cavalry!" said Albert and grinned hugely, folding his arms.

The woman in the car looked thunderous. Victoria craned round in her seat. All she could see through the rear window was an enormous pair of headlights on a radiator, flanked by two massive tyres, pulling up close behind them.

"Wow!" she said, "that's one big tractor!"

"Yep, that's Billy Wildmoor. Good lad."

The BMW was now reversing at speed and screeched to a halt in a driveway about twenty yards back. Albert put the Range Rover into gear and pulled slowly forward, giving a leisurely wave as he passed the red car. In return the woman made a rude gesture.

"Well really!' said Victoria who had somehow believed country people would be more polite than those in London. Clearly this was not the case.

The massive tractor followed them a short way and then ducked into a field. Albert tooted, stuck his arm out the window and waved.

Victoria sat back, confused. "So, was Bill on his way somewhere? Or did you…?" She petered out and looked at Albert. "Did you text him?"

"Might have." He looked innocent and drove on with deliberate care.

"But why?"

"I'm not reversing for that madam! And anyway, rules say,

whoever's in the smallest queue has to back up."

"What rules are those?"

"The rules of polite driving in Devon!" He turned to beam at her. "You'll learn them soon enough!" Victoria grinned. He was such a character.

"Shall we stop off at the pub then?"

"If you don't mind, could we go this evening instead?" she replied. "I'd like to check the few photos I managed to get and write up my notes before I go back again tomorrow. Is that OK?"

"Fine by me. Shall I pick you up about six then?" This seemed to Victoria very early to get to the pub, but perhaps that's what they did in the country. "Yes, that's fine, but couldn't we walk?"

"Walk?" Albert swerved as he turned to look at her. "Walk? Why? I can't remember the last time I walked to the pub! You on a fitness drive or something? No, I'll pick you up and we'll nip down together."

They screeched to a halt inside the barn and Victoria extricated herself, not without difficulty, and untangled her camera bag and tripod and various straps. "So who was 'the madam' then, the one in the red car?" She asked, straightening up as Albert gathered the bags to carry inside for her.

"That was Miss Mandy Parkin of Janner's Jams."

Chapter 4

Sipping her coffee, Victoria browsed through the bookshelves in the kitchen. She expected lots of cookery books – the shelf was in the kitchen, after all – for Aunt Edith had been famous for her wonderful cakes and competition-winning pies. Strangely, she couldn't find a single book on baking. There were plenty on main courses, meat and general farmhouse cookery, but nothing about cakes or puddings. Perhaps a friend had been told she could have all Edith's precious cake books and recipes after the latter's death, and had helped herself? Victoria felt strangely sad at this perceived loss; she'd have loved to share her aunt's secret recipes and tips for making the lightest sponges and the shortest pastry. She rather fancied herself picking up prizes at the local show and, if she was honest, producing some delicious cakes to impress Albert. But perhaps her secrets had died with her.

She jumped as a loud hooting sounded outside the kitchen window. It must be Albert, she thought, wishing the horn on his Range Rover wasn't quite so loud. She stared out of the window and gasped in disbelief. He wasn't in the Range Rover at all: there stood a Jaguar XJS in daffodil yellow. Albert beamed enthusiastically at her through the windscreen and waved. She bit her lip to stifle rising giggles. How many old cars, tractors and assorted vehicles did Albert have, for heaven's sake?

"Two minutes," she shouted out of the back door and rushed

off to grab her handbag, pausing briefly to check her make-up in the mirror. She wasn't at all sure how much effort she should make. Was going down to the pub with him a sort of date? Should she have tried harder with what she was wearing – did she want to try harder? Albert was certainly good looking, but did they really have anything in common? But there again – he did make her smile.

"Sorry, ready now," she said as she opened the passenger door and slid onto the leather seat. "How many cars have you got Albert? And why didn't we use this one for the trip to Primrose Cottage? It's very smart."

"Ah well, that'd be because this old girl can't be relied upon for more than a gallon or so, fuel tank's got a hole in it and she stops after about twelve miles," he stroked the top of the dashboard as if to pacify the vehicle. "So I thought, best take the other, and there'd be room for your cameras and all that business." Albert turned the key a few times and the 'old girl' seemed to be unsure about whether she wanted to start or not. "Come on my lover, it's just a jaunt down the pub, not that far!"

Victoria smiled to herself. Eccentric he may be; endearing, definitely.

Eventually, the Jaguar sprang into life with a deep rumbling purr, indicating she still had plenty of life in her. They made it safely down the hill to the village pub, before the car emitted a spectacularly loud backfire – like a gunshot – and stopped in the car park. "She'll be alright after a bit once she's got her breath back, but if not we can always get a lift home with one of my mates."

As she slid out of the car onto a rough and uneven car park, Victoria reflected on her earlier concerns about dressing up a bit more and decided that high heels would have been a disaster: boots, jeans and sweater had been just the right choice.

Albert ducked through the low entrance and held the door

open for her. She looked around the warm inviting space and wondered if the brewery supplied a standard design sheet on how to make your village pub look 'olde worlde'. A fire blazed in the deep-set hearth and Victoria speculated as to whether it was one of those realistic gas-effect ones, but a loud crackle and spit told her in no uncertain terms that it was the real thing. The beams twinkled with polished horse brasses and framed photos of village events from years gone by sat snug against the magnolia walls. It was charming, genuinely old and well cared for, and obviously a popular spot for a Thursday evening with hardly a spare chair to be seen.

"What a lovely place and it's so busy, must be the real centre of village life," she said to Albert, and then noticed he was frowning.

"Can't say it's usually quite this busy so early, must be some quiz night or something anyway, come on maid." Albert strode purposefully toward the bar and Victoria followed in his wake. "Evening Mudge, full house tonight then!" he said cheerily to the man behind the bar.

Victoria had spotted the landlords' names – 'Roger and Trudy Mudge' – above the door as they came in. Roger Mudge seemed very much a part of the fabric of his pub. His V-necked brown sweater blended nicely with the beams, and his beige cords were an almost perfect match for the walls. The carefully knotted tie was a suitably beery amber colour and sported a crest that could have been military but was more likely the product of a chain-store designer.

"Evening Albert," came the reply.

"So what's happening tonight then, must be quite something to get this lot in here? Trudy got a curry night on?"

Victoria watched as Albert leaned on the bar striking a nonchalant pose, then looked the other way to hide a smile as he stood up, scowling, and removed his elbow from a puddle of beer. Roger Mudge gave a small smile and pretended not to notice as he pulled a pint of beer, not needing to ask what the farmer wanted. "And for the lady?" he asked.

"Small glass of red wine please."

With a nod that seemed to say 'just as I thought', he poured the wine and set it on the bar. Victoria had no idea what it was, having been given no options, but was relieved to find it quite smooth.

Roger Mudge rearranged the bar towels, carefully mopping up the spill at the same time, and said, "Nothing so happy as those ideas of yours Albert, sadly a much more serious reason for a gathering of the clans. Tragedy, gossip and just plain curiosity."

Having failed miserably with the classic 'lean on the bar' pose, Albert attempted to winch himself halfway onto one of the high bar stools. Victoria had a sudden ridiculous vision of him sliding straight off the other side and landing in a heap on the floor. In an attempt to stop herself giggling she let out a sort of strangled hiccup, and both men looked questioningly at her. She returned their look innocently, then blew her nose on a tissue and tried to pretend nothing had happened.

"So what's the juicy gossip then Mudgers?" asked Albert.

Roger paused and seemed about to protest at the misuse of his surname but then thought better of it, adopting a very serious expression. "Sad news indeed," he said leaning forward, "old Henry Simmons was found dead today. Car was up on Haldon Hill. Henry dead as a doornail inside. Seems it was his allergy."

Victoria experienced a rush of heat to her face and a queasy feeling in her stomach. An unexpected death was always a shock, but to happen so soon after they had seen Henry? It didn't seem possible.

"Oh, that's awful!" she said. "We were with him just this

morning. When did this happen? And what allergies and…" she petered out as the full impact of the news hit her. Poor Grace and her two sons.

Roger looked intrigued by what she had said and she realised that the landlord and his pub were probably the epicentre for all local gossip, hence the gathering of locals after all the juicy details. And here she was, a complete newcomer, with first-hand titbits to contribute to this exciting news story.

Roger turned and called into the back. "Trudy, Trudeeeee, come here!" A neat, compact woman, with a typically English complexion, came bustling out of the kitchen. She wore sensible shoes, a tweed skirt and a pale pink blouse complete with a pussycat bow at the neck. Her mousy brown hair looked freshly set by the hairdressers. Although probably only in her late thirties she could have passed for a good ten years older.

"You called, Roger?"

"Come and listen, these two were with Henry just earlier today, they could have been the last ones to see him alive."

A glint of excitement shone in Trudy's eyes and Victoria recognised another enthusiastic gossip hound. "No, were you really?" Trudy looked at Victoria with something akin to respect.

"Haven't introduced you yet – apologies," Albert butted in. "Roger and Trudy Mudge, Victoria West, old Edith's niece, living in her cottage now."

Both Roger and Trudy nodded. "Ah yes, I saw you the other day riding on the back of Albert's tractor," said the latter without any trace of amusement, but Victoria still felt embarrassed.

"So, tell all then!" Roger continued. "Jeff, Ron, come and listen to this!" Roger was beckoning to some others in the bar and Victoria realised she was suddenly the centre of attention. She looked at Albert for help and he interpreted her look accurately and happily stepped into the limelight.

"It was nothing really. Ron, Jeff this is Victoria West by the way, you know, Edith's…," he waved vaguely at her. The two men nodded, and it seemed no further description was necessary.

Victoria wondered briefly if everyone in the pub already knew who she was and, like Trudy, had also enjoyed a view of her split M&S leggings as she'd bounced along the lanes hanging on to Albert. Oh the shame and indignity! She stared into her almost empty wineglass.

"So, why were you there then?" said Trudy, almost glowing with excitement at being so close to the heart of the action.

"Victoria here is doing some articles, she's a journalist you know." Albert said this proudly as if journalists were a rarity, and a few people nodded knowingly. "She's doing a write-up for one of those glossy country magazines, about Primrose Cottage, so she was interviewing the Simmons and taking pictures." This brought a combined mutter of approval; obviously being a journalist was creditworthy, but taking photographs gained extra points.

Victoria decided to brave another question. "So, what was this allergy? Did it cause him to crash the car?"

Roger leaned on the bar and adopted an expression of 'one who knows'. "Well we all knew he had this bee problem, one sting and he was a gonner. Poor chap had to carry one of those pens around with him and stab himself with it at the first hint of a bee! Imagine that… a distant buzzing and you'd feel panic rising in your chest!" He puffed out his cheeks and shook his head. "Poor bugger, obviously didn't have the pen thing on him."

"They are called epipens, Roger dear," said Trudy. "I know that because a cousin of mine has trouble with nuts."

Victoria frowned and started to say, "But…"

Trudy went on. "Peanuts dear, possibly cashews as well, I can't be 100 percent certain. Allergic reaction, you know that anna-fantastic thing where they blow up like a balloon and choke to death!"

Ron coughed and muttered "Bloody 'ell."

"Yes dear, but that's hardly as dangerous is it?" said Roger, gesturing to Victoria to pass him her empty glass, which he refilled without checking if she wanted more of the same or not. "A cashew nut isn't going to zoom over the bar and fly into your mouth now, is it? Night of the killer cashews!" Roger laughed heartily as though he hadn't heard a funnier comment in many a month (which he probably hadn't).

Trudy seemed put out that her link to someone as equally allergic as Henry had been somehow shown to be wanting. "Well, whatever their allergy, people do die if they don't have their epipens. I know at the Tiny Tots Crèche they have to have special training to cope with the number of children that have peanut allergies nowadays." This additional knowledge seemed to restore the status quo and Trudy smiled, looking content.

"So this epipen thing didn't work for poor old Henry then, and he got stung by a bee?" suggested Albert.

"That seems to be the way of it," replied Roger, taking Albert's empty glass and refilling it, also unbidden. "Can't be a pleasant way to go, but then what is?"

"Well, my brother..." began Jeff, but Albert waded in as if he hadn't spoken. "There's certainly plenty bees around at the moment." Trudy nodded in agreement. "Dratted things, conservatory's always full of them! Give me the heebie-jeebies, their great furry bodies and their stings! Killers!"

Jeff decided he'd been left out of things long enough and maligning bees was apparently one comment that had to be addressed. "No, no, I'll not have you puttin' down bees, no, it ain't their fault he was bloody 'lergic to 'em. Bees was 'ere before humans I'm betting. Wonderful things bees, vital part of nature and all, they are." Exhausted by this contribution, he leaned onto the bar and Victoria noticed that his elbow was sitting in a new puddle of beer created by Albert's second pint. Fortunately, she thought, the camouflage-style jacket he wore probably wouldn't ever register any extra dampness or stains.

An older woman with greying hair and pronounced teeth approached the bar and asked Roger for an orange juice and a port and lemon. "Can't think of a nicer way for the old misery to go. Can't say that my Jean and I will miss him one little bit!"

Victoria looked surprised and glanced at Albert for explanation as he slipped off the stool and turned to face the newcomer. "Not blethering on about him and that bleddy recipe again are you Martha Burnicombe? That's old news. You should show some respect for someone who's just died."

Martha sniffed with a great deal of feeling, picked up the two drinks Roger had rapidly produced and flounced off to a table in one of the alcoves.

"Who on earth was that?" Victoria asked in a hushed tone.

Roger and Trudy seemed to vie with each other for who had the most information on the tip of their tongue, then exchanged a silent look that seemed to give Trudy the nod.

"Well, Martha is Jean's sister, talk about peas in a pod! Only difference is that Jean works every hour God sends whereas Martha is a lazy good-for-nothing that just gossips and can't even be bothered to make a decent meal of an evening."

"But why so much animosity towards Henry? I know I only met him for ten minutes, and I'd agree he was a bit overbearing, but that seemed like real venom," said Victoria.

"Oh more bark than bite those two, you don't want to worry

too much about them," replied Trudy. "There's been a long-running spat where Jean says that Henry and Grace stole her grandmother's jam recipe and made a fortune out of it. If you can believe such a thing!" She looked to left and right, then continued. "Even if they had, then they made their money from running a factory and selling it on a big scale, getting the marketing right and all the rest of it, not just the mixture of fruits and sugar in some old recipe!" She rolled her eyes for dramatic effect.

Roger butted in. "My Trudy knows a bit about marketing and finance too, she worked in the bank's sales department. There was many a school leaver got their first bank account thanks to Trudy." He smiled proudly at his wife who looked coy, obviously touched by his endorsement.

Victoria took in the information and thought about poor Henry. He had been so full of the joys of spring only a few hours ago and hinting about that big scoop. And now it was all over. She wondered if she should offer her condolences to Grace and then thought better of the idea; maybe tomorrow, or in a few days.

Trudy was looking thoughtful. "I tell you what, it isn't half going to cause some ructions up at Primrose Cottage."

"Well, course it is, the man's gone and died! Daft beggar as he was, still a tragedy all ways round," said Albert.

"No," said Trudy, leaning forward in a conspiratorial way. "I meant... you know..." she twitched her head and made a moue of distaste. The others leant in too and Victoria wondered what on earth was coming next.

"You know... the power struggle!" she hissed.

Everyone fell back, disappointment expressed through a collective sigh. "Oh that," said Roger, "everyone knows about that, Trudy love!"

Trudy was looking petulant and, thanks to two glasses of wine,

Victoria piped up with, "Well I don't know much about it, other than the boys would like their parents to hand over control. Is that it?"

"Well, there's that but," Trudy went in for the lean again, "there's that Mandy Parkin too. She drew herself up and folded her arms.

"Who?" said Victoria.

"That bleddy woman we met in the lane this afternoon!" said Albert, impatiently.

"Oh her." She paused and then the light seemed to dawn. "Oh, her! The one with the big pair of…"

"Oh yes!" said Albert.

"I was going to say sunglasses!" finished Victoria, trying not to laugh.

Trudy was scowling at Albert for his cheek. "We all know she's got assets Albert, we can't deny that, but who exactly is she flashing them at? That's what I'd like to know!"

"Eh?" Now it was Albert's turn to scowl.

"Well, is she flashing them at Mr William or Mr John? And, of course, it's not just her physical assets. She's got her father's company to play with!"

"Play with my assets anytime she likes!" mumbled Jeff – or was it Ron? Trudy's look shamed them into silence. "That's what I mean when I say power struggle! A right turmoil in the dynasty, and I wouldn't be surprised if it got a bit nasty!" She pursed her lips and gave a satisfied nod.

Roger emitted a low whistle. "What a mind my Trudy's got, very sensitive to people she is. Rarely wrong about such things, you wait and see."

There was a brief hiatus as all pondered this revelation.

"So," said Albert, filling the silence. "What's good on the menu tonight then old Mudgers?"

Roger seemed to come out of a trance and again looked pained at Albert's familiarity before apparently deciding that, as the customer is always right, he'd best just accept it and say nothing. "All my Trudy's dishes are perfection, as you well know Albert."

Trudy basked in the affectionate look Roger gave her and smiled at Albert. "Well, speaking as the cook," she said, "if it was my choice, I'd say the lasagne turned out particularly well today and the steak and kidney pie is delicious as always." With that Trudy turned and left for the kitchen, secure in the knowledge that her cooking was good, her husband adored her and there'd be plenty more gossip to pick up from him later.

"Do you want to look at the menu or do you fancy either of those dishes?" Albert said, looking at Victoria.

Suppressing a smile, Victoria thought of the contrast between the wine bar she'd frequented after work with colleagues in London and the Swaddle Arms. The wine bar's menu had been expensive and pretentious and, when she'd so often just fancied something simple like lasagne, she'd had to choose foie gras or goat's cheese mille feuilles. She fancied having a browse through the full menu but thought she'd better play safe and choose one of the suggested dishes. She could check out the full menu some other night as she felt sure the Swaddle Arms was about to become her 'regular'. She opted for the lasagne as it had, apparently, turned out 'particularly well' today. (What, she wondered, did it turn out like on other days?)

Roger came round the bar and seemed to organise a table for them in seconds. Victoria felt slightly guilty as two aged characters in caps were 'moved on', none too subtly. Albert smiled and nodded to the two old boys. "Bill, Ben, alright?" They nodded enthusiastically and gave huge, toothless grins as they shuffled away to take up positions at the bar.

"Don't you worry about them. Both daft as a brush, but harmless," said Albert and waited for Victoria to settle herself. "So, what do you reckon to our local hostelry then?"

"It's charming! Just how you'd imagine a village pub to be."

Albert nodded. "True. It's been a bit up and down in the past, but with Roger and Trudy here, they know what they're at and they run a tight ship now. Keeps us locals happy and caters for you posh lot too, once the season gets going." Victoria didn't think she liked being bracketed with the 'posh lot' but she let it pass. She was feeling remarkably mellow and realised she'd come to the end of her second glass of wine.

The front door opened and Tufty nipped in and up to the bar, as quick and light on his feet as the red squirrel Victoria still associated him with. She must stop all these animal analogies, but even as she thought it, she noticed how like two wizened old toads Bill and Ben were, with their large eyes, wide gummy mouths and liver-spotted hands.

Roger had a pewter tankard filled and in front of Tufty before he'd even had time to perch on the bar stool.

"Cheers," said Tufty and took a huge swig.

Roger was looking serious. "Bad business," he said, and shook his head.

"What, old Henry?" Tufty fidgeted on his stool. "Too right! I can't understand it! He always had those epipen things on him. Usually at least one in the glove box too, I was always coming across 'em when we did a service."

"How was he when you saw him then?" asked Roger as he emerged from behind the bar to collect Victoria's empty glass.

"Who?" asked Victoria.

"Why, Henry of course!" he went back behind the bar and refilled her glass.

"Oh," she was confused. "Well, he seemed fine, why wouldn't he?"

"Just wondering if he was looking peaky, or if he looked sort of, haunted, you know?"

Victoria didn't and had no idea where this line of questioning was heading.

Albert snorted. "Don't be daft Mudge! How would you know you was about to peg it? You don't get advance warning, especially with something like that. Any of us could drop dead tomorrow, or right here at any second!"

"I do most sincerely hope not!" A cultured and rather mellifluous male voice came from the doorway. "I find funerals such emotionally draining affairs."

"Evening Reverend," said Albert and raised his still half-full glass in the direction of a slightly tubby, red-faced man in a dog collar who had walked up to the bar.

"Good evening Mr Moreton, and to you Tufty, and you Roger," he beamed and nodded his way around his immediate neighbours. A teddy bear, thought Victoria, fair and cuddly and rather sweet – she was doing it again! This animal obsession had to stop.

"Reverend, may I introduce Miss Victoria West?" said Albert rather formally, half rising and indicating Victoria.

"Ah yes, dear Edith's niece, I believe."

The vicar glided across the flagstone floor and shook her hand. She smiled warmly. "How we do miss Edith. She was a stalwart of the church flower rota and always such a voice of reason at testing times."

Victoria digested this information and thought that yes, her plain-speaking aunt probably would have made pithy comments on most issues of the day, but the flower rota was a surprise; she hadn't realised Aunt Edith was into flower arranging.

"Shall we be able to call on you to step into your aunt's shoes with regard to the flower rota?" asked the Reverend, hands clasped across his rather rotund midriff.

"Well, I'm not too sure really, I've no experience of flower arranging, but I'm willing to learn."

The Reverend flapped a hand and giggled. "Oh come now! I don't think Edith would claim any great prowess in that department, but she did like to 'do her bit' and keep some of the more, erm, shall we say, 'effusive' ladies in check!"

"What the Reverend is saying," Albert laughed, "is that Edith was a blooming awful flower arranger, she just used to bung 'em in a vase and hope! But she liked to keep tabs on any local tittle-tattle and make sure anything too way out got nipped firmly in the bud before it got hold!"

"Quite," said the Reverend and chuckled again, then moved back to the bar.

Just then, Trudy sailed out of the kitchen with two enormous plates of food and thumped them down on the table. "Good heavens!" said Victoria as she stared at the huge dish of lasagne in the middle of a plate, with salad on one side and chips piled up on the other.

Albert beamed and tucked his napkin into his collar. "There, proper food, see?" He waved his fork at his vast plate of steak and kidney pie, veg and mash. "That'll make up for you not having any breakfast!"

"That'll make up for a whole week of breakfasts!" said Victoria and wondered where on earth to start her assault on the steaming mountain of food.

From behind the bar, Roger said, "So Reverend, what d'you make of this sad news about Henry?"

The vicar sipped his red wine delicately and then set it down on the bar. "Terrible, terrible business, such a shock for the family, always so difficult to counsel at times like these." He pinched his lower lip between thumb and forefinger. "Such a forceful character too, his absence will be keenly felt." He sipped his wine again. "I shall of course visit the family tomorrow. I fear Grace will need considerable support at this time."

Albert made a sort of 'harrumphing' noise as he shovelled in a forkful of pie and Victoria hoped that she was the only person close enough to notice. They tackled their food in companionable silence. The lasagne was indeed good.

"So how's your old Morris then, Reverend?" said Tufty suddenly. Everyone seemed to perk up at this change of topic.

The Reverend beamed. "Gertrude? She's very well! Very well indeed!"

Another car with a name – are they all mad? thought Victoria. The Reverend was now in full flow discussing clutches, synchromesh gears and the problem of sourcing replacement parts.

"Rev's got an old Moggy Traveller," explained Albert, dabbing his mouth with his napkin, "keeps it tip-top he does."

Victoria noticed his plate was almost cleared. Her own seemed barely touched, although she felt fit to burst. She sat back to try and rearrange the contents of her stomach. "What's his name?"

"Who, the car?" said Albert.

"No! The Reverend, silly!"

"Ruminant."

"I'm sorry?" She sat forward again.

"Ruminant."

Victoria felt her mouth twitch and reached for her napkin to hide her smile. "He's Edwin Ruminant, the Reverend Edwin Ruminant. What's so funny?" Albert looked puzzled.

Victoria was shaking with silent laughter, and Albert gave her a stern look. Fortunately, Tufty and the Reverend were still engrossed in the complexities of maintaining a fifty-year-old car and were oblivious to her mirth. "The Reverend Ruminant?" she eventually managed to squeak, between painfully suppressed gales of laughter.

"Here now, steady on," said Albert jerking his head towards the vicar at the bar.

"I'm sorry," she said hoarsely, "I'm terribly sorry, it's very rude of me… but…" and she dissolved again.

"Now stop that!" said Albert, but his own face was starting to turn red and she could see he too was starting to shake with laughter. The pair of them sat, bent over the table in silent hysteria, neither able to stop. "Oh, I feel weak!" sobbed Victoria and tried to stem the flow. Albert wiped his eyes and cleared his throat, only to collapse again. After about five minutes, exhausted, tear-stained and uncomfortable, they finally managed to control themselves.

"Do you know, it's never struck me as funny before, but now you've brought it up…" Albert shook his head and cleared his throat again. "Dear me, what will folks think!" He ate the last bit of pie, but pushed the remaining vegetables to the side of the plate. "I'm done for, all that bleddy laughing!"

Victoria looked at her plate, a scene of devastation, not even half of it touched. "Oh dear, I can't eat any more. It was very good, I'm just not used to such huge portions."

"Don't you worry, often happens in here. I'll get Trudy to put it in a doggy bag and you can have it for your breakfast."

Cold lasagne for breakfast? Victoria didn't let her mind dwell on this thought or she felt she might well be sick. She already felt ridiculously tiddly after her three glasses of wine. The Reverend Ruminant! She must think of him as Edwin or she would never be able to face him without laughing. She felt she wanted to get to know him better; he seemed a lovely man. He was busy drawing some complex air diagrams and Tufty was nodding avidly. Both seemed oblivious to Victoria's ill-timed hysterics, and she was relieved.

"You want a pud?" asked Albert sitting back and patting his stomach.

"God, no! How can you even suggest it?"

"Nope me neither," he grinned, "but I thought it polite to ask! If you're ready for the off, I'll go and get the bill."

"We'll split it shall we?" she said, scrabbling in her handbag for her purse.

"Nope, you're alright. My treat."

"Oh no really..." she protested. But he held up a large hand. "Don't you worry. Think of it as a welcome dinner!" and strode over to the bar.

"What's the damage then, old Mudgers?" Roger beamed and scribbled out a receipt. He always enjoyed taking a punter's money.

"Doggy bag then?" Victoria jumped as she realised Trudy was clearing their table. "Oh, yes please! It was delicious... but..."

"Ah, don't worry, we're used to it," Trudy laughed. "All you upcountry people, you don't eat like we do. We're always bustling about and need refuelling! I expect you're sitting in front of a computer all day."

"Sadly, that is mostly true," agreed Victoria.

"Reheats very well does the lasagne, you can have it for breakfast!" She winked and trotted off towards the kitchen.

The thought of hot lasagne for breakfast was only slightly less upsetting than cold, but Victoria had to admit it had been very tasty; she just hadn't needed the side orders of chips, salad and hysterics. Gathering herself together, she met Albert at the bar. "That's very kind of you, thank you. My treat next time."

"Maybe," he said and began nodding to everyone and saying

goodbye.

Edwin Ruminant broke off from his conversation with Tufty. "My dear, going already, we've hardly spoken! May I call on you in the next day or so? It will be so pleasant to see April Cottage looking loved and lived in again."

"Of course Reverend, that would be lovely. I'll have the kettle on ready," and she felt she would be genuinely glad to see him. She could picture which chair he'd sit in and imagined he and Edith must have shared many a cup of tea in front of the Rayburn.

"After you," Albert held open the door and Victoria tottered rather unsteadily across the car park toward the bright yellow Jaguar.

"Hang on!" They turned in unison to see Trudy bustling out of the kitchen door brandishing a foil-wrapped package. "Wouldn't want you to go without your lasagne Victoria!" she beamed and pressed the still-warm package into Victoria's hands. "You see if I'm not right – will taste even better reheated tomorrow."

"That's very kind, thank you," said Victoria to the landlady's retreating back.

"Now," said Albert, patting the Jaguar's bonnet gently, "here's the thing. Will she start... or won't she?"

Chapter 5

It may only have been nine o'clock on a May morning, but the sun on Victoria's upturned face had real warmth in it. She took a deep breath and smiled as she surveyed the mass of wildflowers and shrubs in the pretty little garden. Pausing to sip coffee from one of her aunt's bone china cups felt rather wonderful. The peace and tranquillity of April Cottage was making her feel so good. Years of fighting cancer and the strain of keeping up with her London job had taken its toll, and she realised she'd lost the art of stopping and just enjoying the moment.

The garden was a little wild, but in among the colourful chaos various shrubs and plants were starting to burst into flower. She regretted not knowing their names, but they still looked amazing. That bluey-mauve flower climbing over the bank was gorgeous; she must look it up. A small bird landed on the bird table nearby, and again she felt guilty. She wasn't in the habit of leaving food for birds; there had been very few around her London home and it had never crossed her mind. She broke some of her digestive biscuit into pieces and threw them towards the bird table. The little brown bird held its head to one side and regarded her with a suspicious beady eye, then made a dive for the crumbs before anyone else could get to them. Within seconds another bird had joined in, and the crumbs vanished. She made another mental list: bird recognition books and bird food. She'd always dreamt of having pets; she loved animals, but living in a town on her own and working long hours had put paid to all that. Now she could at least learn some names and enjoy the birds living around her.

Her gentle reverie was interrupted by the shrill ring of her phone. She added 'change ring tone' to her mental list, and picked it up.

"Hello?"

"Could I speak with Victoria West please?" said a confident male voice.

"This is Victoria, how can I help?"

"Victoria, hi, this is John Simmons, we met the other..." John trailed off as Victoria jumped in to avoid embarrassment on his part.

"John of course, how are you, I am so sorry about your father."

"Heavens, these things happen. I was ringing you about that interview actually. We never did get everything finished. I think you needed a few more shots of the place, and we are very keen to make sure you meet your deadline."

Victoria paused and felt a little uncomfortable about how matter of fact he appeared to be in light of recent events. Maybe that was just his nature? "Oh, of course, the article. Well yes I am happy to carry on – but are you sure all the family will be OK with that?"

"Why on earth not? It's a marvellous chance for some national PR, I think anyone would be thrilled to have the opportunity. So long as we avoid funeral day, it should be fine – would look a bit disrespectful and all that jazz."

"Fine, OK, if you're happy, when would you like me to come over?"

"Well soon as, really. Are you free, say, this afternoon?"

She took a deep breath and mentally shrugged. "Very well, if that's what you would like. Say two-thirty so I have time to talk to some of the staff before they leave?"

"Yes that would be fine, see you then." The phone immediately went dead and Victoria was left feeling a little sad that a son could be so apparently unaffected by his father's death.

She finished her coffee and threw the remaining pieces of biscuit at the small bird, still hanging about expectantly. The next problem was, of course, how to get to the factory. For heaven's sake she thought: satnav can get you there perfectly well – just get on with it! It was only nine-thirty, so plenty of time to review her notes and get organised. It was really important to make that call to the internet people; she was desperate to get her broadband connection sorted out. And another box or two might get unpacked as well if she made an effort.

It seemed prudent to leave plenty of time for the journey. She tried to remember how long it had taken Albert, but it was all a bit vague. Surely it must have taken at least thirty minutes or even three quarters of an hour. If she was too early she could always park somewhere and read or look at the view. Being late was something she hated with a passion.

Victoria managed to review her notes, unpack two boxes and spend a fruitless twenty minutes on hold on her mobile while the telephone company failed to respond to her enquiry, despite an automated voice repeatedly telling her how important her call was to them. She reheated half of the lasagne and was pleased that Trudy's claim turned out to be true; it did taste even better second time around!

Then, checking her camera equipment was safely stowed and that she had phone, notebook, laptop (in case) and every other possible item, she sat in the car at one-thirty and set the satnav with the correct address. She tutted with irritation as a ten-minute journey was predicted. That's just why you can't rely on satnav in the country, she thought. It probably takes you over some impassable river or via a dead end that may indeed be ten minutes as the crow flies but, as she knew from the last journey, not in reality!

Leaving the satnav settings as they were, she drove slowly along the main lane. White bluebell-like flowers tumbled down the banks and once again she thanked her aunt for enabling this lovely new start in her life. She pottered along, enjoying the quiet road and the peacefulness. Coping with motorways and central London traffic when she next needed to visit the city would be horrible.

A short stretch of dual carriageway surprised Victoria, but in no time the road started to reduce to two lanes. At the very last moment a flashy red sports car tried to overtake – and just succeeded – before the next bend, making her brake sharply. Her heart thudded double time and she glared angrily at the red car. She realised, looking more carefully at its back end as it disappeared into the distance, that it was the same car Albert had forced to back up on their last visit to Primrose Cottage. She muttered various aggressive phrases and then laughed at her grumpiness. Life was too short to get wound up by stupid drivers and yes, if she was honest, she felt a small stab of jealousy at not being a 'flashy red sports car' owner herself.

The annoying voice inside her satnav announced that in 300 yards she would reach her destination. What? Already? She looked at the clock and, sure enough, the journey had taken her just over ten minutes. She couldn't arrive three-quarters of an hour early; and how could it be a really simple ten-minute drive, when Albert had fought with back lanes and byways for over half an hour? Albert! She shook her head, smiling.

It seemed ridiculous to sit and twiddle her thumbs, so she dialled Primrose Cottage and waited. As she did so her eyes travelled across the line of parked cars and alighted upon a red sports car, just like the one that had cut her up.

"Primrose Cottage Preserves, how can we help you?" A nervous little voice recited the well-rehearsed words.

"Could I speak to John Simmons please? It's Victoria West here."

"Oh yes, his two-thirty, just one moment."

"Hi, Victoria." His voice was really rather attractive. He sounded so confident and sure that all was right with his world.

"John I am so sorry, my journey was much quicker than I thought, I'm actually here already. Is there any chance we could start our meeting earlier? I can of course just come back at two-thirty as planned."

After a slight hesitation, he said, "Good Lord, come on in now, you can join us in a spot of lunch, nothing important happening."

"Charming! Don't mind me then!" came a fainter female voice, obviously in the same room.

There was a hurried, "I'll see you shortly then" from John and the phone was put down.

Victoria frowned. Whose was the other voice, and what did she mean? Still, she was pleased to get on with the interview sooner rather than later. If she got back in good time she wanted to explore the village more and perhaps go for a walk.

The receptionist waved Victoria into John's room and instantly she felt glad she had left the cumbersome camera gear in the car and not arrived like a loaded donkey. Opposite John's desk sat a very glamorous brunette. Her dress was red and showed (to Victoria's mind) an inappropriate amount of cleavage for a work environment. She was tapping her fingers in an abstracted way on the desk and, judging by her body language, was not remotely thrilled to see Victoria.

"Victoria, marvellous, do join us, have you met Mandy? Mandy Parkin, Victoria West. Victoria is the journalist who's going to give us some great media coverage. Maybe if you play your cards right she could do the same for your company!" His soft laugh implied he thought this highly unlikely. Victoria detected a hidden agenda and felt uncomfortably excluded.

"John, had I realised you had other plans this lunchtime, I wouldn't have taken up so much of your precious time. Have your little tête-à-tête and I hope you," here she flung a hard look at Victoria, "enjoy the rather sub-standard canteen sandwiches and the cheap bottle of wine more than I did!" She snatched up her handbag and flounced out of the room, leaving Victoria and John looking at each other in embarrassment. A few seconds later there came a loud throaty roar as the red sports car left the car park in a cloud of dust and gravel.

"Ah, slightly awkward," said John. "I do apologise, I didn't think Mandy would mind. Now do sit down. Let's talk while we eat, shall we?"

Feeling distinctly uneasy, Victoria walked over to the chair so recently vacated by Mandy and wondered what to say.

"Girlfriends, who'd have 'em, eh?" John said, perhaps feeling less calm than he appeared. "Now then, ham or corned beef sandwich?"

She could see Mandy's point about canteen sandwiches; she couldn't remember the last time she had eaten corned beef. Taking a ham sandwich she silently bit into the slightly damp white bread. She was glad she hadn't been expecting any food and soon put the sandwich aside. "So John, are you sure you feel up to being interviewed, so soon after your father's death? It could wait a while."

"Oh that, no, my father going won't interrupt things here. It's 'business as usual'. To be frank Victoria, he was more of a hindrance than a help towards the end, so no great loss really."

Victoria winced at his callousness and felt sorry for such a dysfunctional family.

"He had such great pie-in-the-sky plans for the company," continued John.

"Yes," Victoria butted in, "he mentioned a scoop for me, as though there was something truly exciting just around the corner?"

"Ah yes, topic of great debate among the family, not his most popular move to put it politely."

"Really? What had he planned?"

"He wanted out, can't blame him, that many years of jam selling is enough for anyone. But he decided we should sell up to Berry Brothers who are huge, as you know, and they would just swallow up the company, use the brand name and pay him a lot of money."

"Oh right, I see," said Victoria, not knowing quite the right response.

"Well, fine for the old boy and Mother of course, they could swan off into the sunset with shedloads of dosh. But for the lesser mortals like their sons with a minimal amount of shares, there would be barely a brass farthing and no job."

"Oh dear," repeated Victoria now even more unsure about what to say or do.

"No, William and I deserve a damned sight more respect than that and happily we managed to pull the plug on the deal so no harm done. I just couldn't allow that to happen!"

"So, with his death...?" Victoria tailed off. She took a corned beef sandwich and, after one bite, really wished she hadn't.

"I have far better plans for the company long-term, just a case of getting Mother on board, convincing William and we're away. This may still be a scoop for you, but just not the one Father expected to announce." He sat back in his chair and swivelled it, like a fidgeting schoolboy, then sat forward again and looked Victoria in the eyes as if he'd made a decision to trust her. "I am hoping we can negotiate a merger with another local company and it will increase our operation by 150 percent." John slowed and looked to Victoria for an appreciative response.

"Right, I see. Wow!" she floundered, still unsure as to the appropriate reaction.

"Mind you, I may have to smooth troubled waters after today, can't have helped you coming in like that, rather stupid of me." He looked out of the window pensively (probably planning his apology gift, Victoria thought). "I'm sorry," she said. "I've lost the plot a little – why did I cause a problem?"

"Mandy," he said looking amazed, as if she should realise the obvious, "Mandy is the owner – since the death of her father – of Janner's Jams, the local company I was referring to. She's a sensitive soul, so I may have to smooth ruffled feathers later."

"Of course. Well, I'm sorry if my early arrival caused any friction, naturally I had no idea. How about pressing on to get the interview over so you can make amends, and I can wander round the factory and get some photographs to illustrate the article?"

Trying to keep John on a topic was a Herculean task. He was obsessed with statistics and margins, gains and percentages, none of which would be of the slightest interest to a Country Days reader. She managed some useful notes on the history of the company, but felt a further conversation with Grace might get a more reader-friendly version of a long and ultimately successful business struggle. She was hesitant to write anything about future plans as there seemed to be a difference of opinion as to what that was going to be, and she felt a more general upbeat end to the article would be best.

"Right, now for some photos," said Victoria, rising from her seat and trying to hurry John along.

"Oh, do you feel you have enough?" John seemed disappointed that his monologue had been interrupted.

"Masses, you've been endlessly helpful – thank you so much!"

"Well you only have to ask – just ring and get Marilyn to put you through, always available!" John smiled, sure that his charm had carried him through the interview as, no doubt, he thought it did his whole life. A spoilt child, thought Victoria. Grace obviously didn't say 'No!' often enough to either of her boys when they were growing up.

Just at that point Marilyn came bursting into the office without knocking. "Oh Mr John, Mr John! Please forgive me for disturbing your meeting like this but that courier is here again and he is really insistent that the package can only be signed for by you, like last time."

John sighed and waved Marilyn away. "No matter woman, I'll come down and sign; we were just about finished anyway. Now go and tell him to wait. Their ridiculous over-protectiveness really annoys me."

Marilyn scuttled away and Victoria couldn't help herself looking enquiringly at John. "Oh it's no big deal," he said. "Just a consignment of bees. For some ridiculous reason they want to deliver them to an individual addressee, not the company, can't think why but I'd better go and attend to it." He moved quickly past her and went downstairs.

John seemed rattled by the delivery and she wondered why he was ordering bees? How curious to be able to order living things and have them delivered, just like a book or a supermarket order. Victoria assumed it was to boost the hives that produced Primrose Cottage honey; she'd seen them lined up along the edge of the factory's land, backing onto open farmland. But surely they had a specialist beekeeper to handle that – why would the financial director order them? And with a shudder she thought of Henry and his bee allergy. Poor man; had having bees here, near his home, been a constant worry for him and Grace? She suspected she was being an ignorant townie and pushed her concerns aside.

Victoria negotiated her way back to reception and retrieved her camera gear from the car. She walked into the factory, feeling a bit apprehensive, and wondered who to talk to. Then she saw Jean waving and gratefully trotted over to a packing area.

"Hello Jean – how nice to see you."

"Hello Victoria, you after some photographs for this article of yours? You know who you want to take pictures of?"

"Well I'm not really sure," replied Victoria, "you know everyone better than me, I don't suppose you could spare me five minutes to help out?"

Jean seemed to grow a couple of inches taller and puffed out her chest importantly. "Why of course, nothing here that can't wait a while."

"What I would really like is a group shot of some of the workers who've been here the longest, loyal troops sort of thing?"

"Well," said Jean, "ask me that five year ago and I would have had a right gang for you, but Mr Henry has been a bugger for the last year or two and all of us old ones have been put out to pasture or made to go part-time. Valued youth over experience did that man, can't say many will mourn his popping off."

"Oh Jean, the poor man isn't even buried yet."

"Well I say it like it is and he were a bit of a bully." Jean looked a little abashed, but continued, "I know the world laughs about him stealing my Mum's recipe but he did so and he laughed the most of all. He's gone and I can't say I'm sorry, nor I imagine will his sons, every bit as scheming as their Dad they are. They can strut about and rule the roost now instead of being under his thumb, must be the best news they've had in ages."

Victoria was surprised by her attitude. "Oh dear – well, I don't know all the details obviously Jean, but I really don't like to speak ill of the dead." She took a deep breath. "Anyway, let's get a group photo and then I'll take some of the jam saucepan things."

Victoria snapped away including a lovely shot of five somewhat bemused factory workers who didn't quite know why they had been randomly selected, but posed anyway. Victoria suspected that Jean had chosen mates and people who might owe her a favour now they were going to be in a magazine. She also managed some nice close-up action shots of staff working, concentrating on their tasks and ignoring her camera. These were the sort of photos she liked best.

"Thanks Jean, that was really helpful."

"You're welcome my dear," replied Jean.

"I'll be off now. I'm going to drop in on Grace and just make sure she's OK."

"That'll be fun!" said Jean laughing. "I'm sure Grace will have the stage nicely set for her role as the poor widow!"

Unable to think of a reply to such bluntness, Victoria simply said "I'll see you on Tuesday then," swept up her camera equipment and walked back to the car.

It was sad that there was so much antagonism between the Simmons family and one (or was it more?) of their workers. Maybe this was just the management-versus-worker 'them and us' divide, on a greater scale than usual. She settled into the car, having safely stowed all the gear, and felt her tummy rumble. The sandwiches had been really ghastly, and selfishly she wondered if Grace might have any cake if she stayed for tea. She started the car and, feeling rather foolish, drove the fifty yards to Grace's house.

She knocked tentatively on the front door and waited. She was sure Grace would be in, but would she feel up to visitors? She pondered how lonely and terribly empty life must be if you had been married to someone for forty-odd years and then – so unexpectedly – found yourself alone. She was used to living on her own, and rather liked it on a good day, but Grace must be in pieces.

After a few moments Grace opened the door and looked surprisingly good, all things considered. Her hair was immaculate as usual and she wore little make-up, which altered her appearance somewhat. But no red eyes or swollen nose from continuous crying, as Victoria might have expected.

"Grace forgive me, I just wanted to drop over to see if there's anything I can do… some shopping, or bring you some food? I'm so sorry for your loss." Victoria stumbled a little, hating those formulaic words expected at times of great tragedy.

"Oh bless you Victoria, how kind," adding, after a moment, "well, won't you come in?"

They walked through a hallway that was almost surgically clean. The wood laminate floor would not have looked out of place in an operating theatre; there was not a mote of dust in sight. On entering the living room (just as clinical), Victoria thought it was more like a stage set than a house. There was a strategically placed box of tissues next to the chaise longue, dark glasses and a glass and bottle of mineral water on a small table beside it. Victoria hid her smile. So Jean had been right: the stage was set for the role of grieving widow.

Grace reclined on the chaise longue and invited Victoria to sit in the adjacent floral print chair. "It's so very kind of you to come," she said with a slight hint of melodrama. "It has all been so sudden – and such hard news to take in."

Victoria nodded and said, "Yes obviously, it must be the most difficult time for you." She again had to repress a slight smile as Grace put on the dark glasses, adding a dramatic air to her appearance. "Goodness knows, the man had his faults, don't we all? But he was my life, my man. What's that wonderful song – 'Stand by your man'? Well, I did and I always will."

Victoria was getting really annoyed with herself. This was the saddest of times and she was finding it hard not to see the funny side of it. Here was a truly bereaved widow. Be kind, Victoria, she told herself (despite the Dior sunglasses and references to old country songs being a little over the top).

"I truly don't know quite where I will turn now. Henry was my everything and now I am alone."

"I do hope things feel a little easier once the funeral has passed." Victoria wasn't completely sure of the correct thing to say.

"Of course it was a peril we both lived with night and day, his allergy you know. A bee could have taken him at any time. We knew he was living on the edge." This was accompanied by the pressing of a limp hand on her forehead and a pronounced sniff. "I wish dear Edith had still been here. She was always my rock, so comforting and so straightforward. She understood love in all forms and knew just how hard Henry and I had fought to get where we did."

Victoria wished Aunt Edith were here now too; she was feeling very out of her depth. And what was all this 'understanding love in all forms' business?

Grace continued, theatrically wiping her eyes behind her sunglasses. "I looked at him when I identified him you know, and all I could remember was the handsome young man who'd made my heart flutter so many years ago. It was all so exciting."

"What, the identification?" said Victoria, confused once again.

"No dear." Cue another sniff, almost breaking into a sob. "I meant when we met, our love, our life."

"Oh yes, of course. I do sympathise with you over the identification thing. I had to identify my parents after their car accident and I felt unwell for weeks. Every time I closed my eyes the image was there." Even now Victoria felt her stomach lurch at the thought.

"Oh the worst is that they have to do post mortems and goodness knows what. The coroner, the police, the list of intrusions is endless. I explained to them about his allergy and how just one of those wretched creatures could take his life in minutes, but of course they want to check. It seemed so obvious to me, bless him; his face and mouth were so swollen and discoloured."

At this point Victoria felt she had reached the end of her small-talk abilities and thought she should make a move. Poor Grace obviously needed time and space. "Is there anything I can help with? Do you need any food shopping?" she offered.

"Oh no my dear, I simply couldn't eat or drink a thing. I'm just numb really until we can at least bury my beloved Henry." Victoria took this as her cue to leave and felt rather glad to do so.

Back in her car, Victoria set off for the village. After only a few hundred yards, she came to a junction and confidently turned left, recognising the granite post at the corner. After about a mile, she came to a crossroads. There was a signpost pointing back the way she'd come, another pointing toward the town of Westerley and two directions unmarked. Well, neither of those names was any use to her, so she followed her instinct and turned left down an unmarked road.

After about a mile she had to reverse for a very elderly woman in a VW Beetle, who chugged resolutely on at about five miles per hour and, Victoria feared, would have continued at this pace straight into her bonnet had she not reversed very swiftly into a gateway. The old woman drove sedately past without thanks or any obvious acknowledgement of the other vehicle.

Next, Victoria came to a signpost that stated confidently that 'Swaddlecombe' was only two miles. It wasn't. After at least a mile, another post directed her right for a further two miles. Five minutes later Victoria came to the predictable conclusion that she was lost again. Fortunately the lanes were lovely, meandering and almost car-free. She was enjoying the opportunity to let her mind freewheel as she thought about Grace, Aunt Edith, her parents...

Suddenly she popped out between two high banks and found herself in the village street. How on earth had that happened? She caught a glimpse of a small shop and pulled into the kerb. Yes, she was in what passed for Swaddlecombe's high street. About fifty yards away sat the Swaddlecombe Arms; she could see the church down a lane off to her left and Tufty's garage further on along the road.

She had glimpsed the shop before as she'd flashed past with Albert and, having a faded memory of visiting it as a child, was keen to see what it had to offer these days. She got out of her car and looked at the front of Swaddlecombe's 'General Stores'. Interesting. It wasn't clear exactly what it sold but there was a basket of what looked like junk outside the front door waiting to be collected... a rural recycling scheme, perhaps?

An old-fashioned bell above the door tinkled as she walked in. Three pairs of matching blue eyes all blinked at her inquisitively through identical round spectacles, like young owls in a nest box. "Hello," she ventured, "I've just moved in and, as I was passing, I thought I'd pop in and see what you stocked."

"Oh yes dear," said the tallest of the three women. "We knew you would."

An interesting response, Victoria mused. They must be sisters; they were all so similar. If they weren't slightly different heights you'd be hard pressed to tell them apart. Then she noticed each one had a different arrangement of pale grey plaits. The tallest had earphones (Victoria hadn't seen these since her old high school music teacher had worn them). The middle one had one long plait wound into a bun near the top of her head, while the shortest woman wore them coiled around her head like an Alice band.

"My name is…"

"Oh we know who you are dear," said the middle-sized one, "you're Victoria, Edith's niece."

Victoria smiled nervously. "Well, you have me at a disadvantage there, because I'm afraid I don't know your names…?"

"I am Dahlia," said the tallest one.

"I am Iris," said the middle one.

"I am Lavender," said the shortest who, unnervingly, had the deepest voice and spoke in almost a whisper.

"We are the Drewe sisters and yes, before you ask, we are triplets," said Dahlia. And your parents must have been keen gardeners, thought Victoria, with a smile. All three gave her a little bow in unison. Victoria felt at any minute they might burst into a song-and-dance routine, a sort of rustic version of the Beverley sisters.

"So dear, how are you enjoying living in our little corner of Devon?" This from Iris.

"It's a lovely part of the world and everyone is very friendly."

"Yes. Friendly. We saw you on the back of that Albert Moreton's tractor the other day," said Lavender huskily and without a trace of a smile. "You was hanging on well."

"Yes, well you see…" Victoria began, but another sister cut in before she could excuse herself. "That's the trouble with all those trendy outfits dear, you never know when they might let you down," this was Dahlia. "Personally, I don't hold with trousers of any kind. Women were designed for skirts. But there, I know I'm old-fashioned and people laugh at me!" All three trilled with laughter before turning their collective wide-eyed gaze on her again.

"You're probably right," Victoria nodded and felt that if she didn't move the topic away from her choice of clothing she might lose the will to live. Looking around the shop she spotted tins and packets covering essential items from salt to safety pins, custard powder to kitchen roll, all stocked on very traditional shelving behind the counter. There was even a ladder to help the sisters reach the top shelves – it was wonderfully old-fashioned.

There were some nods to the twenty-first century: a chiller cabinet held milk, butter and cream with salad stuff and some vacuum-packed meats, while a freezer stocked ice cream and frozen veg. So, if all else failed or they got snowed in, Victoria thought, they'd probably survive.

At one end, she spotted jars of sweets and was delighted to see sherbet lemons, humbugs and barley sugars. She smiled as so many happy childhood memories flooded back. "Ah yes dear, everyone likes the sweetie corner," said Iris. "Go on, have some sherbet lemons!"

"Do you know, I think I will!" said Victoria and watched, fascinated, as a quarter was tipped into an old-fashioned set of scales, complete with weights. Was that still legal these days? She didn't care; it was lovely. As Iris flipped over the paper bag to twist the corners and handed it to her, she felt about nine again and ready to part with a sixpence.

"Thank you!"

"That Albert, he likes humbugs," said Lavender, nodding earnestly.

"Does he? Well, I'll take him a quarter as a present. He drove me over to Primrose Cottage the other day and I really should say thank you."

Six blue eyes swivelled round to stare at her in perfect unison. "We heard you were there," said Dahlia, "you must have been one of the last people to see him alive."

"Well, I suppose so yes. But Grace was there too as he left, and well…"

"He's dead. The jam man is dead." Lavender, like a slowly tolling bell, stated the obvious, confirming Victoria's rapidly forming opinion that this sister was possibly not the sharpest knife in the box.

"Yes he is, poor man," said Victoria, hoping that might close the discussion.

"He wasn't a poor man. He was a rich man. I didn't like him…" She added as an afterthought "much."

"Yes dear, we know, he was rather sharp with you on occasion but there, we can't all have the patience of a saint!" said Iris brightly.

"He was with that Grace. I don't like her." Victoria waited for the 'much', but it didn't come.

Clearly, Grace was even more unpopular with Lavender Drewe than her late husband had been. "Well of course he was with Grace dear, he was married to her," Dahlia scowled at her sister.

"No. She was with that Janner."

Now Victoria was confused. How could Grace be with Janner?

"The one you said was John's father. You know." Lavender looked at her two sisters challenging them to correct her.

"What are you talking about, Lavender?" Iris patted her bun nervously.

"That man, the one who made jam," she said starting to sound slightly agitated.

"Good lord! That was years ago! That was Janner Parkin! Grace was never married to him. She went out with him when they were young, that's all. Then she married Henry. You're not on form today dear!" laughed Dahlia.

Iris chipped in. "You've got your wires crossed. You've done a Doctor Who and landed your Tardis in the wrong decade!" She gave a squawk like a chicken and she and Dahlia laughed uproariously at the joke. "We like the Doctor," said Iris turning to Victoria.

"Especially that Scottish one, never missed an episode. Dahlia had a 'thing' about his legs, didn't you dear?"

"Oh yes. I do like a man with long legs." She nodded and rearranged some sticks of liquorish. "He had nice thighs."

"We're keen on soaps too. Do you watch any soaps dear? Our favourite is probably Corrie, followed by Emmerdale. But we don't hold with Eastenders. Too common," said Iris, who had started dusting the top of the chiller cabinet.

Victoria realised that if she didn't change the subject she was going to get the giggles. "So, being new here, could you just recap, who was Janner Parkin?"

"Ah well, there's more than one jam dynasty around here dear. The first one was called Janner's Jams and they did quite well. And then Primrose Cottage started up."

"I don't like jam," stated Lavender. "I prefer toffee."

Victoria couldn't quite reason that one out, although she suspected there was a link, but decided to let it go. She popped a sherbet lemon into her mouth the better to contemplate this statement. The sweet sharpness was exquisite and it took all her willpower not to crush it and feel the sherbet explosion on her tongue.

"I've had a good idea!" said Dahlia suddenly, slapping her hand down on the counter and they all, Victoria included, turned to look at her. "Lavender dear, I think it's time you sorted through your special offers, don't you?"

Iris nodded and muttered, "Good idea!"

Lavender nodded slowly as the idea sank in. "You're right. I should check the display. Make sure everything is in the right place. It needs to be properly presented." She walked slowly round behind the counter, lifted the flap and emerged next to Victoria. The floral dress and beige cardigan that Victoria had noticed were now revealed to sit atop a pair of bright pink tights, white ankle socks and yellow Crocs.

"She has such an eye for colour!" said Dahlia, proudly.

"Yes, I can see that. How much do I owe you for these sweets?" said Victoria, savouring the sherbet that had at last seeped through the hard sugary shell. "Oh and I'd better get some milk and other bits and pieces," she said as she crunched up the remainder of the sweet.

Just then the bell tinkled and all three sisters paused and looked around. "Good afternoon Mrs Simmons," said Dahlia reverently.

Victoria turned, expecting to see Grace, but instead faced a short, attractive woman with a mass of auburn hair that fell in loose curls past her shoulders. She had classic redhead colouring: pale, clear skin and green eyes, with a smattering of freckles across her nose. Cleverly applied make-up served to enhance her naturally pretty features still further.

"Hello," said Victoria.

"Hello," said the woman. She looked at Dahlia and smiling, said, "I've come to collect my order, if you'd be so kind Miss Drewe."

"Of course dear," said Dahlia. "Just give me two ticks, I was just finishing serving Miss West here."

"Oh call me Victoria, please. Could I have two pints of milk? Do you have skimmed?"

Dahlia looked like someone had just trodden on her bunion. Victoria heard a giggle and turned to see the redhead trying to hide her smile. "Oh dear that's another strange lady wanting that watery milk! You really will have to order some at this rate! Semi-skimmed is as good as it gets," she smiled, "anything else is a bit avant garde for Swaddlecombe."

Dahlia, still looking pained, said, "Well, there's never been that much call for it, but if Miss West, Victoria, is going to want it too, then maybe…"

"Goodness me! You've only just moved in and already you're making radical changes to our traditional way of life!" She pulled an ironic face and shook her head, laughing. "I'm Nicole Simmons by the way."

"Pleased to meet you! You must be William's wife?"

"For my sins," said Nicole.

Victoria laughed. This woman was fun. Turning back to Dahlia she said, "Well, could I have two pints of your excellent semi-skimmed then, a pack of streaky bacon, four tomatoes and that rather nice-looking loaf please."

"Do I detect a bacon sarnie?" asked Nicole, sotto vocce.

"I'm afraid so! I haven't really got to grips with the Rayburn yet and I'm not a great one for cooking anyway," confessed Victoria.

"Is that the lot dear?" asked Iris who had been adding up the purchases as her sister put them in a bag.

"Yes thank you."

"That's £7.40, but of course as a resident, you are most welcome to have an account with us," said Iris, clasping her hands as if in prayer.

"Well, that's unusual these days. Let me pay this time but I'll let you know." She handed over a tenner, took the change, smiled and prepared to leave, Lavender preceding her through the door. Outside she stopped both to survey the scene and to wait in the hope that Nicole might emerge so they could continue their chat.

She had liked her immediately.

She realised Lavender was painstakingly removing all the bits of junk out of the basket. She inspected each item carefully, as if looking for damage, but as all the items were old (and many broken) this seemed a bit pointless. Sensing Victoria's gaze, she said, without looking up "These are my 'special offers'. You'd be surprised how many people buy them. Last week I sold a lid and a Mills & Boon book. But not the blue slipper. Which was odd."

"I see. Where do you get your special offers from?"

Victoria felt sad for this elderly inadequate woman, but at the same time somehow felt Lavender was probably quite happy in her life. It seemed undemanding and she had her sisters to care for her.

"Every Tuesday, I get on the bus to Westerley and I go to the car boot sale. Other times, I go to jumble sales round about. I love it." She turned to Victoria. "There's nothing I like more than rummaging. I'm very happy when I rummage. Or when I'm making toffee. I like that a lot too."

The shop bell rang and Nicole stepped out with a box of groceries in her arms. "Ah, I see you've been entranced by Lavender's special offers, you lucky thing!"

"Yes, although I'm not sure I need anything just at the moment."

"You say that now, but I guarantee you she'll have something you need before long! A button that matches one you lost years ago, a cup that completes an old teaset or perhaps just an old recipe book that you had when you were a student. You have all sorts, don't you Lavender?"

And then Lavender smiled. It was a slow process, but eventually it stretched across her whole face; and in that moment you could see she was the prettiest of all the sisters. There was a lovely openness and innocence about her.

"Thank you Nicole. I'll keep looking for that bottle top for you."

"Good girl, thank you! Right, we must trot on. Time for a drink?" She began walking slowly down the street. Victoria looked stunned until she realised Nicole was addressing her. "Oh, what, me, now?"

"Well, I certainly didn't mean 'care in the community' back there!" and Nicole laughed again, her slightly unkind comment clearly only said in affectionate jest. "Good God, give dear old Lavender a sniff of the hard stuff and I dread to think what might happen! She's a dear really. They all are, in their funny old way." She stopped. "Surely, it must be getting on for six – can't we justify a quick glass of something white and chilled?" She cocked her head on one side and Victoria knew before it happened that her brain was going to say Nicole, bright-eyed and red-haired, was 'like a robin': and it did. She really was going a bit batty. Must be the country air. Not enough petrol fumes.

Chapter 6

"There you are," said Nicole as she put the two large glasses of white wine down on the table in front of Victoria. "Only Mudge's best Chardonnay I'm afraid, but perfectly drinkable – mind you I'll drink almost any wine if it's cold enough."

"Cheers!" The two women clinked glasses.

"I've met most of the Simmons family over the last few days, it's to do with an article I'm writing about the business," Victoria explained. "I even met Henry, just before, well…"

"Ah yes, poor Henry." Nicole, raised her glass to her late father-in-law, but that was all she said.

"Well, this is very pleasant," said Victoria, smiling at this pretty woman and wishing she had both her figure and that amazing fiery waterfall of hair. She decided ruefully that colour and cut would be outside her budget, so she'd have to make do with her current hairdresser. Then she remembered that using a hairdresser in London, no matter how reasonable, would be far from practical. Perhaps she could ask Nicole about hers?

"Would it be terribly rude," Victoria said tentatively, "if I asked where you had your hair done? I can't take my eyes off it – the colour and the styling are just gorgeous!"

"Not rude at all and thank you for the compliment," smiled back Nicole. "I go to Andrew in Newton Abbot – he's a complete genius. I had to find somewhere half decent when I moved down here. I missed London stylists and fashion – well, just London everything frankly."

"Have you been down here long? I spoke to William and John about the business but really didn't discuss anything too personal with them, so I hadn't realised William's wife would be someone as glamorous as you!"

"Oh get on with you! I just try hard. I hope that if I fight my way to the gym every day and focus on what might be, then I might just find my way back into acting in the not-too-distant future."

"Acting? Wow I was right, very glamorous, might I have seen you in anything?" Victoria felt impressed but at the same time bemused that anyone so vivacious could be married to William, who seemed to her to be one of the most boring men on the planet.

"Christ no," laughed Nicole, "I did rep for quite a while back in the day and then was a regular on a daytime soap that I hope you are way too young and intelligent to have ever stayed in to watch!"

"Oh well, yes soaps have never been my thing really. Tell me more about how you met William, or am I being too nosy?"

"Not nosy, just curious. I'll get my own back in a mo and grill you too." Both women laughed with easy familiarity.

"William and I met at a party, bit run of the mill really," Nicole looked ruefully at Victoria. "I wish I had a romantic story to tell about where we met – by the Trevi Fountain, or tripped over each other by the Eiffel Tower – but no, just introduced at a party. I thought he was good looking, majorly polite and he flattered me big time. When he asked to drive me home I was totally overawed by his car – he had an E-Type Jaguar, and I thought I was in love! A few nights with too much wine and stories of his amazing family business in Devon and I thought I'd captured a big fish with big ambitions. Too late I realised he was just a minnow in a very small pond, a bored, spoilt elder son with a mother who would do anything for him."

Victoria frowned and felt a little embarrassed at her new acquaintance's frankness. "You don't sound very happy."

"That would be because I am not. Not one bit. Life is at a complete standstill for me. I can see thirty fast receding into the distance and forty only a few years away and my acting career will be over." Nicole sighed as though life imprisonment awaited her.

"Did you not want to have a family?" Victoria hesitated as, although she felt very comfortable with Nicole, this might be a step too far.

Nicole looked at her with a puzzled expression. "But I do have a family. We have two girls, Jinny and Em – they're ten and eight. Jinny, in case you hadn't guessed, is the reason I actually married William. These things happen!"

"But…" Victoria tailed off as this was dodgy ground and she wondered if it would be best to steer the conversation towards local events or the weather or something else to play safe.

"But what?" replied Nicole. "Why don't I talk about them non-stop?" She sighed again, this time more deeply, and Victoria thought it sounded almost guilty. "I always felt I might be able to get back into acting you see. If I was going to be working away or at least evenings, then I thought it best to have a nanny from the word go. Trouble is, Annalise the nanny is actually too good at her job, the girls are gloriously happy and don't give a fig whether I am home or not. It really gets to me sometimes."

Both women took a long sip of wine and there was a pause. "So," continued Nicole, "now it's my turn to grill you. You've been down here how long? Tell me all the gory details!"

Victoria laughed. "Sadly nothing gory, just a somewhat pedestrian life."

Nicole interrupted. "Cut the pedestrian bit, I have heard about your exploits on Albert's tractor. Anything but boring." She laughed in a very infectious way and Victoria found herself relaxing even more and really enjoying Nicole's company. "Oh please, surely not you as well. I will never live that down, I could have died when the ladies in the shop mentioned it!"

"Well they're a subject for a whole other evening of wine! I can tell you stories you just would not believe. Now come on, spill the beans!"

Victoria took another sip of wine and realised most of the large glass had gone. "Well, my Aunt Edith died recently, and she kindly left me the cottage."

"She talked about you a lot you know," said Nicole. "There was obviously a very strong bond between you."

"You knew her?"

"I think most people around Swaddlecombe knew Edith. I only knew her to chat to in passing, but I liked her, always forthright, but good fun too."

"She was wonderful and I feel really guilty that I haven't been down as much as I should these last few years. We always wrote but," Victoria paused, "I was diagnosed with breast cancer three years ago, and life got very earnest and grim for quite some time. My parents are dead, so my letters from Aunt Edith were my only support really."

"Oh gosh you poor thing." Nicole briefly laid her hand on Victoria's and gave it a squeeze.

"Well all seems to be OK at the moment, but you can't help worrying it's there waiting to sneak up on you. I feel as though I'm paddling in calm blue seas, but just out of sight there's a big grey shape waiting to swim in and swallow me." Victoria looked up at Nicole and saw real concern on her face, and she smiled. "But enough of this. As my friend Sebastian would say 'Darling, stick a big old fake smile on and before long it'll be a real one.' I'm lucky to have such good friends, crazy though they might be! Apart from Aunt Edith, Gray and Sebastian were the other people that made it all bearable."

"Stop..." said Nicole dramatically, holding her hand up in front of Victoria, like a policeman stopping the traffic. "I need to jump in right now. Tell me you don't have some friends called Gray and Sebastian Fellowes, surely it can't be?"

Victoria frowned. "Yes I do – well that's their surname. Seb changed it by deed poll, as his name was Black – and Gray refused to be known as 'Gray Black' if they got married."

"No," squealed Nicole, "I don't believe it! Small world, it was Sebastian's twenty-first party where I met William. Seb was at art school with my brother. No, no, no I don't believe it!" She laughed and squeezed Victoria's hand. "I am so excited to meet a new friend. I knew as soon as I saw you in the shop we'd get on."

"Really, why?" said Victoria.

"Because you waited patiently while Lavender showed you her 'specials' department and so many people ridicule her. I adore those three and think the world needs more special characters, not less. But Lavender is something else. She once tried to sell me one half of a pair of walking boots. When I said I didn't walk very far, she said yes, that's why she thought one boot would be just right. Come on, let's get another round – are you hungry?"

As they finished their plates of coq au vin (which Victoria thought had a lot more coq than vin), she took another sip of wine and looked over at Nicole. "This has been a great spur of the moment thing for me, thanks so much for asking."

"On the contrary," replied Nicole, "it would have been a terminally boring evening for me. The girls stay late for ballet and Annalise gets them into bed. William will be God knows where. He can't fish at night, so I am assuming he's in a pub somewhere talking about fishing, or back at the office Googling the biggest pike ever found in Devon or some such fascinating piscine fact. If he wasn't just the dullest moron ever I'd suspect he was having an affair but he's not really capable of that, more's the pity as then I could dump him legitimately, grab all the money and run!" She gave a half-hearted laugh and Victoria wondered how near the truth this was.

"Do you really mean that?" Victoria felt saddened by Nicole's life.

"I certainly do," said Nicole, "much as I love the kids, the West End calls and once I have a few thousand to tide me over I'll get my big break. It should be possible now that old man Henry has popped his clogs anyway, should mean the family sells up to Berry Brothers and divides up the spoils."

It didn't shock Victoria that Nicole was so unfazed by Henry's death, but she found it hard to reconcile this grasping Nicole with the woman who laughed and smiled so often. "Do you think that's what will happen?" she asked cautiously, knowing that John had said it wouldn't.

"Oh I hope so, I've been banking on it for a while. There'll be a few dummies spat out of prams, mainly John's I guess, as for some weird reason he actually likes the company. But William and I both have a vote and I'm sure Grace would want to retire as well so he won't stand an earthly. William thinks he's going to retire too but sadly if I take half of what could be quite a good lump that might scupper that one."

They were interrupted by the sound of Victoria's mobile.

"Hello, yes Albert, this is Victoria." She rolled her eyes heavenwards at Nicole and they both smiled. "Oh, what, straight away, well, yes I can yes, is there a problem? A 'bleddy gert problem' – oh and that would be what? Hello?" Victoria was intrigued now and hugely frustrated when Albert rang off. "Forgive me Nicole, apparently Albert has, to quote him, a 'bleddy gert problem' which seems to involve me, so I must go. It's been lovely, thank you."

"Let's just hope the problem doesn't involve leggings and tractors, eh?" Nicole giggled. "Let's do this again soon, it would be fun to have some female company for a change. Here's my mobile number." Nicole handed her a card.

"Thank you, I'll ring you," said Victoria looking down at the flamboyant coppery-coloured business card and smiled. Hoping she could find her way in the dark, she set off back to the cottage and was relieved to find herself at the farm drive after only one wrong turn. She drove into the farmyard and saw lights on in the barn. "Hello?" she made her way over, suddenly a little anxious about what might await her. "Albert, are you there?"

"Yes I bleddy am," came a muffled voice from the depths of the barn.

Victoria ventured a little further into the building and saw something that made her double up with laughter. Albert was looking more rumpled than normal, straw in his hair with what looked suspiciously like chicken droppings down his jacket. He was half sitting, half lying on the floor beside a construction that looked like a cross between a large dolls' house and a dog kennel.

"What's that and what's the matter Albert?"

"What's the bleddy matter, can't you see what the bleddy matter is?" Albert was red in the face, and it didn't take much to see he was not in a good mood. He extracted a very fluffy blonde-coloured chicken from beneath his coat and held it out to her.

"Oh!" Victoria took it gingerly – she wasn't all that fond of feathered things – and held it at arm's length.

"I caught one but the other two are leading me a right dance, damn things should be bred for laying eggs not some flipping beauty contest!" He scowled and lunged into the pile of hay behind him, obviously searching for the 'other two'.

"Umm… why do you need hens? And surely they come in cages, don't they? Why are these running around and at this time of night?"

Albert popped up from under the pile of hay and roared at her. "This bleddy time of night is because you didn't come home! I had this huge package turn up and had to sign for it. Pity I didn't turn them right around when they found you weren't here." With this he disappeared under the hay again, making what Victoria guessed were encouraging chicken noises in an attempt to catch the others.

Victoria frowned. "Albert, ALBERT!" she had to shout to get him to surface again. "Albert – what on earth are you talking about? I don't have chickens, have you lost it, or have I had too much wine and am hallucinating?" She rearranged her grip on the frothy blonde specimen that she was holding as it struggled and, not for the first time, wondered if Devon was in fact part of a parallel universe.

Accompanied by much loud and undignified squawking, Albert emerged, grasping two other hens, both as unusual as the first, but in slightly different honey and toffee tones. "Right then, these are your hens, your problem! I have had enough!"

Victoria quailed before such a fierce Albert; she had only really seen him calm and laid-back. "But, where can I put them? And why are they mine? I've never even fed hens, I mean, what do they eat? Where can they live and do they have to be let out?" Victoria trailed off as Albert gazed at her, probably taking in for the first time her abject look of panic and bemusement.

"So you didn't know then?"

"Know WHAT?" she cried, feeling quite tired and irritable herself now. None of this made sense.

Albert opened the door of the strange gingerbread house and pushed in the two chickens, then grabbed the other from Victoria's outstretched hands. "Now stay in!" he said, banged shut the front door of the hens' cottage and shot the bolt home.

"I'm sorry, I don't understand."

"Ah, well, I can see that now. And I'm sorry I was a bit crabby." He shook his head, and straw dropped out of it. "Bleddy things, chickens." He brushed his hair and more straw fell out. "Well, this huge package arrived with some courier chap in a van, said it had to be signed for as it was perishable goods and as you weren't there I signed. Only when this chap had gone did I hear the chicken pocking and carrying on. So, like a fool, I opened the crate. They must have got free on the journey and out they come! Quick as ninepence and all round the bleddy barn!"

Victoria couldn't help but smile as she envisaged the scene. "Albert, I am sorry. I had no idea, I didn't order these, this, thing!" she gestured at the twee house, painted a duck-egg blue with white shutters and gables and a pale grey door.

"'Tis like a bleddy joke! I mean, who the hell would buy such a thing?"

Victoria thought she had an idea. "Was there a consignment note with it?"

"A what note? I got a scrap of paper here somewhere if that's what you mean." He rummaged in various pockets, unearthing various strange items that Victoria didn't want to try and identify, and eventually brought out a crumpled delivery note. She read it and smiled. "Ah yes, I should have guessed!"

Darling! said the note. We hope these dear little chicky hens will be the finishing touch to your new rural idyll! Gray spent ages choosing the Farrow & Ball paint colours for the coop and I chose the three hens – all in shades of gold, to bring you sunshine, health and happiness. Oodles of love, Gray & Sebastian xxxxx.

"Albert, they are a gift from some very dear friends of mine who know nothing about country life."

"They London types?"

"Guilty as charged."

"Daft buggers."

"Well, yes, probably, but they meant well."

"Daft bleddy thing to send anyone, let alone someone like you who don't know one end of a hen from the other."

"Can't I learn?"

"You're going to have to, I'm not looking after them. Now your aunt, she was a proper country woman and she knew about fowl."

"Ok, don't rub it in! But I'm not a complete idiot! If you could just give me a bit of help initially, I'll get a book and read up on it."

Albert harrumphed and folded his arms. "Bleddy book, what you want with a bleddy book? I'll tell you the basics to keep the poor little beggars alive, but you'd do best to go and see that vicar chap, he's a bit of a fowl fancier. He knows all about them."

"The Reverend Ruminant?" she smiled.

"Now then!" said Albert sternly. "Don't start that again!" but he also smiled and they both started laughing. "Look here maid, I'm starving, I've been running round the barn for the last hour and haven't had me dinner. You coming in for a cup of tea or something to eat?"

"I had dinner in the pub actually." She stopped, realising that might sound a bit rude. "I met Nicole Simmons and we ended up having a drink and then eating."

"Fine woman," he said, pursing his lips. "Fine head of hair. Damned if I know what she ever saw in that half-wit William. Money, I suppose, only she was wrong there." He turned and made off across the barn. "You coming, or what?"

Victoria hurried after him, anxious not to lose sight of him in the dusk. He went out of the barn and disappeared to the left. She followed and saw a square of yellow light as he opened a door, was briefly silhouetted and then went inside. No standing on ceremony then! She noticed the two collies, Nell and Nancy, curled up together in front of a wooden kennel. They lifted their heads and twitched the ends of their tails in acknowledgement.

The house seemed small, square and unprepossessing, certainly not as old as April Cottage. This was her first glimpse of it, tucked in behind the barn and sheltered on all sides by buildings and trees. Half blinded by the light, she stopped, finding herself in a kitchen – and what a kitchen! She thought for a moment she had lost her way and gone into someone else's house altogether.

"Well, shut the damn' door, all the heat will go out else!" No mistake, she was definitely in Albert's house. She shut the 'damned door' and looked around her. "I don't quite know what to say!"

"Nothing is probably best, just sit down and I'll make tea."

She sat at the plain pine table, scrubbed to within an inch of its life, and gazed around. She had only ever seen more gadgets in the kitchen section of John Lewis. A huge chrome food mixer, a breadmaker, a steamer, a smaller mixer, what looked like a juicer, a deep-fat fryer, something she couldn't identify, a mincer, a matching chrome toaster and kettle, pans of every size dangling from one long rail, jelly moulds hung on the wall and a Rayburn thundering away in the midst of it all. In front of her, Albert was cutting into the deepest, most delicious-looking Victoria sponge cake she had ever seen. After a moment or two, she said, "Albert, you are an old fraud!"

Taking a plate from a rack, he carefully placed on it a golden slice of sponge with a thick seam of jam and cream along its centre and said, "I don't know what you mean Miss West."

"You bake cakes! You dark horse! Did Edith teach you?"

He was savouring a mouthful of sponge, but eventually said, "Not exactly. I taught her. Well, I tried to, but she was never much of a one for baking. It's a bit of a knack. She had green fingers and she was good with fowl, but Edith never got the hang of baking."

"But she won prizes at the show, and…" Victoria's mouth formed a perfect 'O' and she pointed at him accusingly. "It was you! All along, it was you!"

"Might've been," he smiled ruefully. "Want some cake?" He pointed at the slice he had placed in front of her. Already full up with Trudy's coq au vin, she really didn't fancy cake, but she bit into it out of politeness. The sponge melted on her tongue. "Albert, this is amazing!" She ate more. "Mmmm!"

"Edith and I, well, we had something of an 'understanding,' you might say." He dabbed his finger in the last few crumbs. "We were always there for each other, but we were never in each other's pockets. I don't know how it all came about, but it did, and it was an arrangement that suited us both fine. I baked the cakes, she entered the competitions."

His hand hovered over the cake and after a brief pause for thought he cut another piece. "I didn't want people chittering about me doing women's work and all that nonsense, so she said they were hers. It was part of her image too. She hated baking and bleddy flower arranging, but it was what she liked to be seen to do. She kept the hens, I used the eggs. I supplied the meat, she grew the veg. She cooked the roasts and savouries, I did the puds."

"Sounds a great partnership!"

He nodded. "Reckon, she was like family to me."

"You must miss her a lot."

"All the time." He turned the sponge around and looked at from different angles. "I still think she'll appear round the corner with her old apron on and a scowl saying 'Albert! What've you bleddy done with so-and-so?' But there, it will pass. You don't forget someone but your mind sort of fills in the gaps and it becomes less painful. Eventually, when you remember them, you just smile." He got up and went to the kettle. "You fancy some tea?"

"Well, I do, but I don't suppose you have Earl Grey?"

"Who?"

"No, I didn't think so, can I scoot home and bring back a few bags?"

"If you must," he snorted and opened a box of PG Tips.

She walked back through the barn and out the other side to April Cottage, unlit and chilly. Damn, she must get the hang of the Rayburn and she must also get broadband sorted out and she still needed to unpack! This was ridiculous! The night was very dark, and she paused and looked up. A few stars were twinkling, the sky like deep velvet. She loved the utter blackness, no ghastly glow of street lamps. Suddenly she shivered and hurried inside. Mostly she thought she was being quite brave, but every now and then she felt just a teeny bit vulnerable out in the wilds on her own. Still, she had Albert nearby.

She grabbed a handful of teabags, and her laptop, thinking Albert might be interested in the photos she'd taken at Primrose Cottage. She left the kitchen and porch lights turned on and made her way back across the yard and through the barn. "It's curious how I've never noticed your house before," she said, setting her laptop on the table and handing him a teabag.

"You want milk with this?" He held the teabag with disdain. "Smells all scented and weird!"

"It's bergamot and citrus and no thank you, just hot water."

They sat opposite each other with their tea.

"So you obviously know Nicole Simmons?"

He huffed. "Well, I know her a bit, but not well. We don't exactly mix in the same circles! I heard she's not too bad. Not happy with that dollop of a husband, but then that's nothing new."

"When we were in the pub the Mudges were dropping all sorts of hints about William and John and that Mandy woman, the one we had the stand-off with in the car, wasn't it?"

"That's her! Right madam she is! How William could prefer her over Nicole, I don't know!"

"You mean it was true what they were saying?" Victoria sat bolt upright.

"Now don't you get all frisky. I don't know! It's all gossip and nonsense. Never did anyone any good."

"But…" Victoria prompted.

"But I have heard from several sources, that there might be something going on with those three, yes." Albert looked vaguely uncomfortable.

Victoria raised her eyebrows. "What do you mean exactly?"

"I suspect Miss Mandy Parkin pulls all the strings. John won't be in it for anything but money and William, daft fool, I expect he's lovestruck and doesn't realise he's being played for a patsy."

Victoria took a swig of tea. "You mean she's playing them off against each other?" Albert shrugged. "Don't know. Like I say, it's idle gossip, but I suspect John knows and doesn't care and William doesn't know and would care. Very much. If he's got the Simmons temper, it could all get quite nasty." He sat back. "Mandy. Her father would be so disappointed."

"Ah, I suppose you were at school with him too, Janner, that's his name isn't it?

"Yep, John, or Janner as we Devonians say. He was a few years ahead of me, same class as old Henry I reckon. He was alright was Janner, bit of a rough diamond. Streetwise, you'd call it nowadays.

Mandy's inherited his brains, she's a smart girl but she missed out on the conscience. Janner was no saint, but he had standards. But not that little minx."

"When I was in the village shop today, the funny one, Iris, is it?"

"Nope, Lavender, strange old girl she is!"

"Well, Lavender then, she as good as implied Janner was John Simmons' father."

Albert scratched his ear. "I don't think I can comment on that. Who knows? Lots of gossip, and of course Grace has made an art of getting people's backs up so they all like to do her down."

"So, not true?"

He folded his arms and let out a sigh that implied enough was enough. "So why did you bring that thing in?" He nodded at her laptop.

"It's my laptop computer."

"I know what it is, we do have them in Devon you know! I just wondered why you'd brought it over?"

She unzipped the case and got out her Macbook. "This is an Apple. It's called an Apple, the type of computer," she explained, using slightly slower speech, as if she were explaining to a child. Albert raised his eyebrows quizzically and drank his tea, saying nothing. "I thought you might like to see the photos I took at Primrose Cottage the other day."

"What, you mean of Henry?"

"Erm, yes?

Albert frowned. "Hmmm, seems a bit, well, you know..."

"I know, but I need to go through them, and I thought you might be able to tell me some of the names of the people on the factory floor."

"I know them all."

The laptop started up and she took a gulp of tea, then frowned. "That's odd. It's asking if I want to join a network."

"So?"

"Um, how can I explain, it's Wifi, so there are no wires, it's sort of 'in the air', it's a way of getting onto the internet using broadband. But I don't understand." The slow, explanatory tone was there again.

Albert had fished in the kitchen table drawer and was pushing a piece of paper towards her. "Here's the password." Victoria felt quite faint. "What?"

"The password to my wireless network."

She looked at him through narrowed eyes. "You look just like Edith when you do that," he said and folded his arms.

"You have broadband?"

"Yep."

"And a wireless connection?"

"Yep."

"And you didn't tell me?"

"You didn't ask. I assumed you'd got one of them mobile dongle thingummies. Didn't think you'd be without broadband, not a city slicker like you!"

She reached across the table and slapped him on the arm.

"Ow! You're getting more like Edith by the minute!"

"Oh Albert! This is amazing! Can I use it?"

"Course, no skin off my nose."

"I had no idea you were such a dark horse! I wonder what else I'm going to discover about you. Wow, this is going to be a godsend."

"I might even have a booster thing, so we could get it across to your cottage if we're lucky."

"Gosh, that's cheered me up no end!" She clapped her hands with glee. Albert laughed and shook his head. "Well, I'll be jiggered if that's not another one of Edith's traits too!"

Victoria resisted the strong urge to check her emails and have a quick scoot round Facebook, and instead opened up the photos. Albert moved his chair round to her side of the table.

"Here we go. Oh goodness, there he is." They both looked at Henry, sleek and smug, unaware that his life was about to be cut so tragically short.

"Makes you bleddy think," muttered Albert and squinted at the images. "You take a good photo, I'll give you that."

Victoria flicked through the shots; there were quite a number.

"Look at him!" Albert snorted with derision as John flashed on the screen. He was leaning back in his chair, a look of utter smugness and arrogance on his face. "Berk," said Albert. "Now, that there is Mavis Pike. She's been with the company since the start, I reckon. And that one there, with the glasses, that's Harvey Stone, daft as a brush." He went on and identified every member of staff.

"Great, I'll have to ask you to tell me again when I've got my notebook with me."

"Notebook? You need an iPad maid."

"It's on my wish list. Why, have you got one?"

He smiled and she sighed. "Oh Albert, I have so misjudged you." They had come to the end of the photos and were back at the beginning, with Henry posing for the camera.

"Poor beggar," murmured Albert and they both studied the photo. "Zoom in a bit," said Albert and she did. "Go left. Bit more." They both peered at the screen. "So, what's that then?" he said quietly and pointed at Henry's suit jacket.

Victoria frowned. "Erm, is it a pen in his pocket?"

"Bit big for an ordinary pen I reckon."

Victoria sat back. She felt rather light-headed. "Oh," she said at last, "you mean it's his epipen."

121

Albert sat back too and they looked at each other.

"But I thought…?" said Victoria.

Albert was frowning. "I don't like it. That puts a whole different thingumajig on it."

"Perspective?"

"That's the bugger."

Victoria felt hot and cold, all at the same time. "Oh dear."

"Hmmm, looks a bit like it," added Albert.

They looked at each other again.

"But everyone said he died because he forgot the epipen, so when he was stung, he couldn't inject himself."

"That's the gist of it."

"So why has he got it, here, as he's leaving the building, just a short time before he died?" She pointed a quivering finger at the blown-up image on the screen.

"I can't answer that my beauty, I'm not Sherlock Holmes."

"Oh Albert, you don't think someone, that someone did him, I mean that, that they murdered him?"

Chapter 7

Victoria felt wonderfully content as she surveyed the view outside the kitchen window. The colours were so vivid; everything seemed to glow. Her little patch of lawn, emerald green in the sunlight, looked badly in need of a cut. Did she possess a lawn mower? Surely her aunt must have had one? Immaculate little white daisies were scattered prettily across the grass, adding to the picture-perfect scene. Taking in deep happy breaths, she realised how quickly she was becoming acclimatised to her new life and how content she was starting to feel.

Suddenly her calm contemplation was interrupted by a loud and raucous squawking and the definite sounds of very unhappy hens. Panicking that a fox or some other predator had breached her new hen-coop's defences, she rushed out of the back door and raced to the barn. The door of the beautifully decorated little hen house was still firmly shut, but the noises continued from inside. Had a rat or some other small creature snuck in last night, or a snake, or…?

Victoria pulled herself together and flung open the door. Immediately the palest of the new hens raced out into the barn, squawking and clucking, being chased by the other two, apparently hell-bent on pecking her to death. "No, no you stop that right now, you nasty things!" She bent down to try and catch the blonde hen and ended up on her face in the hay as she tripped over a coiled rope. "Bugger, damn it and oh that hurt!"

"You OK there?" came Albert's anxious voice.

"Oh just fine!" She sat up. "Do I look fine lying here covered in straw?"

"Keep your hair on, I was just asking!" Albert smiled. "I seem to remember it was acceptable to laugh at me when I was chasing them birds last night, but not so funny now it's you I'm guessing."

"Not so funny at all. And look, they're trying to murder her, are they cannibal hens? Look at her poor little head."

Albert squinted at the pale gold hen and, sure enough, quite a few feathers had been pulled out and she definitely looked the worse for wear. "You know that saying 'pecking order'? Well that's where it comes from. They're sorting out who's number one. A case of finding out who's top hen rather than top dog if you know what I mean."

"Well top hen, top dog whatever, that's cruel. How do I stop it?"

"Can't. It's nature. Just leave them to it and they'll calm down eventually. You need to get a run sorted for them, that house 'thing'," he said, dismissively, almost sneering at it, "that's alright for sleeping in, but for daytime they need space to scratch about and such like."

"Goodness I hadn't thought of that – do you know anyone I can pay to build something for them? Now I've got them I can't just neglect them, and the fresh eggs will be lovely."

"I know just the man for the job, but you'll have to be nice to him for a week afterwards, at least – no, make that two. He's not always available for jobs like this at the drop of a hat."

"Oh absolutely, I understand..." Victoria trailed off as she noticed Albert's huge grin and realised he was teasing her again. "Oh, you mean you! I fall for it every time, don't I?" She laughed. "Well, OK, I will be nice to you for at least two weeks. It's rather your thing, isn't it, helping distressed damsels!"

"Has been known. I can never resist pretty maidens in distress, whether they're hens or humans!" Albert winked at her but she decided to press on. "Yes, well, I need to get food for them and something for them to drink out of too. Would an old dog bowl do for water to start with? I noticed one in the kitchen." Victoria watched as all three hens pecked aimlessly around the barn, quite quiet now and apparently agreeing to a temporary truce.

"Local farming store this side of Westerley, they'll have everything you need for hen keeping. Feed and equipment, but I reckon you'd be best to go and see the Reverend first and get his advice. I do wonder how your posh London friends thought the birds would manage without food, but that's typical townies for you."

"Oh but they meant really well and the hens are gorgeous colours aren't they? I wonder what colour eggs they'll lay?"

"That's easy answered – white with yellow bits in the middle!"

Victoria narrowed her eyes. "Watch it, Albert – comments like that don't go unavenged!" They both laughed, then "Fancy a cup of tea?" he asked.

"Well I would invite you into my kitchen but the cupboard is pretty bare and all I have at the moment is Earl Grey tea or some coffee and I have a feeling neither is to your taste. I must get stocked up properly with food and supplies rather than just coping hand to mouth and nipping down to the village shop."

They walked across to Albert's house. In the kitchen she once again marvelled at the gadgets and smiled to herself. "I still can't believe you and Edith fooled everyone for so many years – and there was me wondering why she didn't have any baking books. Would it be very rude to ask for some more of that lovely cake? I haven't had any breakfast yet – just some tea and I'm starving."

"Aha, first sign that the country air is getting to you. Good appetite, that's very important. Nobody likes skinny maids down here and you could do with adding a pound or two."

"I could not! I spent ages keeping the pounds off, going to the gym and working out."

"Gyms and workouts?" He snorted. "What's the point of all that? Why do a workout when you don't produce nothing useful at the end of it? Daft! You'll keep fit keeping the garden in shape and them hens happy! And what about growing veg? That'd certainly keep you on your toes, all that digging and mulching and such like."

Registering this short lecture, Victoria sipped her tea and took a large mouthful of his amazing cake. A sponge cake was so 'everyday' when anyone else made it, but this was just divine. She sighed, contentedly. "So," she began, not quite knowing how to introduce the subject. "In the cold light of day, how are you feeling about the idea that Henry might have been killed deliberately?" She tried not to speak with her mouth full, but the cake couldn't wait.

Albert stirred his tea and looked thoughtful. "Well I don't know. Seems a bit far-fetched to me." He frowned. "Murder is a foul thing and it's not right to just throw that thought around carelessly, but then you've got that photograph, and that does make you wonder."

"Should we just forget about the whole thing? The police seem pretty sure it was just a nasty accident and we do know he was allergic to bee stings. As a newcomer I don't want to go pushing my nose in and upsetting people. I mean, I hardly know the people involved."

"It's true the police aren't 'investigating' it as such, but then they're busy and only too happy to have an easy answer to clear the books so to speak. But newcomer or not, you and I were around and we have more reason than most to suspect there's something fishy going on." He sat back and added, "Maybe we should just have a general poke about and try and put our minds to rest?"

Victoria took a gulp of tea and thought. "I suppose so. Have you got any idea who could have done it? I can't see what anyone would gain from Henry dying, can you?" She eyed the cake tin and decided that even though they were becoming good friends, she shouldn't push her luck and ask for another slice.

"Well," began Albert, "Jean always did say she'd have his guts for garters for nicking her old Mum's recipe."

They looked at each other, then he shrugged, "No, that's daft, seems a bit of an overreaction for just pinching a jam recipe. Anyway it's too late now, the nicking is done and dusted anyway."

"Anyway how would Jean get access to any bees?" Victoria frowned, deep in thought.

"Well I guess there's the bees kept at the bottom of the land at the factory. They chose a spot as far away from the house as possible obviously. It isn't Jean's job to look after them but I guess she could get hold of some?" Albert didn't seem very convinced.

Victoria pursed her lips. "Maybe she planted a swarm of bees in his car and left it to providence?"

Albert laughed and shook his head, "You can't dump a swarm of bees in a car just like that! Not like an animal in a box, 'tis a great moving mass of buzzing wotsits and could go anywhere." He shuddered. "To tell the truth, I've never been too happy around bees."

"Hmm, I was just thinking aloud really. Have you got a better suggestion?"

There was a pause. "William, he's keen to retire, maybe him and his missus want to go and live in somewhere foreign with big fish and plenty of money, maybe he can sell the business now?"

"Judging from what Nicole said to me the other evening, that's not going to happen. She wants to leave him and possibly the children too and kick-start her acting career up in London." She thought for a while. "I can't see them doing anything as a team anyway, she was too angry and bored with him to co-operate over anything. She just wants to get the money and run. But individually, they would both have a motive, although I am 100 percent sure Nicole would never do anything like that."

"Don't they say that nine times out of ten murderers are family members or partners, so what about Grace?"

Victoria smiled at him pityingly. "I don't think so Albert. 'Let's kill the love of my life because I will get a not-very-much needed life insurance payout.' Really, as if!"

"Just saying," Albert shrugged, "it's often someone close. But yes, you're right – I expect she's pretty distraught and they certainly don't need the money."

"I haven't spent that much time with John so far," Victoria mused. "Is he really as ambitious and pushy as I thought?"

"I reckon," replied Albert, "not a nice chap, that I would say. I remember when Eileen Moore got pregnant, he had her sacked under some pretence rather than do this maternity benefit lark. She was up for taking him to some tribunal or other. Obsessed with the company that one."

"We're not making much progress are we? Is there anyone more blindingly obvious?"

"Well there's Mandy Parkin, a lot of history between those two. She's not an easy woman, but Henry did cross her Dad quite often when he was alive. Maybe she's got revenge in mind after all this time, old Janner Parkin's been dead for quite a few years now."

"Hmmm, interesting. Did anyone in the factory really hate Henry?" asked Victoria. "Any disputes, apart from Jean that is?"

"Can't say that Henry would have dealt with them even if there had been any, that would have been John's domain, or Grace before him. Not keen on getting his hands dirty was Henry."

"We should be writing a list," said Victoria, "tackle it like a proper crime-hunting duo!" Albert rolled his eyes at her and then smiled. "Well you're the girl, you can write the list, women's work I reckon. I need to do the manly stuff and go get timber and netting for three daft little blonde hens that need sorting."

Victoria wondered whether to rise to the bait, and then decided the hen project was more important. As she walked back through the barn, she caught sight of her boxes of 'stuff'. She sighed. Unpacking was so boring, but maybe she'd discover something fun that she had forgotten was tucked away. She picked up one of the lighter crates that seemed to be filled with old letters and photos and treasures that probably could be thinned down and chucked away – who was she kidding?

She sat at the kitchen table and started to sort, hoping she wouldn't get sidetracked and start reading all the old correspondence. She resolutely divided things into 'Of course I want', 'I just might want' and 'Could go but not sure' piles. It was quite hard to differentiate between the latter two; she was really good at hoarding old bits and pieces. When you only have memories of your family, and not flesh and blood, those 'old bits and pieces' become twice as precious.

She traced her finger over her mother's writing on the front of an envelope and felt the familiar ache in her heart. No matter how many years passed the pain of her loss never faded. On an impulse she took the letter out. It had been many years since she had read any of her parents' letters and she had kept almost all of them.

'Darling Tori,' it began. She smiled as nobody before or since had called her Tori; it was a special endearment reserved for her by her mother. She knew her mother had loved her but she'd never really been an openly cuddly sort of Mum, just too busy she supposed. She read the letter through.

Darling Tori

How are things at school? We both miss you dreadfully, but with all the gallivanting we are doing at the moment, I'm sure it's for the best. Are you still in the netball team?

Your father and I are down in Devon visiting Aunt Edith at the moment. It's a strange little house, but your aunt seems very happy and settled. I think your father is eager to get off to New York at the end of the week, the countryside and local yokels are really not his thing, but I am glad we popped in. I quite like it!

A ghastly woman came for tea today. Not your aunt's usual choice of friend! She talked obsessively about jam, can you imagine? Of course, your father was bored rigid.

Apparently she's starting a jam company, but there seemed to be some kind of intrigue with her ex boss going on. She wants to call it Hill Farm Jams, well, I'd change that straight away for something more attractive if she plans to make it a success. I suggested something pretty and flowery, like primrose, or daffodil. But as your father helpfully pointed out, I am not running the jam company.

I did feel a little sorry for her though, when she talked about how many hours she was working and how awkward her husband can be. It makes me realise some women have a much tougher life than I do.

Anyway sweetheart, have a fun rest of term, must dash Edith is calling – see you soon

Much love

Mother

Victoria read the letter again to make sure she wasn't dreaming. It was as if someone had just walked over her grave; her mother had to be writing about Grace. It fitted in with the whole jam thing, and how amazing! Her own mother appeared to have suggested the company's name. Maybe that would be a really fun angle for her article. But no, she imagined Grace wouldn't appreciate having her history rewritten, and certainly not the origin of the name of the company she claimed to have thought up.

She folded the letter carefully and put it back in the envelope. How strange that of all the letters in the box she should choose to read that one. She shook herself out of her reverie – come on Victoria, get a grip! She looked at her watch and realised it was well past lunchtime; no wonder her stomach was complaining. Mind you, cake for breakfast was never a very sensible move. Opening the cupboards she realised there was nothing fresh or edible in the place so she would have to make do and mend yet again and nip down to the village shop.

She drew up outside and tried to decide where to park. Stopping immediately outside the shop seemed rather thoughtless as it blocked their frontage and, looking at Lavender's little display area, she had outdone herself today. There sat a beige plastic bucket with no handle and a pile of old dresses and fabrics tied together with red string and a large label saying 'DIY Patchwork Quilt £5', a rubber duck which appeared to have been loved so much its face had been rubbed off and a black wellington boot.

"Good morning, Victoria," said a perky voice as she entered the shop. Victoria looked closely at the speaker and then said, confidently, "Good morning, Iris."

"Good try my dear, but I'm Dahlia." She elaborately patted the bun at her back of her head, mimicking her sister's nervous gesture, and Victoria smiled as she realised the hair styles were not consistent. Perhaps it was one of the triplets' little jokes, designed to keep everyone on their toes and never quite sure to whom they were speaking. Hmmm, thought Victoria, her detective hat securely in place, that was a good way of confusing people and disguising your identity. But of course, any one of the sisters being involved was ridiculous. What had it to do with them? "I've just popped in to get some bits and pieces for lunch. Have you got any more of that lovely bread? It was so delicious!"

"We have indeed my dear, and some new-laid eggs, best you'll have ever tasted. Nice new potatoes from up along too."

"I've just got some hens of my own, so I hope I'll have my own eggs, but don't worry – I don't think baking bread is going to be on my list any time soon!" Victoria smiled, picked up a wicker shopping basket and started to browse. The bell on the door tinkled and Trudy Mudge came in, humming under her breath.

"Why you seem very 'appy today Trude!" said Dahlia (or was it really Iris?).

"Yes I am," smiled Trudy, "a man from the brewery came and did an inspection and they passed us with flying colours and are really pleased with the way business is going. He even commented on how delicious my lasagne was when he stayed for a spot of lunch. I told him I like to have a few more exotic choices on the menu now and again, not just casseroles and pasties."

Having sampled the lasagne herself Victoria felt she was qualified to join in the conversation. "And very tasty it is too Trudy, I can vouch for that." She smiled at Trudy and hoped she wasn't being too pushy for a newcomer.

"Oh hello Victoria, how lovely to see you, thank you kindly. I expect being from the city you'll have a much more discerning taste than some of our more local customers, so that's very nice of you to say. You all comfortable with Albert and settling down in Edith's lovely cottage?"

Victoria wondered whether there was a hidden meaning in either of those comments. Was she meant to be 'with' Albert now?

Did the words 'Edith's lovely cottage' imply it wasn't rightfully hers? She was getting paranoid! "Yes I'm fine thank you, just getting some odds and ends to try and make a spot of lunch."

"Oh you should have brought Albert to the pub and not bothered with cooking for him yourself."

Victoria bridled at that, now certain Trudy was fishing for gossip. "Heavens no, lunch is just for me. I've no idea where Albert is – I expect he's rushed off his feet at this time of year. I'll have to find out next time I see him."

Dahlia (or was it Iris?) looked across at Trudy and they exchanged a meaningful look. "Talking of coming in for a spot of something to eat, John Simmons was in after you and Nicole left last night, with that Mandy Parkin again." Turning to Dahlia, Trudy said pointedly, "Making a bit of a regular thing of it they are now."

Both ladies nodded as though that meant something significant; maybe it was a local custom that three visits to the pub in consecutive weeks meant you were betrothed? Victoria was racking her brain for ways to join in and prolong the conversation, her detective instincts in full flow again. "I bet they tried some of your lovely lasagne?" was the best she could come up with.

Trudy looked at her in amazement. "Lasagne, beef lasagne? Heavens no, that Mandy doesn't touch flesh or fowl – and how many thousands of times does she have to mention it?" Trudy struck a pose, threw back her head and mimicked, "Darling, I couldn't touch anything with eyes, it's just so, so... peasant like!"

Dahlia and Trudy laughed in unison and Victoria could only assume that this was a first-class imitation of Mandy. "Oh, so she's a vegetarian – well lots of people are nowadays, being kind to animals and all that," said Victoria.

"Kind to animals my arse, excuse my French," replied Trudy. "Old man Jacobs was in with his dog last night. Sweet little thing, rescue dog, but friendly as anything and greets the world like her best friend. Ran over to her ladyship and was only sniffing. Going to say 'Hello' and flaming woman kicked her out the way enough to make her squeal. Then just swanned off to the ladies, not a second thought. Left that John to apologise, and he had to buy the old man a pint. Kind to animals? Pah!"

Dahlia had been nodding all through this diatribe. "Well, I've never liked her, not since she were a tiddy thing and came in with her Dad for sweets. Always had a ruse to make him buy more than he wanted to – too clever by half she was even then. Could twist him round her little finger."

"She and John had plenty to talk about, deep discussions they were in all night. Something's afoot, that's for sure!" added Trudy, folding her arms triumphantly.

Victoria thought this might be a good point to pay for her items and make a move. She realised the shop was a mine of gossip and intrigue and somewhere to be monitored. She spotted some milk and added that to her basket and marvelled yet again at the total when Dahlia told her. Everything seemed so much cheaper here than a similar lunchtime trip to a supermarket would have been in central London.

She had now perfected her route back home and was getting quite confident in the narrow lanes. There was no sign of Albert, so she sat down for a quick, solitary lunch. The article was preying on her mind. Could she realistically finish it, given Henry's death? But at the same time, she didn't want to mess up this first commission; it could well scupper her future chances. Friend or not, Georgie didn't have time for people who couldn't deliver a decent job to a deadline.

Victoria got out her laptop and opened up her notes. She really needed some more detail; no, not detail – she already had too much of that and it was dull – she needed colour. She thought Henry might have provided that, or even Grace, but one was impossible and the other unlikely. What about Jean? She'd worked there probably from the first; she'd have lots of stories about the early days and how tough it had been, and would probably be a whole lot less discreet and happy to tell it like it really was. This thought cheered Victoria up. She sat down and worked on what she had got so far and was quite engrossed when she heard a knock at the door.

"Only me," said Albert and sauntered in.

Victoria felt disproportionately pleased to see him. He flopped down in a chair and she noticed he was rather smartly dressed, in a tweed jacket, equally tweedy tie and ochre-coloured cords. A proper country gent, she thought, and rather dashing.

"I thought you'd vanished!"

"No chance of that my lover, the only way I'll be leaving here is feet first."

"Oh don't say that!" Victoria felt a slight panic at the thought.

Albert laughed. "Don't be daft! Only my joke. Anyway, let's have a cup of tea. I've got some news for you, Miss Marple!" Victoria hurried to reboil the kettle and made his tea, strong, with sugar, as he liked it. She sat down opposite him, looking expectant, and waited... and waited... "Well?"

"I'm drinking my tea!"

"Don't be so annoying! What have you discovered?"

"Any chance of a biscuit?"

"What?"

"Not very hospitable, you townies. Have you got any biscuits?"

"Erm, no I'm afraid not, I don't eat them."

"Well I do! You won't get on too well down here if you don't keep biscuits or cake in stock, I can tell you."

Victoria fidgeted in her seat. "Oh do come on!"

"By the way, I bought some wood and netting for the chickens. I can knock up a temporary run for them, should get it done before dark, if you can lend a hand?"

"Me? Well, OK, I'll try. But WHAT have you found out?"

He beamed and leaned forward. "I've been to a farmers' meeting at the White Hart, this side of Westerley. And who do you think I saw?"

"The Queen and Prince Philip, how should I know?"

"Now, now, steady on." He was clearly enjoying winding her up. "I spotted Mandy Parkin and William Simmons, closeted together in a booth in the hotel bar. We were in another room, having a lunchtime meeting, and I spotted them through the door." He looked smug and sat back, arms folded.

"Oh, well that's interesting, but is that it?"

"Not quite. The barman, he used to go with the sister of one of my exes."

"Not one of your relatives then?"

"No, anyway, he said..."

"...and not someone you went to school with either?"

"No – do you want to hear this or not?"

"Get on with it," she grinned, pleased to have wound him up in return.

"Well, he said they were quite regular visitors and had been known to book a room for a few hours at a time, if you see what I mean."

"Gosh. That really does sound like William is playing away from home then."

"That's what I thought too. So Mandy Parkin seems to have a leg in both camps."

"Well, that's one way of putting it!" she giggled.

"You know what I mean. She's a saucy minx and seems like

she's hedging her bets. I wonder if John knows? I'm damned sure William doesn't. He's the sort who'd get all fightable if he knew his brother was supping at the same table."

"Do you think she…?" Victoria trailed off and looked uncomfortable.

"What? Do I think that she could have bumped old Henry off?"

"Well, yes."

"I don't think I'd put it past her. She's a very determined young woman."

"But, what would she gain?" Victoria pondered.

"She's got her father's company, Janner's Jams and maybe, with Henry out of the way, she thinks she can join forces with Primrose Cottage and either brother will do."

"Well, that would fit in with John's idea too. Would you kill someone for that?" Albert snorted. "People have killed for less, believe me. They'd have a very nice little dynasty there."

Victoria drank her tea and looked thoughtful. "Want to tell me?" asked Albert quietly.

"Well, it's all a bit odd, but I found a letter from my mother when I was going through one of my many boxes of stuff, kindly stored in your barn thank you. It was from over thirty years ago." She recounted the letter to Albert and he nodded.

"Yes, that would be right. Grace started off working for old Janner Parkin, she was very good as his secretary and things. Very bright is Grace, she encouraged him and they made quite a team and the business got going quite well. Then Henry makes a move. Bit of a better 'class' of person was Henry, well in Grace's eyes anyway, so she jumped ship and before you can say jam jar, she'd got Henry starting their own jam enterprise and outdoing Janner at his own game. As you can imagine, that didn't go down too well. Lots of hostility for many years, but I always reckon Grace had a soft spot for old Janner."

Victoria cleared her throat. "So when they were saying in the shop that John Simmons might be Janner's son…?"

"As I said before, that's nothing new, people have been saying that for years. I don't know, but I reckon both boys are a chip off the old Henry block, and it's a load of hooey if you ask me." He stood up. "Right, I'll get changed out of me gladrags and get those hens sorted out. Oh, and I picked this up in a computer place near Westerley." He fished a small box out of his jacket pocket and shoved it across the table towards her. "It's a booster for the Wifi, you have a fiddle with that and see if you can't get it sorted, then come and give me a hand banging in posts – soon get you working like a proper farm girl!" and he was gone.

There was certainly more to Albert than met the eye, Victoria thought – and not for the first time.

After installing the booster, which worked brilliantly, Victoria helped move the chicken coop. Fortunately it was on wheels and looked like a sweet gypsy caravan as they trundled it into her front garden. "You really want to be able to see them, good to keep an eye out as I expect Mr Fox will come around. They are quite amusing things really, they chitter and flap, your aunt and I used to watch them for hours." He smiled. "But they'll soon eat the grass, so best put them up this end."

"I'm not a great fan of lawns and the less I have to mow the better, so that's fine."

In no time a grassy area, with an old apple tree to one side, was made secure and the chickens rounded up and put inside. "There, that'll do for now. The tree will give them some welcome shade, they'll be happy as larks. Probably need to get an electric fence and then you can move them around as suits, they like a bit of fresh grass, keeps the yolks nice and yellow."

"Oh does it?"

"Yep, that's why all the barn-reared ones are so pale, poor beggars don't get grass, well, not enough of it anyway."

Victoria wasn't at all sure about an electric fence. She envisaged something akin to Colditz and feared she'd end up electrocuting herself, but never mind; she was sure Albert would help her sort it out if she played the 'dim townie' role again. Admiring the hens, now all happily chattering and scratching about in the grass, she said, "Albert, I was thinking I might go back to Primrose Cottage again on Monday and chat to John, see if I can't find out a bit more."

He scratched is head. "Do you think that's wise?"

"I need a bit more stuff for the article anyway and, well, I thought I might probe a bit."

"Hmmm, I'm not sure…"

"And I also want to speak to Jean. Has she worked there from the beginning?"

"I reckon."

"So she'll know all the details about when they started up? That would be really useful."

"She'll be in to clean again Tuesday won't she?"

"Oh yes, gosh I can't get used to having a cleaner, you're right, I could ask her then."

"Right, well 'tis dimperty and I need to go and do some paperwork before bed."

"Dimperty?"

"Dimperty, dimpsy, dusk – don't you town folks know nothing?" He grinned at her in the twilight.

"It seems not," she said, and grinned back. "Night then."

"Night."

Victoria settled down to an evening of Googling and Facebooking and enjoyed catching up with her friends and updating them on her new life. She posted a few photos and was gratified to see all the 'likes' she generated. In bed by ten (unheard of on a Saturday night), she just had time to start thinking about all the unpacking she could get done the next day, and where on earth was she going to put everything, before she fell sound asleep.

* * * * *

After a productive but exhausting Sunday of unpacking, Victoria woke early on the Monday morning. Unlike her London life when her first thought was of work, this morning it was of her hens. She went outside to let them out, opened the nestbox and threw them some bread. Albert had found some things called layers pellets, presumably left over from her aunt's time. The chickens seemed happy to tuck in and drank water from the dog bowl. During her unpacking marathon, she'd sat and watched them whenever she'd stopped for a coffee break and found them wonderfully restful. To her surprise, they were going to be a positive addition to her country life. She must try and see the Reverend this afternoon as she needed to get equipped. She also needed to say 'Thank you' to Gray and Sebastian. She fired off a quick email to her London friends, effusive with thanks, then gathered her laptop, notebook and camera equipment and got in her car.

Victoria set off for Primrose Cottage. It was a beautiful morning. The hedgerows glistened with early dew and bluebells were starting to appear, as was a really pretty pink flower which her flower book had identified as red campion. She opened the sunroof to enjoy the birdsong as she navigated her way around the lanes. There was a wonderful smell of onions (or was it garlic?) in the air too; she must ask Albert about it. Victoria only had to reverse once, for the elderly lady in the VW again, who was as resolute as before.

John was surprised to see her, but ushered her into his office. Now she was there, Victoria felt quite flustered and unsure.

"Did I forget something?" he asked, striking a pose of casual confidence behind his desk, but not without glancing at his watch first. "No no, not at all, you've been really generous with your time. I just wondered about a few things…" she began.

"Fire away."

"Well, this deal that your father mentioned."

"I thought I'd dealt with that?" His tone was brusque.

"Well, sort of. Wasn't he about to sign a deal with Berry Brothers the morning of…"

"Yes, yes, but what has that to do with anything?" Now he was frowning. "I told you, that wasn't anything we needed to concern ourselves with anymore, we have other plans."

"Right. It's just a bit of a major change of course and I wondered if that might cause some ripples in the industry?"

"Ripples in the industry?" He almost shouted. "I don't know where you've got that idea from. Certainly not! And what's this to do with your article, anyway?"

"Well, it's all quite relevant to where you are now, and what your next move might be."

"I have no intention of discussing that with you." His tone was icy. He sat forward in his chair, arms braced against the top of his desk as if he might spring up out of his seat at any moment. "Oh, right," said Victoria trying to sound casual, rather than terrified, which in reality she was. "So you can't tell me what your next move will be?"

"No." The statement was final, and he got to his feet. "I have a meeting starting in ten minutes and I need to prepare, so I'm sorry, but you need to leave."

"Of course, that's fine. I just wondered if Janner's Jams were still anything to do with your future plans?" The temperature in the room seemed to drop about ten degrees and Victoria felt her breathing quicken. John Simmons was stony-faced. He held her gaze fixedly and she finally knew exactly what the phrase 'rabbit in the headlights' meant. He crossed the room and held the door open. "Goodbye," he said.

The door slammed shut behind her and, trying not to run, Victoria made her way down the stairs and out the front door. Marilyn's timid brown eyes followed her all the way, like a frightened puppy.

"Breathe," Victoria told herself as she sat in her car, holding the steering wheel very tightly. She started the engine, backed out and began her journey home. The wind had got up, and the sun had gone behind a cloud; everything looked slightly bleak now. She hesitated at a crossroads, but remembered the way and turned left.

She negotiated a tight right-hand bend and was just entering a narrow straight stretch when she saw a red car coming towards her at speed. "My God!' she cried as she realised that braking was no use; the red car was not stopping for her or anyone, and the lane didn't seem wide enough for two cars.

She wrenched the steering wheel left towards a field entrance. She saw the gate splinter like matchwood as her car struck it; then the back end of the vehicle clipped the granite gatepost and she was shot into the field. For a terrible moment she thought the car was going to turn over, but instead it bucked, then slewed to a halt and the engine cut out.

Victoria found she was shaking uncontrollably. Her camera, handbag and pad were jumbled in the foot well and great gobbets of mud were sliding down the windscreen. She realised she was making a strange gulping, sobbing noise and she took deep breaths to try and calm herself. Then she started to cry. A face appeared at the passenger window, then another, and another, until she was surrounded by large, inquisitive cows, all peering in at her with wide brown eyes. A huge tongue slurped up the driver's window and she half laughed.

"Only in Devon," she muttered and reached for her phone, lodged somewhere under her seat. By some miracle she had a signal. By some other miracle, Albert answered on the first ring. "Hello," she said shakily.

"Victoria? You alright?"

"Not really, could you possibly bring your tractor? I seem to be stuck in a field with some cows," and she started crying again.

Chapter 8

Victoria sighed as she climbed out of the scruffy enamel bath – long gone were the days of glorious power showers – and placed her feet carefully onto a folded towel. The bathroom lino was so far past its sell-by date she felt a bit uncomfortable standing on it. She knew Jean scrubbed it regularly (amazingly, she appeared to scrub all the floors), but despite that it always looked slightly grubby and as though bacteria might feel very at home in the cracks and crevices. She reminded herself that she needed to think about talking to builders and plumbers sooner rather than later.

She luxuriated in the feel of her soft bath towel and tried not to wince as she dried the bruised and tender areas resulting from last night's car accident. It still seemed like a bad dream: had Mandy really run her off the road and not even stopped? True, she was basically unhurt – apart from a nasty graze on her right arm and a bruise all the way down her right thigh – but still...

Turning a blind eye to the rust patches around the taps she felt comforted that she had lovely towels and body lotions to make bath-time a bit less Spartan. She was just reaching out for her Dior moisturiser (another generous gift from Gray and Sebastian) when she heard a noise downstairs and a woman's voice yelling abuse at something (or someone). She flinched, feeling vulnerable in her nakedness... and then remembered it was Tuesday, Jean's day for cleaning.

She rushed through getting dressed and got downstairs as fast as she could. As she approached the kitchen, the abuse started again and she came upon Jean flapping a tea towel at Betty, the serious-eyed ewe that had given her such a fright a few days earlier.

"Oh no, not again!" said Victoria.

"It's Edith's fault," replied Jean, "she was always feeding things. Sheep, birds, cows… wouldn't surprise me if she fed the mice too."

Victoria felt a lot less frightened this time and remembered Albert's herding technique. She spread her arms wide, saying "Go on, get out of it!" and making a shushing noise. The ewe looked at her adoringly. Jean flapped a tea towel at her. "Get out, you gert big, dirty thing!"

"Go on, scram!" Victoria clapped her hands and moved towards the ewe. Slowly she turned and wandered out of the back door. Victoria closed it quickly.

"It crept up behind me like a ghost!" said Jean, patting her chest. "Gave me a right fright it did! Dunno how something so big can walk so soft!"

"Here, have a seat and get your breath back."

"Oh right – frightens me, big animals do," said Jean, "and as for cows, well, don't start me! Talking of cows, I hear you had a bit of a close encounter with some last night?"

"Well, the cows were incidental really, I don't suppose they were expecting me to land in the middle of their field. I am alright, but I'm not sure about my poor little car. It's down at Tufty's. Albert came to the rescue and did the knight in shining armour thing."

Jean nodded knowingly, as if this information implied far more than Victoria intended. "So what happened then, did you hit a bank or summat? They's very narrow these lanes for a newcomer."

"I'll just get the kettle on and we can have a cuppa. I was just about to have breakfast – I wasn't expecting you quite so early."

"Early! Why goodness me, it's close to half past eight, I've been up since five – today's the day I do all out under my beds. Can't let dust lie you know, makes me cough in the night."

Victoria pondered whether she was wrong to never really consider 'doing out' under her bed, or if it was Jean's cleaning obsession that was the problem. Probably a bit of both, truth be told. She saw Jean eyeing her peppermint teabag suspiciously and so very deliberately produced the standard brand she'd stocked up on for Albert. She thought Jean's shoulders relaxed a little when she recognised 'proper' tea. "It was a bit of a nasty accident actually."

"No!" replied Jean, now agog for new gossip.

"I was just driving along by that farm that has the flowers and veggies outside on a table."

"Hmm yes, that's Jacobs, lovely swede."

Victoria paused, took this in, and ploughed on. "I was just driving, as I said, and along came Mandy Parkin in that sporty red car of hers and just pushed past for want of a better way of saying it. I had to swerve and went right off the lane and crashed into a field. The worst of it was the damn woman didn't even stop. I was just so shocked, luckily my mobile worked so I rang Albert and asked for help. Lucky he was in," she nodded slowly to confirm the point.

"He came and sorted you out then," said Jean (no doubt memorising every word, thought Victoria, to pass on in the shop).

"He did, bless him. I must admit I was a bit tearful and very grateful someone could take charge of the whole mess. I think I might have been in shock."

"I bet you was, feeling better this morning I hope? That Mandy Parkin is a right one, no manners, no charm. Not like her Dad, her Dad used to be right nice to me, I always had time for him." She leaned forward and looked around, furtively, her eyes magnified by the lenses in her glasses. "In my opinion, Grace made a mistake changing 'orses so to speak, she should have stuck with old Janner, he were lovely."

"Is that so? Well I definitely owe Albert a big thank you for last night, it would have been much more long-winded if I'd had to call out the AA."

"I'm sure he'll find a way to get a favour back," said Jean, her big horsey teeth showing as she grinned hugely. "I always laughed with Edith about how useful Albert was as her toy boy!"

Victoria decided it was time to change tack. "I would be very grateful Jean," Victoria said as she put the mugs on the table, "if you could spare some of your time this morning to talk to me about the early days of Primrose Cottage. I have to get the article finished in the next few days and it's been a bit chaotic around here as you can imagine."

"So long as I gets time to do my cupboards and skirting, third Tuesday of the month, we always did cupboards and skirting." Jean nodded to ensure Victoria understood the vital importance of a regular cleaning schedule.

"I'll make sure there's plenty of time – and don't worry if something has to wait till next week." The look on Jean's face made it plain that nothing, under any circumstance, could wait until next week. Victoria decided to just get on with talking through the points for the article.

"When did you first go and work for Primrose Cottage then?" Victoria picked up her laptop from the worktop and created a file which she labelled 'Jean'.

"Oh it weren't called anything fancy like that when I was first helping out!" Jean wrapped her hands around her mug of tea and sat back in her chair. "I answered an advert, matter of fact, down at the shop. There was a postcard in the window asking for cleaning help and a little light packing. I never mind a bit of hard work and it sounded just the thing as my lot were all off at school."

Victoria tried to input the words as fast as she could, to get down most of what Jean was saying.

"Grace worked with old Janner you see and funny, most of us thought she was going to marry him the way they were. She virtually ran the old place and Janner seemed pretty gone on her we all thought. But then Henry appeared, come back from some jaunt overseas and she seemed to go right off Janner and thought Henry was the bee's knees so to speak." Jean stopped and put her hand over her mouth. "Oh dear! That were a real wrong thing to say, pardon me."

Victoria tried hard not to smile at Jean's unfortunate bee reference and encouraged her to continue.

"Then she fell pregnant with young William and it all seemed to happen quite fast after that. Grace married Henry afore the bump showed too much and she gave her notice at Janners and was out within a couple of weeks."

Victoria realised that, as interesting as all this was, none of it would be of any use for her article. "So, you did what in the early days then, packing and a spot of cleaning?"

"Well it wasn't that long after William was born that they had this idea to open a jam company, Primrose Cottage was the name she came up with. Bit daft but she was dead set on it." Victoria smiled, remembering her mother's input. "The job was just what it said in the advert, helping her in the house with a spot of cleaning and keeping the kitchen spotless on jam-making days and then helping pack a few jars into boxes when they started getting local shops wanting an order."

"Oh so Grace started in her own kitchen. Goodness! That's a real rags-to-riches story."

Jean pushed her mug a little further towards her and Victoria recognised the sign for another cuppa. Refilling both mugs she tried to push the story on a bit. "So once it was really established, what sort of jobs did you do then?"

"Oh took a while before they was 'stablished," continued Jean, and Victoria resigned herself to not being able to move things along any faster. "Grace worked hard, I'll give her that, she was a grafter. Of course things was a lot more popular once Henry took my Mum's recipe, daylight robbery that was and that's a fact!" Victoria nodded, unsure as to the correct response. "Not as I likes to speak ill of the dead, but it were right underhand what he done."

"Underhand, in what way?"

"Well he were one of the judges on the village show that year, he judged on currant buns and three fruit jams. Though how he ever persuaded anyone he knew anything about buns and jams was a mystery to me, never raised a spoon in the kitchen his whole life he didn't. Grace did everything. She can bake a fine cake that one."

"So what happened?" Victoria wondered how judging at a show had lead to the now legendary stealing of the family recipe.

"Well it was in the rules, no arguing, just was the rules!"

"Sorry," said Victoria, "I don't follow."

"For the cup for the three fruit jams, the rules was 'Three fruit jams presented in matching dishes with spoons and the full recipe'. S'pose it was to check you weren't cheating and hadn't just gone and bought them, like."

"Oh so you had to display the recipes with the jams in the competition!" Light dawned at last.

"Yes, and he stole 'em, all the lot, whole class came in after the judging and there they were, gone."

"What – the jams were gone?" Victoria sensed the plot getting away from her again.

"No, no, the recipes. All the entries was there, jams on plates with spoons but NO recipes. All of us went to the committee and asked but no one had seen them go. Of course we all had proper copies at home so not much lost, but I know he got away with them all!"

"What made you think it was Henry who stole them?" asked Victoria. "Well was just after that when their jams changed colours, that was the final proof," Jean nodded wisely.

"Sorry, changed colours?"

"Yes, they always done red jam and then, all of sudden, there was yellow and even a greengage, same as my Mum's."

"Oh they made more varieties, I see, but are you sure they used your mother's recipe?"

"Well who else in the village ever made greengage jam, we were the only ones with the trees you see!" Jean made her point triumphantly as though there was no other solution.

"So Grace and Henry bought the fruit from you?"

"Oh no!" said Jean with as much scorn as she could muster. "I s'pect they went to some cash-and-carry somewhere, never did speak much to Henry after that, never have forgive him!"

"Oh I see." Victoria felt that if she had been on a jury deciding the case Jean would not have convinced her of Henry's guilt, but she guessed it had become something of a local legend and could never be disproved.

"Mind you, wicked man though he was, I'm not sure I would have wished him dead like that, nasty way to go."

"Yes," said Victoria tentatively, "allergic to bee stings I gather?"

"Must have been badly 'lergic the way 'is face blew up." Jean gave another all-knowing nod.

"I hadn't heard much detail, except that it was a bee sting." Victoria almost held her breath and hoped Jean had more information than she and Albert had already gathered.

"Well Dot, her that's in the darts team with me on a Thursday, Dot works down at Westerley General Hospital, the one they took him to when he had the accident and that. Anyway, she said she was just passing when he came in on a trolley and they was still trying to revive him and he looked something chronic."

"Really?" Victoria quietly refilled Jean's mug in an attempt to keep the conversation flowing (and before the grubby skirting boards pricked her conscience).

"Yes really bad," Jean's eyes grew even larger as she relished the ghoulish details. "His mouth particular was all swelled up, he were real blue-coloured and his eyes wide-staring, mad like. 'parrently when the allergy takes you it stops you breathing and is a bit like suffocating. Nasty way to go."

"Poor Henry," said Victoria

"Yes. Dot said he had red wheals and a rash all over 'is cheeks, and his mouth were stuck open like he were gasping. Nasty sight, she says she hasn't slept a good night since, she's even thinking of going to the doctor for some of that Prozac stuff people have in the magazines."

"Oh dear that does sound nasty, poor man."

"But all this chatting won't get your skirtings sorted, now will it?" Jean put down her mug. "Still it was nice for you to have a sit down after that nasty carry on last night, calming you down is probably more important than they skirtings!"

Victoria considered the description of Henry's death had been anything but calming, but she could tell Jean had said all she was going to on the subject. Victoria left her to her skirtings and decided to walk to the village and see what state her poor car was in. It was currently residing at Tufty's garage looking like it had been through a hedge backwards which, in a way, it had.

The walk was heavenly. The birdsong was almost deafening.

A wren hopped along in the hedgerow singing its heart out, seemingly keeping her company. Spring had clearly sprung, and all the male birds were doing their best to woo the females with their impressive singing and puffed-out chests.

Victoria realised she was always alert to the sound of a car engine. She was following the footpath, but every now and again had to cross the road or walk a short way alongside it before going over a stile or through a gate, and she felt poised to fling herself into the hedge at any moment in case mad Mandy was behind the wheel.

She must check which were Albert's fields and try and find a route that avoided the roads completely. Soon the edge of the village came into view and she was safely on the pavement. She waved at Iris, Dahlia or Lavender (she had no idea which one was behind the counter) as she passed the shop and made her way to the garage.

"Well, you're a lucky one," said Tufty in greeting.

"Really, why do you say that?"

"State of your car, by rights you should have had broken bones and all sorts."

"I see what you mean." She looked at her forlorn car, smeared in mud and with clods of earth wedged in the wheel arches and even sitting on the roof. One front wheel was askew and both front and rear panels on the passenger side were crumpled. It did look very sorry for itself. As a final insult, the cows had done a fine job of licking and dribbling on everything so that it had the look of an impressionist art installation. She could probably sell it for a fortune in London, Victoria thought ruefully. "Is it very bad...?"

Tufty pursed his lips. "It isn't good, to be truthful. I reckon you might have damaged the chassis. Insurers might write it off. Bit borderline I'd think."

"I rang the insurance people just before I left, so I expect their assessor will be round any day."

"Reckon."

"I suppose we'd better just wait and see then…" She smiled, turned to leave and almost bumped into Grace. "Oh I'm sorry – Grace, how are you?" Victoria worked hard to rearrange her face from a look of astonishment – Grace looked wonderful, radiant even – to one of concern as befitted the situation.

"Well, you know…" Grace brushed her immaculate blonde bob back behind one ear.

"You seem to be bearing up very well, but if there's anything I can do…?"

Grace gave a tight smile and patted Victoria's arm. "You are sweet, thank you, but no. I am at my best when I'm busy doing and coping. If I sit down and think for too long, I shall simply fall apart."

Victoria doubted that very much but perhaps there was some truth in Grace's need to keep busy. She knew that feeling herself. She sneaked another look. The woman looked younger than when she'd last seen her, never mind drawn and haggard through grief. How extraordinary – maybe Albert was right about botox?

"My goodness, is that your car?" asked Grace.

"I'm afraid it is."

"What on earth happened?"

"Well, not to put too fine a point on it, I was driven off the road by someone coming the other way who had no intention of stopping."

"Good lord, how very ill-mannered of them. An aggressive young man I assume?"

Victoria pulled a face. "No, an aggressive young woman actually. Mandy Parkin."

"Well! Whatever next!" Grace snorted. "That young woman is a liability! Are you alright, your car looks ruined?"

"Yes, thanks, I'm fine, just a bit bruised."

"Well, I'm here to look at Henry's car. Tufty, have you heard anything from the police? Can we advertise it yet?"

"No Mrs Simmons, sorry. I haven't heard nothin'. They've been and looked at it, obviously, but they haven't said they're done with it." Grace turned to look at the Jaguar, parked to the side of the forecourt. "But there's nothing much wrong with it, is there?"

"No Mrs Simmons, 'tis fine. Mr Henry can't have been going very fast, or even moving, when…" he tailed off. "No, you're right." Grace nodded. "The car seems fine. Excellent, we'll get a good price for it then!"

Victoria felt slightly shocked – but then why be sentimental about a car? She somehow thought it was a little disrespectful to be selling it on so quickly, but then she was too soft-hearted and, to her detriment, rarely made decisions based on economics.

"You don't want to buy it, do you? It looks like you might be needing a new car!" Grace turned to her, bright-eyed and inquisitive.

"Me? Good lord, no! It's much too new and smart for me. I am strictly a 'needs must' car owner. I shall be going for something plain and practical." Then she thought she'd better add, "But the Jaguar is lovely, I'm sure you'll sell it easily."

A distant ringing could be heard and Tufty said "Oh, s'cuse me, that's the office phone!" He scuttled back to the garage workshop, or 'office'.

"Decent chap," said Grace. "Well, I ought to be going really. I need to buy a birthday card for one of my granddaughters."

"Nicole's children?"

"Yes, have you met?"

"Not the children, no, but I've met Nicole. I thought she was lovely."

"Did you?" Grace's fine eyebrows arched and she smiled. "Yes, I suppose you two would have some common interests. She is a dear, but not quite daughter-in-law material I'm afraid. No, that sounds bad." She sighed. "She is a nice woman, but I fear she is dissatisfied with her lot. And that's never a good thing."

"Oh, I see. I don't know her that well, but she seems very... bright and bubbly!"

"Yes, she is, that's true – and such a pretty girl. Of course, she should have pursued her acting career. Not really cut out for country living, poor thing. But there, you make your bed and you have to lie in it. I don't believe in people just 'opting out' of marriages because they are bored. Especially when there are children."

Is that the voice of experience speaking? Victoria wondered.

"Have you ever been married dear?"

Well, that's to the point, thought Victoria. "No, I haven't, always managed to shy away at the last minute!" she laughed and tried to make it sound casual.

"I admire an independent spirit, good for you! You'd better keep your eye on Albert though, well known for the ladies!" Grace looked at her watch. "Oh dear, I really must fly."

"Grace, I'm sorry to mention it again – and please say no if it's all too difficult – but I really do need to finish my article on Primrose Cottage. It's got to be submitted on Friday."

"Ah, good job you mentioned that. We're having an important meeting tomorrow, looking at where the company is heading now, so if you could come in tomorrow afternoon we should be able to give you a 'stop press' update. Does that sound OK?"

"It sounds wonderful," said Victoria, marvelling at the woman's enthusiasm and energy only five days after her husband's death.

"Say, three o'clock?"

"I'll be there!"

Grace was already backing away and waved briefly before heading off to her car.

"Funny woman," said Tufty and Victoria gave a start.

"Oh! I didn't hear you come back – you made me jump!"

"Sorry 'bout that. Thought I'd keep out the way while you were chatting."

He wiped his hands on an appropriately oily rag and then stuffed it into a pocket in his overalls. "You sure you don't want that Jag? Lovely car." He wandered towards the car and peered inside.

"It is lovely but firstly, I can't afford it and, secondly, given the roads around here, I'll be looking for something smaller, older and more practical."

"I thought all you London people had loads of money!" He turned and grinned at her.

"Not me! Working girl, with no rich husband to lavish posh cars on me."

He peered back inside the Jag. "Still think that's weird though."

"Sorry? What is?"

"Them epipens. Henry always had them dotted about. One in the glovebox, one in the door pocket, even found one under the seat once! Then that very day when he needed it, not one in sight. Poor bugger." Tufty straightened up. "Well, best be getting on. I'll let you know if I hear from the insurers."

"Thank you."

"Want me to keep an eye out for another car for you in case yours has had it?"

"That's not a bad idea."

"I reckon a small four by four would suit you. Not too big, lots of grip, and you sit higher up so you gets a better view of what's coming. And then when you get a dog, great for carting that round too."

Victoria was puzzled. "Who said anything about a dog?"

"Well, I heard you'd got chickens already, so the next thing is always a dog!"

"Oh dear – are we 'incomers' so predictable?" she laughed.

"Yep!" He gave her his funny little forelock-tug-cum-salute gesture and trotted off back into the workshop.

Victoria wandered along the road, realising she now had to walk back home again. Not exactly a hardship, but it all took time. She lengthened her stride; the exercise was good for her. A car hooted and she turned to see the Reverend Ruminant's Morris Traveller. "Miss West! Would you like a lift? I heard about your little mishap."

"Goodness, news does travel fast around here, doesn't it? A lift would be lovely, thank you." She tugged open the door and slipped inside. The smell of leather and the distinctive sound of the engine instantly transported her back to her childhood. "What a lovely car. I feel about eight years old again."

"It does seem to have that effect on people." The Reverend beamed and pulled out with an elaborate hand signal. Victoria laughed. "I haven't seen anyone do that in years!"

He wound up the window. "I feel it befits the vehicle. But then I am a bit of a professional old fogey." He gave the infectious giggle Victoria had so loved when she'd first met him. "People are always in such a rush these days they don't always see the rather lovely indicator flippers that Gertrude has," he gestured towards the top of the door, "so I find a clear indication of intent is quite beneficial. On the whole."

"Oh yes, I loved those funny little flippers when I was little, I always thought they made the cars look so sweet. But yes, I am sure they are easy to miss in today's hurly-burly."

"Whenever I venture into Westerley I feel as if I am under siege and find myself driving in a most defensive manner, really quite alarming!" He changed gear and pottered along at twenty-five miles an hour. Lovely, thought Victoria, as long as you weren't stuck behind him and in a rush. "In case you are wondering, yes, this is my normal speed for processing along the highway, but I do pull over at regular intervals – I know how tedious it can be if you are in a hurry."

Victoria hid her smile and murmured sympathetically.

"Actually, Reverend…"

"Edwin, please!"

"Edwin, I've been meaning to call on you. I find myself the rather puzzled owner of three hens with no idea really how to care for them, and I'm told you're the man to ask."

"Goodness, my fame precedes me! I do know a little about keeping fowl and I will be only too delighted to help." He wound down the window again and made another expansive gesture to indicate he was turning left. As far as Victoria could see, there was no one else on the road at all. "I have half an hour to spare now and could give you a quick rundown on a few vital things, if that would suit?" They turned into the drive to Victoria's cottage with another flourish of his right hand.

"That would be perfect, I'll make some tea."

"Splendid."

Once in the kitchen, Edwin looked momentarily saddened. "Ah, this is the first time I have been here since Edith passed away."

"Oh, I'm sorry, I should have thought. I haven't changed anything really, so far, but I expect it all feels rather odd."

"It does, but I'm sure once you have made your mark on it all will be well again. And Edith would be so pleased to know you were going to be here permanently."

"I am very, very lucky that she decided to leave it to me."

"Oh, I don't think there was ever any doubt about that. Unlike some families, yours, small though it was, did seem grounded on genuine love and affection."

"Thank you." She got down two mugs. "It's Earl Grey – is that OK?"

"My preferred tipple, sans milk, thank you."

"Same as me!"

"Same as Edith!"

"Really? I don't remember that."

"I think she kept it under her hat – Albert doesn't approve. I think the Earl Grey came out when I called, that and a piece of cake."

"Oh dear, now there I have failed you. I'm afraid I am no baker."

Edwin's eyebrows did a strange manoeuvre as he looked at her over the rim of the mug. "How interesting," he said quietly, "even more like your aunt then."

Victoria put down her mug. "Ah. So does this mean... you knew?"

"It does, and it seems you now know too."

"I do." They exchanged secretive smiles. "Does Albert know that you know?"

"No, I rather think he doesn't. And I think it's probably best to keep it that way."

Victoria paused, and then nodded. "Fine, then we'll go on as before."

"Excellent, so I'll expect to see your entries in the village fête baking classes then?"

Victoria laughed. "My goodness! Well yes, I suppose so. As long as you don't hold me to the flower rota too?"

"Oh but I must. You need to be my 'eyes and ears' among the ladies. Edith was marvellous at it. And you never know, you might actually find you enjoy the flower-arranging side. You look to me like a creative person and, heaven help us, we could do with some decent arrangements every now and again. Edith's were rather, well, random!" He giggled, and Victoria laughed too. "Now then, let's go and see your chickens and I'll give you the benefit of my wisdom!"

Chapter 9

With a sigh, Victoria rebooted her laptop yet again. She and technology would never be best friends. It was fabulously useful and she couldn't imagine life without email, but some days she wondered if there was a chip implanted in most computers whose sole purpose in life was to annoy her.

The article was due in a couple of days and she needed to get it finished and take this weight off her shoulders, and earn some money too. Much as she loved writing and researching, Henry's death had complicated things and left her feeling agitated. Murders didn't happen in real people's lives. She felt sure there was a vital piece of the jigsaw missing and, if she could just find out enough, it would all slot neatly together.

Scanning through the pictures she had taken on the day Henry died, she stared intently at each one hoping they would tell her something. The epipen seemed glaringly obvious now – was there anything else in the shots that might help? Feeling frustrated she flicked back to the article and read through what she had written so far. It was OK, but not special enough to fire the reader's imagination and, more importantly, to get the magazine interested in hiring her again.

Life seemed to be one big frustration at the moment. She'd spent hours last night unpacking bits and then not being able to find a suitable home for them. It was amazing that Aunt Edith had left her this house and she felt a huge debt of gratitude. It seemed ungracious to want to put away, dare she say it, even sell some of her aunt's bits and pieces, but she wanted to make the cottage her own; living among someone else's possessions didn't make it feel like home. Finally she had decided that she would just tackle one room at a time and see how that worked.

The kitchen was the first room she thought her aunt would have no problem with her changing. It seemed that although Aunt Edith had been interested in food and cooking – just not cakes – she had seen the kitchen as a means to an end rather than the centre of her home, which was what Victoria wanted it to be.

She'd unpacked box after box of her favourite cooking paraphernalia, from plates to saucepans to casserole dishes that she'd treasured for years. She'd smiled at the matching set of china that Gray and Sebastian had bought her as a house-warming present when she'd moved into her last flat. She had such lovely memories of dinner parties and happy times together. One important piece of equipment was her slow cooker. After a long day in the office it was so comforting to come home to a warm and filling casserole or curry. Her aunt had some interesting old kitchen gadgets, and some lovely pieces of china, not valuable, but traditional, like some blue-and-cream-striped Cornishware. Victoria was fast coming to the conclusion that she'd end up with an 'eclectic mix' – to coin a trendy term – and would keep quite a lot of her aunt's 'kitchenalia'.

Almost in reaction to the foodie memories her stomach rumbled. She needed a trip to a large supermarket and a big spend on basics and freezer contents. It was fine using the local shop but – fun though it was to visit – the choice was too restricting.

"Halloo! Anybody around?" Albert's voice boomed up the stairs.

"I'm up here just trying to get on with the article, be right down!"

"Don't you worry I'll get that kettle on – I know where everything is."

Victoria smiled. Finding a neighbour like Albert had been the best start ever to her new life. How on earth would she have managed without him? Walking downstairs into the kitchen she couldn't miss the wonderful array on the table; it was covered with plates of stunningly irresistible food. "Albert? What's all this?"

"Well I just started cooking and carried on really. It gets me like that sometimes. Anything you don't want to eat straight away I reckon you can freeze."

The choice of cakes, breads and cookies was just out of this world. She spotted chocolate brownies, plus another pillow of a sponge, chocolate this time, and what looked like chocolate-dipped flapjacks. "Albert – there's quite a chocolate theme going on here?"

"Well I know you girls, chocolate's a safe bet I reckon."

Further along the table was apparently the pastry corner. There were sausage rolls, a quiche and a covered pie. "I'm just speechless Albert! Thank you very, very much. This must have taken you ages. I will be stocked up for weeks."

"Have you eaten any lunch yet then?"

"Now you come to mention it no, I hadn't got round to lunch or much breakfast come to that. I keep meaning to stock up but it's been so manic I haven't got it sorted yet."

"Well I've not had lunch either so let's have a bit to eat and then you can tell me what you found out now we seem to be a detecting duo."

"Oh I'm not sure about that," said Victoria. "I don't really see myself as the 'elderly but insightful village lady.'"

"Well no you're not one of them, that's for sure – maybe a new breed of young village lady." Albert smiled at her and – not for the first time – she felt her stomach flutter a little. She distracted herself by taking one of the amazing looking sausage rolls and wished she had some nice conveniently bagged packs of green salad to serve with it. "I'm sorry I haven't got any pretty salad leaves or some tomatoes to have with your lovely offerings."

"I always reckon the best thing to go with a sausage roll is another sausage roll, so don't go worrying on my account!" Albert poured some hot water onto the mugs with teabags and they munched on the home-baked feast.

"So, you learn anything yesterday that might shed any light?" Albert was talking with his mouth full and it was even harder than usual to detect what he was saying.

"Oh about Henry. Yes and no I guess," she bit into the sausage roll, still warm from the oven, and the rich flaky pastry melted in her mouth. She sighed, swallowed and continued her tale. "I had a chat with Jean about how Primrose Cottage started and, having heard it straight from the horse's mouth regarding the legendary 'stolen recipe', I really don't think Henry is going to suffer in eternal damnation for anything he may or may not have done. It sounded to me like a mix-up with judging and someone removing the recipes when they shouldn't. But I guess Jean will forever think of herself as wronged and her mother the secret ingredient that made Primrose Cottage such a success."

"'Exactly what Trudy said the other night, hard woman to dissuade that Jean." Albert waved the remains of his sausage roll at her. "She made her point to Henry many a time, but he just ducked into nearby doorways when he saw her coming, he were a wily old fox. Anything else she said?"

"Her friend Dot was at the hospital when he was brought in, and Jean managed to relay a very gory description of what he looked like. Major allergic reaction I would have said. Apparently his mouth was hugely swollen and he was a bluish colour, red wheals and a rash on his face too. Must have been a horrible way to die."

"I reckon, he was an old bugger but didn't deserve to go like that."

Victoria's phone gave a piercing trill and she jumped. "Oh! I must change that ring tone. I was fiddling around with it and thought that was an improvement, but it isn't." She looked at the screen: 'Caller unknown'. "Excuse me Albert." She pressed the button. "Hello? Oh yes that's me yes, yes yesterday, I spoke to the garage again this morning."

Albert quietly moved over to the quiche, cut a large slice and took another sausage roll.

"What, completely? But how much? £800! You can't be serious. I realise you are just doing your job but how am I meant to replace a car with that sort of... is there someone in charge I can speak to? You are in charge, oh." Victoria looked up at the sky through the window and tried to stop her eyes filling with tears. "Yes I do realise there is an appeal procedure, thank you for that, yes, that's the correct address for the paperwork. Thank you, yes I'll be in touch." She placed the phone on the kitchen table and tried to steady herself. She hated crying in front of people and right now the tears were very close.

Albert gazed at her and seemed perplexed. "Plenty we can do with the spare vehicles I've got standing idle on the farm. No need to get too upset, eh?"

Victoria blew out a long breath and then thumped the table. "It's just not fair, that horrible Mandy has no concern for anyone but herself and now my car's a write-off and I have no way of replacing it, if they'll only give me £800 for it. If I were a witch I'd cast a hex on that nasty red car of hers. Can't we report her for dangerous driving?"

Albert put a chocolate brownie on a plate and tentatively pushed it towards her. "Doesn't mend your car, but it might make things feel better for a while." He smiled at her. "But Mandy'll just say you were too far over on the road or something, your word against hers on these country lanes." He looked at her sympathetically and Victoria felt even nearer to tears.

"I'm sorry to be so pathetic," she said. "It's just I haven't got any spare cash at the moment to sort out a car and the plan was for that one to last me a few years yet." With that she swallowed hard and got up to switch the kettle on again.

"Well I'm sure I could lend you a car if you'd be willing to take it?" Albert looked a little tentative, in case his offer was rejected.

Victoria paused, looked down at the floor for a moment and wondered what she ought to say. It was going to be really hard in this rural environment with no car but the cost of hiring something or buying a new car was completely beyond her for now. Having said that, the thought of driving someone else's car – especially one like Albert's Jag that barely made it from one petrol station to the next, or a Range Rover with doors that didn't open – was not something she felt comfortable about. "You're very generous Albert, but it's a huge favour to take from anyone, I mean we've known each other for really no time at all. I feel I would be abusing your kind nature."

"Indeed you are not!" Albert stood up and seemed almost offended. "I'd known your Aunt Edith for over thirty years, and she was like a mother to me and always a friend to listen to me and share life with. If she knew I didn't help you out she'd be mad as all hell with me. I'd like to lend you something, but if you won't take it for yourself, then maybe you'll take it for your aunt?" He sat down again, affronted, and looked at her. His fierce face was so endearing

Victoria wanted to laugh.

"Oh Albert you are such a kind man and already I can see why Aunt Edith treasured you as a friend. Thank you, it's more than my life's worth to say no. Thank you, it's a lovely gesture." Despite her words Victoria was filled with dread as to what type of vehicle she might have landed herself with. Her mind ranged from ex-army tanks through farm trucks to her worst-case scenario: a motorbike.

"Well once you've finished that cuppa – let's be off and find her."

"Find her?" said Victoria.

"Yup" Albert nodded seriously, "I think you better meet Gloria."

Victoria now felt totally confused and wondered if perhaps she was to borrow one of his friend's cars. Well, at least Gloria might have something down-to-earth and sensible. The panic began to subside and she braced herself for whatever was about to come. She could hear her aunt describing it as 'all part of life's rich pattern' and phrases like 'what doesn't kill you makes you stronger'. Aunt Edith had been a great one for sayings.

Victoria grabbed her jacket, buttoning it right up to the neck as they went out to the farmyard. The weather today was unusually cold for May, with a bitter wind. She neatly avoided the muddiest parts of the yard and marvelled at how much her life had changed in the last fortnight. Albert strode ahead to the furthest barn that stood a little separate from the others and turned to wait for her.

"Come on – it's cold out here."

Stating the flippin' obvious, thought Victoria. "OK, I'm trying to keep up!"

Albert was struggling with the sliding doors, apparently unwilling to move on their rusty runners. Suddenly they admitted defeat with a jerk and gave a squeal of indignation as he pushed them back, letting light flood into the barn. There sat a car. It seemed quite small from what little she could see, and totally covered with a dust sheet. Albert whipped the sheet off with a practised flourish, then turned to her. "Victoria, meet Gloria. She's a good girl if you treat her right and could be just the job I reckons."

Victoria's eyes widened with surprise. "Oh Albert, I couldn't!"

"She's a good car. I told you, Edith would have my guts for garters if I didn't help."

There, in all its glory, was a classic MGB sports car. She couldn't judge from the number plate what year it was but the condition was like new. This was no old runabout: it must be something special to Albert. She looked up at Albert, unable to frame any words. Running her hand over the pale yellow paintwork she fought back those tears again. She remembered these cars from her childhood, always the choice of the heroine in a TV show or a star in a film. The roof was black fabric and then she realised that it was a convertible. Oh my, how she'd always wanted a convertible car!

"That'll show Mandy Parkin she's not the only woman on the road!" said Albert with a note of challenge in his voice.

"Are you sure you're happy for me to drive this? It must be really valuable."

"Don't know, worth a bit I suppose, but no point in having lovely things if you never use them I say. Gloria just sits here, sometimes Tufty and I give her a run but mainly she just sits."

"But she's so beautiful," said Victoria. "You must have completely rebuilt her?"

"We've whiled away many an hour here rebuilding, searching out new parts and reconditioned ones. It was a labour of love you might say. It was your aunt that named her Gloria. 'You two boys coming in for a cup of tea or you spending all night out there with Gloria?' she'd say." Albert smiled fondly at both the car and the memories.

"I can't wait to take her for a drive. I was going to suggest we went to the farmer's store to get the bits Reverend Ruminant suggested for the chickens, but I guess this isn't the best vehicle for an errand like that! But Grace did suggest I went over to Primrose Cottage later today."

"You leave chicken stuff to me and take little Gloria out for a run and see how you like her. She'll be 100 percent reliable, we only looked at her the other weekend, went for a bit of a blast we did, so she's all fit to go. Taxed and MOT'd the lot, and she's on my fleet insurance, so you're covered to drive her."

"Oh Albert, thank you!" Impulsively she gave him a quick hug and then stroked the car again. "She's amazing."

"Yes, well," said Albert scratching his head and looking a little bashful, "that's all fine, but now I need to go and see a man about a dog."

Victoria raised her eyebrows. "Oh, I see, well don't let me hold you up!"

"No, no really," said Albert laughing. "I've got to go and see a bloke over Hattersley way about training up a new collie, so I'll give you the keys and leave you to get on." He rummaged in his pocket and handed the keys to her. "None of your central locking mind, you'll need to lock each door individually. She's got four gears and overdrive, but unless you're going far, don't worry about that. Oh, and no power steering or ABS either, so make sure you allow a bit more time to stop." He smiled and headed off towards his house.

"Thank you so much!" Victoria shouted after him. He waved but kept going.

Twenty minutes later she was sitting in Gloria, familiarising herself with how the controls worked, giggling at the antiquated heater and the funny little windscreen wipers that flip-flopped in small arcs across the screen. She had all her work bits and pieces in the boot – just – and was relieved to find it functioned normally. She was ready to set off for Primrose Cottage.

Gloria started first time, but pulling out of the barn took several attempts as Victoria stalled the engine, the clutch seeming to be a bit tricky. She soon got the hang of it and made her way, rather cautiously, along the drive. It was a good job Albert had reminded her about the car's old-fashioned brakes and steering; it was totally different from a modern car and needed some getting used to. She found she rather liked the immediacy of it, feeling 'at one' with the car rather than detached and cocooned by technology as was more usually the case these days. At the end of the drive she cautiously did a three-point turn then drove back, turning in the farmyard and heading out again. She felt more relaxed having hauled the steering wheel around a bit and gone through the gears. Now she headed out onto the open road.

As she approached Primrose Cottage, she spotted a distant flash of red. Oh no, she thought; it would be too cruel to meet that vile woman in her red monster again and damage poor Albert's car on their first trip out together. Deftly, she pulled the little car into a driveway immediately on the left. A few seconds later Mandy's sports car sped past, but not before Victoria had caught a glimpse of her flushed face and mouth drawn into a furious line. Well, well; all was not happy in the world of Mandy Parkin.

She wound the window down – a rather slow process as the MGB had manual winders – and stuck her head out to check the road ahead. A blue convertible Mercedes was approaching, more slowly than Mandy's BMW, but still travelling at quite a lick. Victoria registered the auburn mass of Nicole Simmons' hair and her face looking small, white and pinched. Curiouser and curiouser. Victoria tapped the leather steering wheel and pondered. Was it a coincidence that the two women were driving down the road from the farm just a minute or so apart?

She checked the road again and pulled out, the rest of her journey being uneventful. Gloria buzzed along smoothly with a few endearing little squeaks and rattles as befits a car of her vintage and character and, Victoria had to admit, she was already a little bit in love. She pulled into the now familiar car park, gathered her belongings and went inside the building. She waited at the reception desk and, after a few seconds, heard quick light footsteps pattering down the stairs. Marilyn crept into view.

"Hello, can I help you?" she asked, anxiously, as if they had never met before, her timid face and anxiously clasped hands reinforcing Victoria's original view of a small timid rodent. Victoria smiled warmly, resisting the urge to either say "Boo!" and terrify the woman, or to stroke her, or to offer a lump of cheese.

"Victoria West, here to see Grace – again," she said brightly, feeling the need to remind the mousy woman that they had met before.

Marilyn's paws flew to her mouth. "Oh my!" she said. "Yes, yes, of course, you came before, you came that day when Mr Henry..." She gave a small squeak and swallowed audibly. "And then you came another time too, I remember now. Sorry, I'm a bit muddly just now."

Thinking she might be stranded in reception the whole day with this poor creature on the edge of hysteria, Victoria prompted her. "I've an appointment to see Grace at three o'clock."

"Oh dear! I don't rightly know!" She moved forward and clutched Victoria's arm in a surprisingly tight grip, "there's been such a to-do!"

"Really?" Victoria's detective antennae twitched into life. "What exactly?"

Marilyn glanced about her nervously. "I don't know if I should say. But, well, they all had a big meeting, all the family and Mandy Parkin and," she glanced around again and Victoria felt like giving her a nudge to get on with it. "Well, t'was after about twenty minutes. There was a lot of shouting and I heard all sorts of things… and the language!" Her eyes were like saucers. "Then that Mandy went stormin' out. Slammin' the door like you can't imagine!"

Victoria thought she could.

"Then there was a bit more shouting and," she dipped her head slightly as if avoiding a blow, "I'm sure I heard a loud slap!"

Victoria was on alert now.

"The next thing, Mrs William, Nicole, her comes running out, tears all down her pretty face and that mouse-cara stuff all black and running! Proper shame I thought."

A door banged upstairs, causing Marilyn to shriek and almost hide behind Victoria. Down the stairs thundered John Simmons, his face white with rage. He did a double take when he saw Victoria, hesitated as if he was going to speak, then shook his head angrily and barged out of the front door. He flung himself into his Porsche and roared off, spraying dirt and gravel across the front of the building.

"Oh my!" said Marilyn again, from behind Victoria's left shoulder. "Mr John didn't look too happy, did he?"

Understatement of the year, thought Victoria. The poor woman was almost quaking with fear. Victoria thought she might as well try and make the best of the situation. "Marilyn, why don't you sit down for a moment?" She steered her to the small couch in the corner of the reception area and perched next to her.

"I do feel a bit queer I must say," the receptionist produced an old-fashioned lace handkerchief from her cardigan pocket and dabbed her brow. Gosh, did people still use such things? Victoria watched, fascinated. "Grace said they were having a big meeting to finalise the future direction of the business," she said casually.

"Yes, that's right," murmured Marilyn, "I typed the agenda for Mr John. When Mr William saw it, he wanted to change it, so I did."

"Really?"

"Odd that was, he wanted me to take out the bit about Mandy Parkin becoming a director and changed it to a merger with Janner's Jams, I don't know why." She was now chewing the corner of her handkerchief.

"And then what happened?" Victoria was feeling quite a thrill at her own audacity and nosiness; she wasn't usually so good at subterfuge.

"Well, then Mrs Simmons saw it and she got right cross with me!" Marilyn shook slightly. "She said was I mad and what did I mean by it? I just said I didn't mean anything and it was what Mr John and then Mr William had said." Victoria murmured in an understanding way. "Then she sort of shook herself and apologised to me, she's a very decent woman is Mrs Simmons, and she said to retype it again and to take all the Janner's stuff out and to put in about calling a proper board meeting to appoint her as managing director."

"Really? Well, that is interesting," said Victoria and patted her hand.

"Is it? I do hope I haven't said anything out of turn," Marilyn was looking terrified again.

"No, no, it's fine, that's exactly what Grace and I are going to talk about now." Victoria got to her feet. "Why don't you go and have a glass of water and get your equilibrium back?"

"Oh, right," said Marilyn, looking not entirely sure.

"I'll see myself upstairs." Gathering up her bits and pieces,

Victoria made her way up the stairs and looked around to locate Grace. She guessed she'd be in Henry's old office, so tapped on the door and went in.

"Victoria! Ah yes, I said to call in didn't I?" Grace seemed confused, half rising from behind the desk. "Erm, sit down, please."

Victoria tried to hide her surprise. Grace looked haggard; the youthful bloom witnessed yesterday seemed to have vanished. "Grace, are you OK?" Victoria leaned forward, concerned at the other woman's changed appearance. "You look exhausted."

"Yes, yes, I expect I do!" She smoothed her hands over her bobbed hair. "It's been something of a…" she searched for a suitable word, "momentous day."

"Oh dear," Victoria said as she opened her notebook and settled back into the chair.

"Oh lord, that damned article!" Grace groaned, as if she'd forgotten that Victoria was there in a work capacity rather than a personal one. "I really don't know what I can tell you just now. Frankly, it's all a bit of a mess."

Victoria looked enquiringly at her and said innocently, "Really? I thought today was all about the future direction of the company?"

"So did I, but it seems my family is more intent on tearing itself apart. I'm sorry, that's not very professional of me, but I think I'm still trying to come to terms with it at the moment," said Grace, "I need a moment." She took a deep breath. "You think you know your own children and then suddenly you find that you don't know them at all. You even wonder if you like them very much." Grace had picked up a paper knife and was turning it over and over in her hands.

Victoria felt a knot growing in her stomach. She thought she'd been clever trying to get details from Marilyn, but now here was Grace almost unravelling before her. This was very personal, and obviously very painful, and she suddenly felt like an intruder.

"My sons, Victoria, are spineless. It's a very hard thing for a mother to say, but there we are. I cannot begin to tell you how disappointed I am. Bitterly disappointed. I've given up so much for this business, done so much." The paper knife was jabbing now, accentuating Grace's words, making small indents in the old-fashioned blotter on the desk. Victoria wondered if the woman was on the edge of tears. "Mandy Parkin, that common, scheming, conniving little bitch has been rutting with BOTH my sons, if you please!"

The paper knife stabbed the blotter as if Mandy herself were pinioned to the desk. Victoria realised Grace was nowhere near tears; she was absolutely seething with rage. "That guttersnipe thinks she can take over this business, or at the very least 'merge' with us. How dare she suggest such a thing!"

Victoria opened her mouth to speak, but thought better of it. Instead she nodded and looked understanding, hoping Grace's unchecked and furious outburst would continue.

"Both of my sons think she wants them, that they actually matter, that she actually cares for them. They are too stupid and too arrogant to see she does not want either of them. What she wants is the business. MY business." The paper knife was stuck now, having passed through the blotter and jabbed into the wood. Grace wrenched it out.

"And that useless, disorganised, bleating daughter-in-law of mine, all she can think about is the money. Money, money, money. How can she survive? What will she do? Where will she go? She wanted a payout from William, if you please! She thinks he has money to pay her off and divorce her and let her run back to London! Over my dead body." The paper knife was now bent. Grace stopped and looked it, as if surprised to see it in her hands.

She suddenly threw it towards the wastepaper basket.

Down the corridor, Victoria heard a door flung open. A heavy tread thudded along the carpet and then William was in the room. "Mother?" he bellowed, then stopped on seeing Victoria. "Oh, it's you. What do you want?" He put his hands on his hips and looked like a petulant child.

"No, what do YOU want William?" snapped Grace. "I told you to go home. Go home and sort your wife out, sort your priorities out and get back in here tomorrow morning to start afresh, as if none of this ever happened. Do I make myself clear?" Her tone was icy. Victoria wished she was invisible. This was heavy life-changing family stuff and she should not be here.

William swayed, contemplating bluster or dignified retreat. He chose the latter (wisely, Victoria thought), turned and left. The silence seemed interminable and Victoria was aware of the blood pounding in her ears. She sucked the end of her pen and eventually looked up. Grace had her eyes closed; her eyebrows were raised and she seemed to be concentrating on deep breathing. When she opened her eyes a few moments later they were clear and focussed, and her usual serene demeanour had returned. Wow, thought Victoria, this is one strong lady!

"And so, Victoria, for the conclusion of your article, you can say that I am taking over, from my late, lamented husband Henry, as managing director of the company. Primrose Cottage Preserves will be looking to expand, possibly buying out some other local jam producers as part of that expansion and looking to export more of our products." She stopped to take a breath. "We will be introducing more of our popular 'seasonal specials' and I can confirm that, despite recent very sad events, Primrose Cottage Preserves is entering a new and exciting era of growth."

Chapter 10

Well, Grace certainly knows what she wants, thought Victoria as she walked slowly to the car. It wasn't how she had originally seen the older woman; she appeared to have acquired a much more businesslike persona since Henry's death. But maybe that was how she was dealing with a future without him. Victoria pondered the contradictory aspects of loving someone so much that you went on to make a life with them. It would be wonderful to be married and immensely happy but, of course, for so many people it wasn't a 'happy ever after' ending.

As she fiddled with the old-fashioned seat belt, she imagined herself rushing home to cook someone's dinner, juggling school runs and cleaning dirty shoes. A slight feeling of claustrophobia began to engulf her. Yes, a family life and a loving husband would be wonderful, but there were definite drawbacks too. It had been her choice to say 'No' to several boyfriends in the past when they had proposed something more permanent and, on balance, she felt it had probably been the right decision – but doubts were always there, waiting to catch her out.

Come along Victoria: get a grip. Food – lots of it, from a supermarket – seemed an excellent idea. She enjoyed popping in to see Lavender and the others, but she needed to discover where the local supermarket was to stock up on the things that the quaint village shop would never sell. How hard can it be to find a large supermarket? She looked on her phone – yes! she had a signal! – and typed in 'supermarket Westerley'. It quickly announced that there were four in the area. She smiled and started the engine.

She put the car into reverse – she couldn't quite bring herself to think of it as 'Gloria' – and realised she was enjoying driving now she had a feel for 'her' strange quirks. Slowly she headed down the lanes towards Westerley, enjoying the flowers that sprinkled the banks, savouring the novelty of living in the countryside.

An hour later, getting her breath back after her mammoth shop, Victoria realised why the modern day five-door hatchbacks with an economic engine made such good sense. With the boot full of her camera equipment, she had a nine-pack of loo rolls pushed in the back of the car and two large packets of cereal wedged beside it. Her passenger seat just about held three carrier bags (although any sudden stops would make the contents cascade into the footwell where she had put the wine bottles).

She took the approach to the farm slowly as it was almost dark now, and the last thing she needed was a stray pothole to throw her shopping into disarray. Security lights, that was something she ought to organise; it would make life much easier if a light automatically came on as you approached the cottage, but maybe Albert would object as it would disturb the animals, or some other eco-friendly reason. As she got out of the car (easier twenty years ago, she thought, as her back twinged), she spotted a large parcel left near her door. Oh Sebastian – what have you sent now? Please tell me it isn't a matching dovecote to go with the chicken house! Peering through the gloom she realised it wasn't a delivery at all. It was a person wearing dark clothes, making him (or her?) all the more difficult to spot.

"Hello?" she called out tentatively. The dark shape jumped, and as Victoria approached she realised it was Nicole.

"Nicole? Are you OK, did I forget a date we had?" she said, knowing full well that her diary was completely empty.

"Oh Victoria, I'm so glad you're here – I thought maybe you'd gone to London." She sounded weary and unhappy.

Pushing the key into the lock, Victoria switched on the porch light, deciding that yes, a security light seemed very sensible indeed. She turned to Nicole and couldn't stifle a gasp. "Oh my God – what happened?"

Nicole's face was bruised and her left eye badly swollen. A patch of blood matted her hair on that same side and her eyes were reddened from crying. "Oh yes, umm…" Nicole hesitated, then realised an explanation would have to be forthcoming. "William was angry. I've never seen him so passionate about anything. We got into an argument and he pushed me and I fell against the fireplace. I think I have some grazes along my arm too."

"Look come on in, let's get you a hot drink and cleaned up. Oh my God you must feel terrible – it all looks really painful." Nicole looked at her and the tears welled again. "I'm so sorry to bother you, I just didn't know where else to go. I don't really have any friends nearby that I can talk to."

"Right, you sit there," said Victoria, pulling out a kitchen chair, "and let me get the kettle on. I am pretty sure I know where my first aid box is." She half ran into the barn and managed, as luck would have it, to go straight to the right box. It was her 'grown up' box of sensible things like fire blanket and first aid kit, that she'd bought in a fit of practicality after a health and safety talk at work some years back. As she returned to the kitchen she saw again in the overhead light just how bad Nicole's face looked and wondered if they needed to go to the local hospital. "Are you sure you don't need to see a doctor?" she asked.

"No honestly, I think it just looks worse than it is and I'm feeling a bit shocked and upset. I'm sure I'll be fine after a hot mug of something. I won't be in your way for long, I was wondering if you could give me a phone number for Gray and Sebastian. I thought I might get in touch as I suspect I will be going back to London now."

"In my way? Don't be so ridiculous. You know I am happy to help – tell me you'll stay the night. I can even cook you a meal as I've just been to the supermarket and my wine stocks are at their best. I just need to stick a bottle in the fridge to chill."

She thought Nicole smiled and she wondered how true the falling against a fireplace story was. "Here, take some aspirin – are you OK with aspirin? I might have ibuprofen upstairs."

"No aspirin's fine, thank you."

Victoria made them both a strong coffee and then filled a small bowl with warm water and some disinfectant from her first aid kit. Sitting beside Nicole she said, "I have a feeling this might hurt but I think your face should be cleaned up a bit. Would you like me to do it – or I can fetch a mirror?"

"To be honest," replied Nicole, "I can't be bothered to do anything at the moment, even thinking."

Victoria started wiping the blood away with a cotton wool ball soaked in what she hoped was the right strength of disinfectant-laced water. Nicole winced with every touch, but not as badly as Victoria had feared. Once Nicole's face was clean it became obvious that things were not beyond hope. Victoria assumed Nicole might have been worried about scarring, given her career hopes, but it was really just a very nasty graze down the left side of her face and quite a cut above her left eye.

"There, now have some coffee – maybe you should have sugar in it?" Nicole nodded mutely, then wrapped her hands around the mug once Victoria had stirred the contents and passed it over. "Do you want to talk about it? Is there anything I can do to help?"

Nicole looked up miserably and shook her head slightly. "No, nobody can help really. It's partly the same problem that we talked about in the pub. William, apart from being a totally lazy mummy's boy, doesn't like anything not going his way. He wanted the business sold for loads of money and he had his sights on a comfortable retirement, doing nothing but fishing all day. Now things seem to have changed and he is mad as heck."

"So the meeting today changed how William saw the future then?" Victoria wondered if she was pushing too hard, but she hadn't really grasped from Grace what the meeting had triggered. All she knew was that it had left several people very, very angry.

"Oh it was a real humdinger of a family meeting today." Nicole tightened her hands around the coffee mug till Victoria could see her knuckles whiten. "It seems," continued Nicole, "that William is capable of more than just fishing in his spare time and has been having an affair with Mandy Parkin. I'm not sure what I felt when I heard, surprise at the affair or amusement that anyone would want to spend time in bed with him."

"Mandy?" said Victoria, trying to sound surprised. "So she was going out publicly with John and then having a quiet affair with William. Do you think that was because she fancied them both or, as seems far more likely to me, was related to the business?"

"Oh the business, definitely. We were discussing the future of Primrose Cottage and Grace made it obvious that putting the business up for sale so Janner's could acquire it was simply not going to happen. Mandy got angrier and angrier and started shouting about what a waste of time the last three years had been. How she should have known better than to put up with ridiculous groping from Grace's two useless sons and how she had invested a lot of time and effort into this family making sure the business would be hers."

"Wow," said Victoria, not quite sure of the appropriate thing to say.

"It was impressive though, seeing Grace turn from Mrs Nice-Guy to Mother Tiger when someone insulted her boys! She shouted back that Mandy knew full well that Henry was against selling the business to Janner's and would always have blocked anything because of his feelings towards her father."

"Oh because Grace used to go out with Janner, her father, oh right." Victoria wondered if she would be able to remember all this to tell Albert.

"Mandy replied that his sons wouldn't have blocked anything that made them some money. William thought he would sell and retire and John had massive delusions of grandeur and thought he could build an empire with us working together, and then she turned towards John and laughed. He was really mad at that." Nicole sighed as if remembering the whole thing was too stressful for her.

"I can see that Mandy would be angry, as she thought she would come to the meeting and discuss buying Primrose Cottage and things didn't go her way. Was William really this angry?" Victoria said, pointing to Nicole's face.

"Oh that was his usual reaction when criticised by one of his parents. Grace turned on both of her sons and gave them a very large piece of her mind – she was so cross. Funnily enough, it didn't seem to be so much the goings-on with Mandy she was angry about, but their plans for the business. Almost as though she was disappointed with them."

"So William was angry because Grace was angry?"

"If Grace says 'Jump!' he usually does. I think both his parents bullied him as a child and now he hates being told off or being in the wrong with his mother. I must say I haven't seen him react with violence much before. His father's death may have affected him – just before he died Henry was being particularly vile to him – and to me, come to that."

"To you?" Victoria felt shocked.

"Oh, Henry was one of the original dirty old men. He grabbed your bottom soon as look at it. How Marilyn coped with working with him all day I'll never know – but maybe she was grateful for the attention."

"Did you discuss this with William?"

"Well I mentioned it, but he just laughed it off and said I should stop being such a baby and there was no harm done."

"What about telling Grace, would that have helped?" Victoria moved across to the fridge to get the wine out, and found two glasses.

"Somehow," replied Nicole, "I don't think that would have been news to Grace. I reckon she knew what he was like. Local gossip says he had multiple affairs and it seems she always just put up with it. I reckon that may be why she wasn't overly mad at William for the affair with Mandy. She sees it as all Mandy's fault rather than her saintly son's."

"Then why did she get so angry with William?"

"I'm afraid that was my fault." Nicole looked down at her wineglass sheepishly. "I'd just had enough and somehow this affair was the last straw. You know I wanted to escape back to London, and I refused to back down on that one. I told them all I didn't care whether they sold the business or not but I would be divorcing William and asking for my half of his share value."

"Oh I see… is that a lot?"

"Well I went to see a solicitor in Westerley yesterday – obviously I'll need to find a specialist divorce lawyer when I get to London

– but he said he thought I should ask for about a million and just see what happens. So I told them all that's what I would be doing and walked out. Mandy was close behind me; with me pushing for a sale to raise that much money they might go back to Henry's plan of selling to Berry Brothers. It's a fail all round for her."

Victoria remembered the two cars speeding past her as she'd arrived. "Did William tell you what his mother said?" she asked.

"Just told him to sort me out, I guess. He was angrier than I have ever seen him before. I don't think he's mad about me leaving, just angry about the money and losing face to everyone if I force a sale. Or maybe they have enough in the bank between them – I really don't know."

"So you're not flavour of the month with any of the family at the moment then?"

"Tell me about it. I've had numerous texts from John, really quite nasty. He and William have always been rivals for everything in life and he is too angry to speak to William directly about Mandy, but is mad at me for the whole money thing."

Victoria noticed that it was getting late, and carefully stifled a yawn. "Shall we sleep on it?" she suggested. "Maybe things will look less bleak in the morning" (or maybe not, she thought). "The spare room is presentable thanks to Jean's wonderful cleaning skills, but I'm not sure about bed linen." She paused and wondered if she should offer Nicole her bedroom for the night.

"Heavens no! If you've got a spare duvet or a blanket I am more than happy to sleep on the sofa. To be honest I am so exhausted I could sleep sitting up in a chair, never mind the luxury of lying down!"

Victoria looked at her new friend and felt sad for her. To be contemplating leaving your family, and having so few friends to turn to, must be a very lonely prospect – and was the dream of being on the stage really worth all this angst? "I've got lots of blankets and I'll cook you a nice breakfast in the morning and we'll see what can be done."

She showed Nicole the sofa and made sure she had a toothbrush and toothpaste, (without which Victoria couldn't face a night's sleep). She wrote out Gray and Sebastian's details and added the number of a good divorce lawyer who was a friend of a friend up in London. Back in the kitchen she aimlessly poured the last bit of wine into her glass and headed up to bed.

* * * * *

Victoria woke with a jolt. The room was already light and she suddenly remembered she had a houseguest and ought to be making coffee and lending a sympathetic ear. But almost immediately she became aware of the utter stillness in the cottage and knew that she was alone. She got up, pulled on her dressing gown and padded downstairs.

Her instincts were right. A note in what could only be Nicole's large theatrical hand was in the middle of the kitchen table, held down by a vase.

Victoria, thanks so much for your kindness last night, I cannot tell you how much I appreciate it. A text woke me at 5am and that was it! I couldn't get back to sleep! Sorry to sneak off, but I need to get packing and sort myself out. A new life beckons!! You are right, I need a good solicitor and to mount an organised campaign of attack!!! Will give you a call later sweetie. Love Nicole xxxxx

PS Thanks SO much for Gray and Sebastian's details!!!

Victoria smiled. It was very 'Nicole' with all those exclamations and kisses. She hoped her new friend had managed to do some serious thinking in those early hours and wouldn't do anything too impulsive.

It was only seven and Victoria needed coffee, badly. She filled the kettle and switched it on, recalling how she had had to rummage to find it when she'd first arrived and had failed miserably with the Rayburn. The Rayburn was still a mystery, but at least the good old electric kettle did the job! She smiled as she thought of Albert and his 'gadgets', and felt a little glow of something like excitement. There was turning out to be a lot more to Albert than she'd originally thought, and she wasn't sure yet where it might all lead.

With a large cafetière of coffee brewed, she took a mug upstairs with her, to wash and get dressed. Today was the day she must finish the Primrose Cottage article and she needed a solid few hours of uninterrupted writing time. She hoped Albert wouldn't appear until it was done. He didn't seem to understand deadlines or any degree of urgency, but then that wasn't his lifestyle. Farmers worked with the seasons, not in hours and minutes.

She finished just before noon. By some peculiar good luck, she had not received one interrupting email, phone call or visitor. The photos were already sorted; she had a reasonable selection and the article had come together well. As ever, she had been far more worried about it than she needed to be. Once she'd got her opening paragraph down and set the tone for the whole piece, the rest had flowed quite well. She pressed 'send' on her email to Georgie and let out a long sigh. She stretched in her chair and then went out into the garden.

The sky was really blue, but the day not overly warm. She went back in and pulled on a fleece, then went out to visit the hens. To her surprise she was finding them immensely restful and also fascinating. She could sit and watch them for ages, studying their individual character traits and funny little quirks. The largest chicken had quite a deep voice and burbled. The smallest, predictably, had a much higher twiddly voice and liked to skip about like a young girl. The middle-sized one was more serious and actually seemed to be the one in charge. She would admonish the other two with quite savage pecks, which made them squawk, and generally seemed to dictate the state of play.

Their background chatter was very soothing and Victoria looked forward to sitting outside and eating her lunch next to them in the warm summer days ahead. She wandered out towards Albert's house, but all was quiet. Both collies were asleep in the sun, but not completely – she saw their ears twitch as they heard her approach. Victoria smiled. She thought she might like a dog eventually. She was a little wary of the commitment, but she thought she might enjoy the company.

Just as she was contemplating fetching her camera to take some shots of the spring flowers dotted around the farm, she heard a great squawking from the hens. Rushing back, she was relieved to see there were no interlopers in the run. Instead, the largest hen was standing in the doorway of the coop almost on tiptoe, her head thrust forward, making a repetitive and very loud cry, almost like a cockerel's crow.

"What are you doing?" said Victoria.

The hen stopped abruptly at the sound of her voice, shook her feathers into place and stepped arrogantly out of the doorway, almost strutting her way over to the water bowl, where she drank heartily. How very odd. The other hens seemed uninterested and continued with their pecking and scratching and chattering. Victoria was puzzled. The big hen seemed excessively pleased with herself and was now preening one wing with great concentration.

Victoria went back into the run and, tentatively, opened the nestbox. She gave a cry of joy and carefully picked up the still-warm egg. "Oh you clever girl!" she said and inspected the egg closely. It was mid-brown and the most beautiful egg she had ever seen (not that she was biased). "You clever, clever hen!"

The chicken had obviously been crowing proudly at her egg-laying efforts (or, Victoria thought wincing, perhaps she was really saying "Ouch! Ouch! Ouch!" – laying an egg probably took quite a lot of effort). "Right, now that's a good example for the rest of you to follow," she said, holding the egg up in front of the others, who ignored it. She felt she wanted to celebrate. Her article was written and now she had her first egg!

As if on cue, Albert ambled into view, whistling. "Hello my beauty! How are you today?" "Look!" Victoria walked carefully towards him cradling the egg as if it were a priceless piece of porcelain. "Our first egg!"

"Yep, that's definitely an egg," confirmed Albert, peering into her cupped hands with exaggerated interest. "About time. Those pampered chickens need to spend less time eating and more time working. If they were mine, they'd be getting their necks wrung in a week or so if they didn't buck their ideas up."

Victoria looked appalled. "I'm only joking maid!" said Albert with a wink.

"I should think so! They obviously needed time to settle down. I ought to look up the breeds. I think Edwin said the big one that's laid the egg was a Buff Orpington. I can't remember the other two."

"Different breeds lay different amounts of eggs through the year," said Albert. "I don't know about those posh things, I expect you might get half a dozen or so a week if they're young and keen. Maybe more – of course they don't like it if it's too wet or cold, or when the days are short."

"They sound a bit like me then," she laughed.

"I reckon. Temperamental women!"

Victoria pretended to swat at him and almost dropped the egg.

"Steady on! Tell you what, shall I nip down the shop and get some bacon and a few more eggs and we can celebrate your first egg in the proper manner?"

Victoria had been planning something green and healthy for her lunch, but suddenly the thought of a fry-up seemed very appealing. "Oh go on then! I've just sent off my article so we have two reasons to celebrate."

"Sounds perfect! I'll just nip down to the village, I'll only be ten minutes. You get the kettle on."

"Could you pick up some milk too please? Get yourself some of the blue-topped stuff, I know you hate my skinny milk."

Victoria trotted back to the cottage. Life was good. Life was very good. For the first time in ages she was enjoying herself, and worries about her health and stress levels seemed remote. She laid the table and got the crusty loaf out of the bread bin. She boiled the kettle and made a cafetière; she could make tea for Albert once he was back. She put a bottle of white wine in the fridge for later. She'd rustle up something for them both this evening; that would be a rather nice end to the day.

Victoria sat down and looked at her watch. He'd been a good ten minutes. She sighed and poured herself a cup of coffee while she waited, smiling as she thought about Albert probably chatting away to half the village in the shop and forgetting what he'd gone in for.

After twenty minutes she felt slightly irritated and was just about to pour a second cup but then she heard the roar of the Range Rover's powerful engine as he drove into the barn. And suddenly, there he was in the doorway, carrying neither bacon nor eggs.

Victoria stood up, hands on hips, ready to chide him in a light-hearted way. "Albert, what…?" she began, but stopped as she saw his face. "What on earth has happened?"

"I think you'd better sit down," he said and walked into the room, flopping down into one of the kitchen chairs. Something in his expression made her do as she as told, and she sat down opposite him. "Tell me what's happened?"

He rubbed his face with both hands and then blew out his cheeks. In a timid voice Victoria said, "Please tell me Albert, you're frightening me."

"I don't rightly know how to say it. It's Nicole Simmons. She's dead. Murdered I reckon."

Victoria actually felt her jaw drop. She felt sick and lightheaded and was aware that she was sitting, like an idiot, with her mouth open. Aunt Edith's voice popped into her head as clear as a bell saying 'If the wind changes you'll be stuck like that' and she snapped her mouth shut.

"But… she can't be!"

"She is – was all they would talk about in the shop. Round and bleddy round they all went, saying the same thing over and over. Apparently, she was found in one of the big vats of jam at the factory."

"No!" Victoria almost shouted. "That's grotesque! Is this all some kind of sick joke?" Albert shook his head and reached for the coffee pot. "And I forgot the bleddy milk." He swallowed the coffee black and screwed his face up. "Bugger, that's awful!" He sat back. "I'm afraid it's true."

"But she was here last night, she actually spent the night here!" Victoria picked up the note that she had moved onto the worktop. Albert read it through. He looked immensely sad. "What a bleddy waste." Victoria felt numb now. She wanted to cry but couldn't. She leant against the worktop and hugged herself.

"Well, reckon you'd better phone the police. Looks like you might have been the last person to see her alive and this note," he brandished it at her, "could prove very important."

"Oh my goodness, I suppose you're right."

Albert got to his feet. "I'll drive you to the station if you like, not easy to find in Westerley."

"Oh Albert, this is awful – and I'm scared!" He looked at her levelly. "Here we've been talking about whether Henry was murdered," she looked up at him, "and now this!"

"I know. It's no joke. But don't you worry, there's no need for you to feel scared maid – I'm here." Without any further thought, Victoria flung herself at him and was comforted to feel him embrace her. She rested her cheek on his chest and closed her eyes. She could feel his strong, slow heartbeat, and somehow that made her feel a lot better.

Chapter 11

"Albert, would you mind?" said Victoria. "I feel really nervous about contacting the police and I don't want to do the wrong thing – but maybe I should ring rather than go down to the station?"

"Can't hurt, they'll soon put you right."

Victoria reached over for her phone and then hesitated. "When you ring a local police station you don't dial 999 any more, do you? I don't know the number for the Westerley police."

"No problem, I have it in my phone. Always pays to be prepared and we had some nasty cattle rustling in the area not so long back, needed to ring them for updates."

Victoria tried hard to stifle a giggle. "What's your problem?" said Albert. "You laughing at me for knowing how to store a number in my phone?"

"No, really not that, truly." Despite the seriousness of the situation, Victoria gave in to the urge to laugh. "I was just tickled by the thought of cattle rustling in this tiny little village, seems a bit surreal."

"It was no laughing matter – there were plenty farmers back in the day lost a lot of money to those cattle thieves." Albert passed his phone over and gestured that the number was already keyed in.

"Good morning Westerley police station, Constable Moore speakin."

"Oh right yes, umm it's Victoria West here." Unexpectedly,

Victoria found her voice had gone all croaky and she felt really nervous. "I er, wanted to speak to someone handling the death of Nicole Simmons?"

There was a cough and a rustle of papers at the other end of the line. "And why would that be madam? They are very busy with this h'investigation," came the reply. "Well, I do think this is pretty urgent, I mean, it's a really important fact they need to know as I suspect I was the last person to see Nicole before…" Victoria paused, a lump coming to her throat. "I mean Nicole stayed at my house last night so I think they need to know that."

"Deed they do madam, very crucial part of the evidence. I'll contact the team immediately. Could you hold the line please?"

"Yes, of course I will." Victoria wondered if there would be tinkly music while she waited. 'Greensleeves' perhaps? Then she smiled as she thought maybe 'Greatest Hits' by Police, but decided she was being too flippant. In the end, there was no incidental music and she just waited till the voice came back.

"Hello Miss, are you there?"

"Yes, I'm here."

"Right I'm going to take down your particulars and the team'll send someone out presently."

Victoria wondered when presently was but hesitated to ask. She gave the policeman her address and mobile number and said yes, she would be available for the rest of the day. "Right ho, well one of the team will be over to see you as soon as they can but t'will be an hour or two at least. Not usual for Westerley to be handling fatal accidents, all hands on deck if you see what I mean."

Victoria nodded and then (realising he couldn't see her nodding) replied. "Thank you officer, I'll expect someone later today." She clicked off the phone and took a deep breath.

"Phew, Albert that really made me nervous, why should I be so nervous talking to the police, it's not as if I've ever done anything wrong, well nothing too bad. I did get caught speeding once and I got off a bus without paying accidentally..." Victoria stopped as she saw Albert's raised eyebrows. "Sorry – am I babbling? I often do that when I am nervous. This feels terrible – I can't believe that last night she was sitting here and I was comforting her and now she's gone."

"Well why not make a start by telling me what went on last night? And in the meantime I'll get the kettle on and you can have a cup of sweet tea." Victoria winced. "Could we make that a cafetière of strong coffee, no sugar, instead? I think sweet tea might make me feel a bit sick."

"Oh you bleddy women, picky picky. Right I'll put the kettle on and you make yer own coffee and I'll make some tea – assuming you still have decent teabags, not just that herbal rubbish?"

Albert started searching the cupboards, obviously expecting to find something. Victoria suspected he thought she would have cake. "Sorry, we ate it all last night and drank all the wine too and I put everything else in the freezer. I could run down to the shop?"

"Tssk, as if our shop sells any cake worth eating! Give me a second." With that Albert disappeared out of the back door, clearly on a mission. Victoria smiled to herself. A man who makes chocolate cake: what's not to love!

Albert came back triumphantly bearing two large cake tins and a bulging carrier bag. "Didn't know how long we might be holed up waiting for the police, so I brought supplies." The word 'supplies' was delivered with more raising of the eyebrows. Victoria looked on with amusement as he unpacked a large chocolate cake – she had been banking on that one – and some scones from the second tin. In the carrier bag was clotted cream, jam and a packet of digestive biscuits. Victoria looked questioningly at the biscuits.

"What – not home-made, Albert? But surely…?" she smiled as he looked a little sheepish. "Well there are just some things, and home-made digestives is one of them, that are just better bought. Mine just don't dunk in tea like the bought ones. Thought we might be getting through quite a few cups today." They settled companionably at the table, sampling the cake and Albert enthusiastically dolloping cream and jam onto several scones. Victoria could feel her waistline expanding just watching him.

"Mmm – what happmm then maid, tell mm?" Albert spoke with such a large mouthful of scone and cream that Victoria had to guess at some of his words.

"Well, Nicole was sitting on the back doorstep when I got back from Primrose Cottage yesterday. I'd been to the supermarket in Westerley and didn't rush home so it was dark when I drove in. To be honest she gave me a bit of a turn as it looked like a big sack of something was on the step, not a person. Anyway she told me that William had been really angry with her and had shoved her about when they argued."

"Mmm, I have heard he has a bit of a temper on him when things don't go his way, but then all the men in that family are a bit prone to throwing a tantrum – old Henry punched a man at the country fayre one year, all because of some misunderstanding about judging cows or something. Though what old Henry knew about cows was a bit debatable… guess he was as near as they could find to a celebrity."

"Nicole was in a real state. When I first saw her there was blood everywhere and I was really worried. But once I had bathed it all and cleaned her up, I could see it was a nasty cut over her eye but just grazing on her face and arm. I think she fell against their stone fireplace when he shoved her and that's how she got her injuries. At least that's what she said."

"Well poor lass, that can't have been easy for her. What brought that on then?" said Albert.

"Oh the meeting they had earlier in the day, definitely. Apparently Grace was very angry with both boys. It came out that Mandy Parkin had been having an affair with William and then Nicole dropped her bombshell that she wanted her share of William's money and was leaving him. Nicole said William was upset that his mother had shouted at him."

"Never did have any backbone that one, not my favourite young men either of those Simmons boys," said Albert, frowning.

"So we stayed in and I tried to calm her. She wanted Gray and Sebastian's phone number as she was planning to leave for London – today, I think she said."

Albert looked puzzled, "Who's this Gray and…?" Light dawned and he grew serious as he realised. "Oh the idiots that sent you that hen palace, daft buggers."

"Yes, it seems we have those friends in common. Nicole met William at one of Sebastian's parties many years back. So I guess she thought they might be a useful port in a storm as she'll be pretty much on her own to start with in London," Victoria faltered. "Oh dear, I mean would have been on her own."

Victoria felt her eyes welling up. She felt so sad that she would never see Nicole again. She didn't imagine they would ever have become bosom buddies, but Nicole was as near to a friend as she had made in ages. She had dealt with people dying before, but they had all been elderly, never someone young and in such tragic circumstances.

She looked up at Albert with tears in her eyes. "Please tell me this couldn't be murder… could it? But then again how on earth could it be anything else? There would be no reason for her to go to the factory in the middle of the night." She sat back and blew her nose. "To think, I came down here to have a calm, unstressful life. It seems to me that I've come across more violence here than I've ever seen in London!"

Albert put his large, comforting hand over hers. "Now come on, you don't know what's what, there may be a good reason why – though blessed if I can think of any way it's just an accident."

At that moment there was a firm knock on the door and Albert showed in a uniformed policeman and a woman police officer. The man was medium height and had fair receding hair. "Is Miss West at home please? Sergeant Butler – and this is WPC Woods, Westerley police." Albert indicated Victoria. "The station told me that you rang in with information about the whereabouts of Nicole Simmons last night."

"Yes officer," replied Victoria, again feeling her stomach flip with nerves. "Nicole spent last night here with me and left early this morning."

"I'll get that kettle on again," said Albert firmly. Both police officers looked at him. "And you are, sir?" said Sergeant Butler. "Albert is my friend and neighbour," said Victoria hurriedly. "Is it OK if he stays, only he knows as much about the case as I do really?"

Butler looked unsure, but then shrugged. "By all means – and I have to say a cup of something wouldn't go amiss, it's turning into a long day. Now can you just run through the details clearly for me, Miss West?"

The police officers settled down at the kitchen table, notebooks open and Albert provided mugs of tea and offered cake and the digestive biscuits. It amused Victoria that the sergeant took a biscuit and immediately started dunking, but the WPC refused anything but the tea.

"Nicole was here waiting for me when I arrived home last

night."

"That would be at what time Miss West?"

"I'm not completely sure – but around eight-thirty-ish I think, it was pretty dark. I saw she was bleeding and spent the next hour cleaning her up and calming her."

"Bleeding? Can you be more specific?"

"There had been a huge family row at the Primrose Cottage factory yesterday and her husband, William, was angry with her. They had an argument at home and she said he pushed her and she stumbled against their stone fireplace. She had a cut above her left eye and bad grazes to her face and arm."

The WPC flipped back a few pages of her notebook and nodded at Sergeant Butler. "Seems that tallies with injuries found on the body this morning. So what did you both do while you were 'cleaning her up'?"

Victoria frowned. "Do? I don't understand you – we just sat here, I bathed her face and put some ointment on it. Then we opened a bottle of wine as we'd both had a nasty shock."

"So you both drank wine then?" said Butler.

"Well yes of course, I had just been to the supermarket so luckily I had quite a good stock. Since moving here I haven't had time to build up a collection!"

"Regular drinker are we, Miss West?" Victoria frowned again. What had this to do with anything? "Yes I enjoy a glass or two of wine, same as a man might have a beer at the end of the day, just to relax."

"This Nicole Simmons, was she a regular wine drinker too?" Butler was furiously writing notes in his book, as was his colleague. At this point Albert intervened. "I would have thought the details of yesterday's argument at Primrose Cottage was a lot more important than whether Miss West drinks wine or not."

Butler ignored him and continued. "So what happened as the evening progressed?"

"Well Nicole poured out all her worries about how unhappy she was with William and her plans to move back up to London."

"So things were unhappy at home then? She drink much in her own home?"

Victoria felt hugely frustrated, What was all this focus on drinking for? "I really don't know how much she drank at home, I only met her a couple of times – we'd only just begun to get to know each other." Her throat tightened a little as she said the words and felt overwhelmed by sadness. Oblivious to her discomfort, Butler continued. "So when was the first time you met Mrs Simmons?"

"We met a few days ago and spent an evening together at the Swaddlecombe Arms, it was fun to find we had friends in common up in London."

"Drinking wine again that night then?" said Butler with a slight gleam of triumph in his eyes. "For heaven's sake yes!" replied Victoria. "Now can we get back to last night?"

"What happened next, Miss West, that you want to tell us about?"

"Well, obviously after such a traumatic evening, Nicole was tired and she had drunk too much to drive herself home."

"So she was quite drunk by then?"

"She'd had a few glasses of wine, so had I for that matter. Nothing excessive but neither of us are," she paused, "were, irresponsible enough to drink and drive, so I offered her a bed for the night."

"Do you often have these parties where people have to stay the night? Or coming from London I expect you're used to having taxis to call on at all hours?"

Victoria registered the anti-Londoner comment and decided to ignore it. "So," she continued, "I gave her a blanket for the sofa.

She said she would be happy on that as she was finding it hard to stay awake and I haven't got the spare room sorted properly yet. I only moved in a week or so ago."

"So she fell asleep on the sofa, yes? And when did you realise she had left?"

"When I got up this morning. I found this." Victoria handed him Nicole's note. "As you see she says she was woken by a text. That has to be important – surely that can be checked?"

"Yes Miss, we'll be checking everything thoroughly. I am very grateful for all your information. I think we probably have all the details we need now. Thank you very much – and for the tea." The two police officers stood up and, almost in a trance, Victoria showed them to the door. Was that all they needed? Why hadn't they asked more questions?

She returned to the kitchen table and flopped down dejectedly in her chair. "Well," said Albert, folding his arms. "I didn't reckon much to the long arm of the law! Silly buggers didn't seem much interested in the important stuff."

"I know – that's just what I felt. It seems like they'd already drawn their conclusions." Victoria sighed and pushed some biscuit crumbs around the tabletop with her finger. "Poor Nicole, I feel I've let her down somehow."

"Now don't be so daft, and don't get all maudlin. That won't do any good at all," said Albert sitting up straight and wagging a knowing finger at her. "I tell you what, how about a trip to the Swaddle Arms for lunch, on me?"

Victoria shrugged. "I don't know Albert, I'm not sure I feel like being very sociable and I'm truly not hungry."

"Nonsense! I'm not having you brooding like a bleddy old hen. You need to get out, and I want a pint, none of your fancy wine stuff. Get your coat maid, you've pulled!" Dear Albert – he managed to make her smile even at the blackest moments. She shrugged on her jacket, gave her hair a quick brush and said, "Will I do?" "I suppose so," he replied, and grinned at her. "Let's take Gloria, I'll drive."

They climbed into the sports car that suddenly seemed rather small with Albert crammed into the driving seat. They shot off at a rate and Victoria was amused at how she had been handling the car with kid gloves, whereas Albert was throwing it into corners and double declutching, or something equally impressive, when changing gear.

The pub car park was almost full and they managed to find a space in a corner. "Cars were a bit smaller when this beauty was made," Albert remarked, unfolding himself from the seat and climbing out, "always find a space to slot her in." As he pulled open the pub door for Victoria a wall of noise and warmth hit her, the air full of chatter and laughter, mixed with wood smoke and the smell of delicious food. "Goodness, it's busy Albert, I'm not sure I'm up to this."

"You'll be fine, just stick with me." Albert beat a path to the bar and leaned heavily on the counter. Victoria looked anxiously for spilled beer but the bar seemed freshly wiped, so she too rested her elbows.

"Albert, Miss West, what can I do for you?" beamed Roger Mudge, immaculate in fawn sweater, cream shirt and chinos, hands clasped expectantly. "A pint of Farmer's Fancy and Victoria, what's your poison?"

"Erm… whatever red wine I had last time please, it was very nice."

"Coming right up!" Roger bustled away.

Albert was nodding and waving to people and the general hubbub was immense. "Is there a party on or something?" Victoria asked. She felt herself squashed against the bar as a large chap in farmer's overalls rocked back into her when he laughed at a joke. "Oi, Bramley, watch where you're leaning!" barked Albert.

The large man turned and, for a moment Victoria felt fearful. "Albert Moreton, you old beggar! Not seen you in a few weeks! How you be?" Albert's acquaintance was ruddy faced, smiling broadly and the size of a barn. He even had straw in his hair, Victoria was amused to see. "Bramley, this is my new neighbour Victoria West," said Albert.

"Ooh my," said Bramley and turned to shake her hand, not an easy feat in the crush at the bar, "you'm a cutie! Where's he been hiding you?"

Victoria felt herself blush, but it was said in such a charming way and he looked so exactly like a caricature that all her feminist instincts dissolved as she said slightly coyly, "I'm Edith's niece, I live in her cottage now."

Bramley nodded and continued to shake her hand. "Very pleased to meet you my dear, very pleased." Victoria rescued her semi-crushed hand and picked up her glass of wine. "Cheers!" bellowed Bramley raising his pint mug in their direction, before turning back to his mates.

Albert smiled and shook his head. "Don't worry, soft as butter that one. Anyway, look here Mudge, any chance of a table?"

"There is if you want to eat Albert, I'll turf someone off that's just drinking – but if you're just after a comfy seat, you'll have to fight for it, not literally of course!" Roger looked slightly shocked at his own words and then laughed.

"We'd like to eat, no rush," said Albert.

"Fine, I'll go and ask that lot in the corner to shift in ten minutes or so. That OK?"

"That would be lovely, thank you," said Victoria. "Why is it so busy in here?"

"Well, surely you've heard?" Roger leaned forward, one hand on a beer pump, the other resting on the bar, in what Victoria was starting to realise was his 'confidential' pose.

"What?"

"About Nicole Simmons?"

"Oh! Yes, of course, but is that why everyone's…" she trailed off, feeling slightly sick. "That's rather ghoulish, isn't it?"

"Don't be daft!" Albert joined in. "Down here, the pub is the centre of the community. You wouldn't get that up where you come from I don't suppose. This is the old-fashioned version of what's now called 'social networking', only we actually do it face to face!" He raised his eyebrows at Roger, who nodded in agreement. Victoria sipped her wine. "I still think it's in rather bad taste," she said quietly.

Roger moved off to get some menus. Albert had somehow found them two bar stools and signalled to her to climb up. "You don't want to be so stuffy maid," he said quietly. "It's been a shock of course, but it's just what people always do – they want to gossip about it, tell what they know – or don't, as is more usually the case. They want to be part of it somehow."

"I know what you mean I suppose, but still…" Victoria sighed, took a large swig of wine and looked at the menu Roger had put in front of them. Just then she caught sight of Jean with her sister and a group of women of a similar age huddled round a table. "You can guarantee they'll be making the most of it!" remarked Albert, following her gaze.

Trudy Mudge pushed her way through the throng to deliver food to a nearby table. After she'd plonked down the plates she made a beeline for Victoria. "Isn't it awful?" she said in hushed tones, clutching Victoria's arm, "and you getting right friendly with her too! You poor thing, must be upsetting."

Victoria nodded. "Yes, it has been a shock, poor Nicole." She shuddered and sipped her wine. Trudy was watching her avidly.

"When did you last see her then?"

"Nicole? She stayed at my house last night actually." As soon as she'd said it, she wished she hadn't. "No!" said Trudy, her eyes as round as saucers. "You were with her last night?"

"Well, yes. Actually, she stayed the night as we'd had some wine and she left very early this morning."

"No!" said Trudy again, looking like she might burst at any minute. "Roger? Did you hear that?"

Roger came over. "What's that dear?"

"Nicole spent the night at Victoria's cottage. And she only left early this morning!" She made it sound the most thrilling pronouncement she had ever made. Several people had tuned in to her comments and eyes were now turning in Victoria's direction.

Victoria felt, yet again, like the rabbit in the headlights. "It's OK. I've told the police about it," she said in a small voice.

"Of course you have! My goodness Victoria, you were one of the last people to see Henry alive, and now it looks like you were the last person to see Nicole!" Trudy's face was a picture. "We'd better keep an eye on you!" Several people nearby laughed and nodded their agreement.

Victoria sat with a fixed smile on her face, swallowed the last of her wine and wished she could disappear through a trapdoor into the cellar. Fully aware of her discomfort, Albert stood up. "Mudgers, can you get that table sorted please? We'd like to go and sit and have a quiet drink while we choose our food." He looked pointedly at Trudy, who was oblivious, and then helped Victoria off her stool. They followed Roger through the busy bar as he politely asked the drinkers to move, which they did without fuss – although Victoria was aware of people nudging each other and commenting as she passed.

"Oh dear Albert, I think this was a mistake. I feel like an exhibit."

"I'm sorry," said Albert settling himself down and signalling to Roger that they wanted the same again from the bar. "Trudy can be as subtle as a brick sometimes." He looked at the menu. "Might be something in what she said, though."

"What do you mean?"

"About you being the last person to see them both. I might need to keep an eye on you just in case there is skulduggery going on."

Victoria looked at him. "I don't understand."

"Well, think about it. You might be in danger yourself at this rate." He nodded to Roger as he delivered their drinks. "Do you know what you want to eat?"

"Oh Lord, no, not really. I'll have whatever you have."

"Right, that's easy. Two pasties with chips on the side please, and a salad for the lady." He closed the menu with a snap and handed it to Roger, who looked discomfited by his wife's lack of tact. "Will do Albert, sorry about that." He gave Victoria a sheepish grin and gathered up her menu.

"Albert, you are sort of scaring me," said Victoria quietly.

"It's probably nothing, but for all her tittle-tattle Trudy might have made a valid point. If someone is going round doing awful things, they might just be getting concerned about how you keep popping up." He took a mouthful of beer. "I'm probably being a silly old fool but, well, I'd hate anything nasty to happen to you."

Victoria smiled, in spite of herself. It was so sweet to know that he cared about her. "After all, you've only been here five minutes and it wouldn't look good!" he beamed, and she grinned back.

Victoria became aware of someone going "Pssst!" in a very

theatrical way. She looked around and saw Jean waving at her from a few tables away. She gestured that she wanted to come over.

"Oh Lord," said Victoria, but nodded encouragingly nonetheless. "Look out, here comes Jean," she said quietly.

"Gordon Bennett!" said Albert. "They're all in here today!"

Clutching her glass in both hands, Jean was weaving her way through the crowd with exaggerated care. "Well my dears, what a thing to 'appen," she said as she sat down at their table, leaning forward and looking conspiratorially from left to right, "'tis terrible, terrible!"

"It certainly is," agreed Albert. "Poor bleddy woman, no age at all."

"I know! I said to me sister, what a tragedy!" Her birdlike movements were slightly slower than usual and her cheeks were flushed, and Victoria realised that Jean was tipsy. "What's that you're drinking Jean?" she asked, looking at the reddish liquid in the older woman's glass.

"Port and lemon, thank you, I will have another!"

Albert gave a snort of laughter, waved at Roger Mudge and pointed at Jean's glass. Roger rolled his eyes again and went to prepare the drink.

"I said to me sister, that Victoria, she was just getting pally with Nicole. And now I hears she was with you last night!"

"My goodness, news does travel fast," said Victoria dryly. "Yes, she was, left my house early this morning. I was still asleep, sadly. Not that I suppose I could have changed what happened. She received a text, she said in her note, and then she was found at the factory, so I don't know what that all means."

"Well, I reckon it must be that William. He could be a beast when he was roused!" She shook her head vehemently. "A beast!"

"I spoke to him a few times and he didn't strike me like that –

a thwarted and unhappy man, perhaps, but he didn't strike me as violent, but shows what I know. He'd certainly pushed Nicole about a bit before she came to my cottage."

"Really?" Jean's eyes were huge behind her magnifying spectacles. "That would fit in with what happened, wouldn't it?"

"I don't know, what did happen? I've been rather too afraid to ask," said Victoria timidly. She felt Albert pat her arm consolingly.

"Well, everyone has said she fell into a vat of jam!" Jean peered at them both, making sure this registered. Then she leaned forward further. "But 'tis all gossip and nonsense. Poor woman, her fell off them wooden steps, broke the banister when she fell an' went head first into a vat that is true, but t'was empty of course. We never leave jam sitting there like that, t'isn't hygienic."

Victoria felt a sense of relief knowing that Nicole hadn't drowned in a ghastly bath of suffocating jam.

"I spec' it was instant and her broke her neck when she fell in. Never knew nothing about it, poor maid," finished Jean, sitting back triumphantly. "That sounds a more plausible account," said Victoria. "I wonder why or how she fell?"

"Course my dear, that's the big question!" Jean sipped her fresh drink and raised her glass. "Cheers then! I'd better get back to the girls," she cocked her head in the direction of her sister's table. "Tell 'em about Nicole being at yours. They all think she must have been tipsy to fall, so maybe there is some truth in it after all!" With that, she got to her feet, a little unsteadily, and tottered back across the bar.

The crowd had thinned slightly, and it felt less oppressive. Victoria and Albert sipped their drinks in silence for a while. "Seems clear which way the police are thinking then," said Albert at last. "With her falling like that. They obviously think she was drunk and it's an accident, plain and simple."

"Yes, but why go to the factory in the middle of the night? The text must have been from someone asking her to go there. And anyway, I know she wasn't roaring drunk, just not legal to drive. She must have been pushed."

Just then, Trudy hove into view with their food. "Here you are then my dears!" she plonked the plates down with a flourish. "I hope you enjoy it!"

They smiled blandly, managing to be polite but at the same time dismissive. Trudy, clearly after some more gossip, looked disappointed and retreated to the kitchen leaving Victoria and Albert to ponder on what had really happened at Primrose Cottage earlier that day.

Chapter 12

All Victoria could see was a pair of grubby overall-clad legs sticking out from under an elderly estate car. The radio was blaring out an old rock song and someone, Tufty she assumed, was joining in on the chorus.

"All right now ow ow."

Victoria tentatively tapped her foot against one of the dirty trainers moving rhythmically in time to the music. "Excuse me, Tufty, is that you?" The legs grew a little longer and even grubbier as they emerged from under the car. It was indeed Tufty. "Oh 'ello Miss, and how are you this nice sunny day?"

Victoria smiled. She was really getting to like the 'olde worlde' courtesy of rural life; at the garage back in London she'd have got a grunt at most, and possibly a swear word if she'd picked a bad time. "Hi Tufty. I just came to see what we can do about my poor little car. I've settled with the insurance company and accepted the £800. They're going to come and collect it, I assume?"

"Well 'tis here when they want it," replied Tufty, brushing his oily hand through his hair and making it stand up even more than usual. "Right shame, nice little runabout like that should be scrapped, but maybe it's for the best."

"Yes but best for who? I really loved my little car, I've had it for years now and it just makes me so mad." Victoria tailed off as a figure blocked the doorway. She shaded her eyes against the sun and realised it was Mandy Parkin.

"Talk of the devil," muttered Tufty.

Victoria realised that all three of them were staring at each other but not saying a word. As happened so often she had to stifle a giggle as she imagined a sort of High Noon situation with her and Mandy as gunslingers in the old Wild West. "Mandy," she nodded.

"Good morning Victoria, morning Tufty," said Mandy. "I saw Victoria's new little sports car outside and wondered if I could have a word?"

Victoria wanted to make a clever comeback – "Which word would that be?" or "I'm not sure there are any words, polite ones that is" – but her wit failed her and all she could say was "Oh did you?"

"Tufty if you could make yourself scarce – it was a private chat I was hoping for." Mandy gave Tufty a look that would have scared most people, but Tufty was such a laid-back character he merely shrugged. Victoria thought he was a lot braver than she was, or thicker skinned; if she'd been on the receiving end of that glare she'd have turned to jelly. Not for the first time, she told herself to get a grip and be more assertive.

Tufty simply said, "Suits me, I was just off to the shop anyhow to get milk, tea break time about now." With that he grabbed a towel, did a perfunctory job of wiping the grease from his hands, finished them off on his overalls and strode outside.

Victoria realised that, left alone with Mandy, she felt quite anxious. She waited for the other woman to make the first move. "Nice little runabout you've got there." Mandy looked towards the MGB.

"That's not mine, I've just got it on loan from Albert my neighbour. Losing my own car left me in quite a mess." Victoria wondered whether to drive her point home, but decided to see what Mandy had to say.

"Well I suppose you feel it was my fault, just assuming you would be experienced enough to judge the width of your car. These lanes can be tricky." Mandy faltered and Victoria noticed how tense she appeared. She looked pale and the shadows under her eyes were very pronounced.

Victoria gave Mandy one of the raised-eyebrow looks that worked so well with Albert, but she felt sure it wouldn't have the same effect on Mandy. "So, basically you stopped off to tell me it was my fault for misjudging the width of the road when you drove at me the other day? Very thoughtful, thank you." Standing up to a bully often paid off, Victoria told herself, and swallowed.

"No actually..." Mandy hesitated, and if Victoria hadn't known better she might have thought that she too was a little nervous. "I really wanted to offer you some help, without prejudice of course, towards the cost of replacing your car."

Victoria tried not to gawp and gathered her thoughts as swiftly as she could. "I'm sorry? You want to give me money towards another car?"

"Totally without prejudice of course," repeated Mandy. "I felt sure any driver would have been able to get past at that point in the road, but then I do know the route pretty well."

"Well 'totally without prejudice', I felt you were driving far too fast even if you do know the road pretty well, as you put it. Any number of other factors – quite apart from a newly arrived townie – could have caused a major accident – an animal could have wandered across the road, anything!" Victoria felt a bit defensive as she knew she was still overly cautious about the distance between her car and passing vehicles. These tiny lanes were unnerving, but no doubt she would get used to them. "So thank you for the offer but no, I wouldn't be prepared to accept any money from you. I will manage perfectly well."

Mandy shrugged. "OK – the offer's there. I didn't want you to blame me forever just because I drive a little too fast occasionally." Victoria thought that every time she had spotted the red sports car it was being driven too fast, but decided to say nothing. Neither woman spoke for a moment. "Also," Mandy said, then paused again, "I wanted to ask about Nicole."

"What about Nicole?" Victoria frowned.

"She was with you just before she died I think?"

Ah, thought Victoria, so she didn't really stop to discuss the car situation at all. How had Mandy found out that she'd been with Nicole? Then she remembered that village grapevine. "She might have been, but why do you want to know?"

Mandy looked uncomfortable but continued. "I know this may sound selfish, but the rumours are going round that William beat her up before throwing her out and that she came to you because she had nowhere else to go. I was just worried."

"Worried about Nicole? Why would you be worried? I would have thought not having an affair with her husband would have been more helpful if you were worried about her?"

"Oh no, not Nicole, worried about William!"

Victoria smiled ruefully and thought how stupid it had been even to contemplate that Mandy would be concerned about Nicole. "I'm sure William is just fine. He obviously thought it was acceptable to lose his temper and push Nicole around – he probably doesn't even realise how much he upset her."

"No you misunderstand me, I'm not concerned about whether William is fine or not, I'm just concerned about his state of mind. I'm a bit surprised at how angry both William and John seem to be about everything."

"Surely it's not a huge surprise that both men should feel

somewhat aggrieved that you've been two-timing them, especially John as he thought you were a couple. Finding out you were also sleeping with his brother must have really made his day!" Victoria said, doing the raised-eyebrow thing again.

"Well, I suppose if you put it like that... yes, I guess they may feel a bit put out." Mandy looked at the floor as she contemplated the point. "There's still no cause to come round to my house and threaten me though."

"William came round to your house and threatened you? Was this before or after the row with Nicole?"

"Not William, John. He came round not long after the meeting at the factory and was very unpleasant, quite over the top I thought."

Victoria realised Mandy plainly had no idea of the emotional turmoil her two-timing actions had caused, and thought that whatever John had said she probably deserved it. "Well, John did have a right to be angry, having just found out about your affair with William."

Mandy seemed to consider the idea. "Possibly, but surely there's never any excuse for violence? He slammed the front door so hard I'm going to have to get a man to come and look at it. And, frankly, if the cat hadn't moved fast enough the kick he aimed at it would have caused real injury."

"Can I ask why, though? I mean, why you thought it was acceptable to sleep with both brothers despite the possible consequences?" queried Victoria.

Mandy shrugged. "I just thought both of them could be useful. Temporarily Nicole scuppered those plans as her taking the money away from William would have meant selling the business and, at the moment, I suspect the buyer they'd all choose would be Berry Brothers. I need longer to show them how a takeover from Janner's would be the best move. Hopefully that still stands as an option now."

Victoria realised that, far from being sad about Nicole's death, it was actually in Mandy's interest. "Have you spoken to William since Nicole's death?" she asked.

Mandy stared at her. "No, I tried to ring him after John came round and threatened me. Stupidly I thought maybe William would be kinder to me, but there was no reply all evening on his mobile – I left messages and numerous texts. So what did Nicole say when she was with you – did William really beat her up? I just wondered if I should get some protection."

Victoria was feeling very confused. Mandy obviously needed some information from her but she couldn't quite get her head around what it was. Was she worried about William? Was she concerned that Nicole had said something to her and was fishing for information, or was she just selfishly worrying about getting hurt herself?

"Nicole and William had a row, and to be honest I think William just pushed her too hard rather than actually hitting her. She fell onto their stone fireplace and so was badly grazed and had a cut above her eye. She did mention that there had been some fights before but I can't think William would be the type to hit a woman, surely?"

Mandy looked at her through narrowed eyes. "The quiet ones are often the most dangerous – I wouldn't assume anything about those two men. Both brothers are as bad as each other. The only person they both fear is their mother – oh and their father when he was alive. I gather he made their lives hell. So you didn't speak to Nicole in the morning as she was leaving?"

There was a loud whistling and Tufty came back swinging a plastic-wrapped loaf of bread in one hand and a pint of milk in the other. "Gossip time over now ladies?" He grinned, revealing a gap in the teeth on one side of his mouth and a flash of gold on the other. Victoria was still trying to get used to the chauvinist comments that went hand-in-hand with the old-fashioned chivalry down in the country. She itched to make a caustic comment in reply, but held herself back.

Mandy smiled at Tufty, but the smile definitely didn't reach her eyes. "Oh quite finished thank you Tufty, I only stopped by to say hello to Victoria. I must be on my way now – I have so much to do." With this she swept out and the loud roar from the exhaust proved yet again she was speeding off far too fast for these lanes.

"Alright?" asked Tufty, head cocked to one side and a look of concern on his face.

"I think so, yes," said Victoria. "But slightly confused."

"Her's a funny one," he said and shook his head. "Her old man was OK, but with her, you're never quite sure all the chicks are in the nest. And if they are, whether they're the right way up."

Victoria frowned, mulling that one over. She assumed it was something similar to being a sandwich short of a picnic, or having a screw loose. "I see," she said eventually. "She does have a certain, strange detachment."

Now Tufty looked puzzled and said "Yeah, right" and turned back to the car he was working on.

"Well, I'll leave you to get on Tufty. Let me know if you hear from my insurers. And if you hear of any nice little cars coming up that might suit me, will you give me a call?" "Sure thing!" He did the strange salute-cum-forelock tug thing again and disappeared under the car.

Victoria drove home slowly, her mind full of what Mandy hadn't said, rather than what she had. Pulling into the drive, she found herself hoping Albert was around as she wanted to tell him about Mandy and, she realised, she just wanted to see him. She parked and went into the cottage, flicking the switch on the kettle before removing her fleece jacket. As if on cue, there was a knock at the door.

"Alright to come in?" asked Albert, sticking his head around the door.

"Of course. I was hoping you'd pop in. I've had an interesting experience with Mandy Parkin," Victoria smiled.

A number of different expressions passed across Albert's face, not all of them entirely pure, Victoria thought, so she gave him a look. "Oh really! Have a seat while I make some tea."

"Well, I have some news too," said Albert and sat down, reaching for the cake tin that seemed to have become a permanent fixture on the kitchen table. "Got a knife?" he asked, and was soon carving off a sizeable slice of chocolate cake. "You having some too?"

"Yes please, but about half the size of your piece!" she laughed, then put the teapot, mugs and plates on the table and sat down. "Mmmm, this cake stays moist doesn't it?" she said, savouring the rich chocolate flavour and the light sponge.

"Will do in an airtight tin, or one of those plastic container things," nodded Albert, sagely. "Come on then, tell all about young Mandy."

Victoria fortified herself with another mouthful of cake and a gulp of tea, then recounted what had happened. "Seems a bit bleddy odd," said Albert when she'd finished. He sat back and folded his arms. "Can't believe she offered you money for the car – maybe she has got a conscience after all."

"I don't think so – I think she was trying to butter me up to get information."

"I reckon she's nervous," Albert nodded. "I think she realises she's gone too far and maybe put herself in danger." He pursed his lips. "She might have a point I suppose." He sat forward and, waving the teaspoon about for added effect, said, "But then, as you said, definite advantage to her to have Nicole out of the way. So perhaps it's a double bluff on her part and she's the one who did it!"

Victoria looked shocked. "No! Surely not. That never crossed my mind! You mean she might be exaggerating, or even lying, about the two brothers being aggressive with her – and it's her all along?"

"Well, the bit about John and William might be true or it might not, and she's just mentioning it to make herself look vulnerable."

Victoria studied the scrubbed pine of the table top. "I assume the police will talk to her?"

"I assume so. And has she got an alibi? She wouldn't have been with either of the brothers, so maybe she was on her own, or maybe she was waiting at the factory."

Victoria shuddered. "Don't! I was only saying to Tufty that she seems weirdly detached and he agreed. Maybe she's a psychopath… or do I mean sociopath? Oh I don't know! I write articles, I'm kind to animals and small children and lead a law-abiding life – I'm out of my depth with all this horrid stuff." She wrapped her arms around herself. "Honestly, Albert, it is a bit scary."

He nodded. "I know maid, it is that."

Victoria watched in amazement as he cut another piece of cake. It was smaller than the first piece, admittedly, but still… he gestured to her, asking if she wanted another piece, but she shook her head. "Anyway," she remembered, "you said you had some news?"

"I went to the shop earlier and of course everyone was agog with it all and that's where I heard that they've arrested William." Victoria's head shot up and she met Albert's gaze. "Really? Crikey! Why?"

"Apparently, they couldn't get hold of him to tell him Nicole was dead, and he can't produce an alibi."

"I don't suppose fish make very good witnesses," Victoria mused.

"You reckon that's where he was?"

She shrugged. "No idea, just guessing. If he wasn't at home I imagine he'd either be fishing or with Mandy – and he wasn't with the latter as he and John are somewhat cross with her just now, as we know."

Albert frowned. "You don't think he's got another woman on the go, do you?"

"Good grief, surely not!"

Albert sighed. "Yes, I suppose you're right. Such a boring chap – can't believe he was even at it with Mandy."

"Yes, but she wasn't attracted by his dynamic personality or immense good looks, was she?" Victoria pointed out.

Albert shook his head. "Ridiculous carry-on really, I can't quite get my head around it. That poor Nicole killed off so young, it's not right."

"Oh don't, you'll start me off again," said Victoria as her chin started to wobble. 'So, William arrested. Oh dear, I suppose that's all down to me and what I told them about the state Nicole was in when she came here."

"I reckon it didn't help his cause, but it was the evidence of your own eyes and what she actually told you – assuming she wasn't lying."

"Why would Nicole lie? Who on earth else would have done that to her?"

"No idea – who knows what goes on behind closed doors. And neither of us knew her that well, did we?"

"You are right, sadly no," Victoria sighed. "I hadn't had a chance to get to know her well before..." she trailed off. "Do you think I ought to say anything to the police about Mandy?"

Albert shrugged. "I don't think so – surely they'll interview her and work things out for themselves?"

"I suppose you're right. I think I've watched too many TV series where Miss Marple or some other amateur sleuth has more idea than the dim plods. I am sure it's not like that in real life."

Albert snorted with laughter. "I don't rightly know about that. The few times I've had anything to do with the local boys in blue I haven't been too impressed, but then that's been petty stuff, people stealing bits of farm machinery, or your favourite one, cattle rustling!"

Victoria smiled, but her mind had already gone off on another tack. "There's always John, of course."

"What do you mean, John?"

"Well, Mandy said he'd threatened her, didn't she, so he's obviously really riled. From what I've seen of him, he seems terribly pushy and far more driven than that dopey old fisherman William. I reckon he could have lashed out at Nicole if he thought her divorce demands would wreck everything."

Albert was nodding slowly. "Well, yes, you might have a point there – no one's really thought much about him yet."

"And men's egos and pride, especially when it involves both sex and money, can be very fragile things. Maybe he just lost it with her. Poor Nicole, she was quite a small woman – it would have been easy to overpower her."

She shuddered again and Albert patted her arm. "Now, now, let's not go too far down that route." He fiddled with the teaspoon. "You know, I was thinking... and I wouldn't like you to take this the wrong way... but..." Victoria looked at his bowed head and wondered what on earth he was about to say. "I did wonder if it might be better if I came and slept on the sofa here until, you know, things have been resolved. Might make you rest easier?"

She smiled and felt a gooeyness in her stomach that had nothing to do with tea and cake. "Oh Albert, that's terribly sweet of you. I don't think the sofa is very comfortable, but there are a couple of spare bedrooms upstairs as I'm sure you know... I mean..."

"It's alright!" Albert laughed. "I know this house almost as well as me own, it's true. I reckon one of the beds up there must be serviceable, so I'm happy to do that if it would help."

"I feel a bit of a baby but, do you know, I think it would."

"That's agreed then, I'll bring over some bedding and bits and pieces later, if that's alright?"

"That will be fine, thank you." She was trying hard to stop the fluttering in her stomach and the ludicrous feelings of a teenage crush that seemed to be invading her. This was ridiculous; she was a mature woman, and Albert a very mature man!

"I'll cook us some dinner later. I bought some steak in the supermarket and..." As soon as the words were out of her mouth she knew it was the wrong thing to say.

"From the supermarket? I'm not eating supermarket steak! You're living among some of the finest reared cattle in this country! A bit of Ruby Devon is hard to beat and it's supporting the local economy. I thought you were into all that sort of 'green' stuff? No air miles and all that old nonsense?" He looked quite fierce and Victoria had to reassess her opinion of him yet again. "Anyways round, if you've bought the bleddy stuff, we'd better eat it. But I think it's time I took you along to the butchers in Higher Coombe and you can see some proper meat prepared by a proper butcher and not a bit of plastic wrapping in sight!" He slapped the table and stood up.

Victoria felt desolate – had she really upset him? "And now I will go and get my duvet," he grinned. "There's no need to look so worried. I've got to check the cows first so I'll be half an hour or so I expect."

Victoria breathed a sigh of relief, stupidly pleased that she hadn't mortally offended him. She decided to spend the time rootling through a few more of her still unpacked boxes. She was on all fours backing inelegantly out of a corner cupboard in the kitchen, where she had decided to store some of her aunt's old china, when she heard a loud "Ahem!" and promptly jumped, banging her head on the doorframe.

"Ouch!" she stood up stiffly and rubbed her head. "Well, goodness, that's a surprise!" She was amazed to see John Simmons standing in the doorway looking even taller and more imposing than normal, his smart dark suit incongruous in her rather ramshackle kitchen.

"Indeed," he said with a sardonically raised eyebrow, while managing to look her up and down appraisingly at the same time. Victoria felt herself shudder; she hadn't realised before quite how creepy he was. "What on earth would bring you out here to my humble abode?" she said self-consciously, smoothing her rumpled hair into place.

"It's rather charming, in a rustic way," he smiled and again Victoria was reminded of something vaguely reptilian (if reptiles were capable of condescension, of course). "Would you like a cup of tea, or something?"

"No, thank you, I was just passing and thought I'd pop in, a few things I wanted to chat about." He folded his arms and leant against the dresser.

"Oh, really?" Victoria's heart was thudding, but she refused to be intimidated; this was her house. "Well, sit down at least, I don't like people 'looming' in my kitchen."

John managed a tight smile, and sat in the chair recently vacated by Albert. "I wondered... have you come across Nicole's phone?"

Victoria stared at him. "What?"

"She was here wasn't she? I understand a jolly girls' night in over plenty of wine was the order of the day?"

"We shared a bottle of wine, yes, but I'm getting a bit fed up with all this hinting that poor Nicole was drunk. She'd had about three glasses of wine, technically too much to drive and she decided to sleep on the sofa – not that it's really any business of yours."

John nodded and traced his finger around a knot in the wood of the table top, raised, yet smooth, after years of Edith's diligent scrubbing. "But you see it is my business, Victoria, it's family business." His eyes flashed at her below his dark brows. "And we really don't like other people getting involved."

Victoria swallowed and, fearing her voice would come out as a squeak, decided to keep silent, merely returning his stare defiantly.

"I wondered if she'd dropped her phone here, if it had slipped down the sofa or something, as it wasn't found on her body."

"That would concern you, wouldn't it?" Victoria said quietly. "Because you'd been harassing her with nasty texts, and I expect you wouldn't want the police to see those, would you?" She felt quite calm and was pleased to see a spasm of fear cross his face. You're a coward, she thought, and in the next heartbeat wondered if she had just made a major error in telling him that she knew. What if he were the murderer? She concentrated on keeping her breathing steady, and watched as he sat back and folded his long legs in an attempt at a nonchalant pose.

"I see. Is that what she told you? Such a drama queen! I merely suggested she ought to think carefully about her actions."

"Well, it's too late now, isn't it? Someone decided she was

too much of a threat and the poor woman is dead," Victoria said sharply.

"Yes and my brother is under arrest thanks to you!" John said suddenly losing his cool and jumping to his feet. "Why ever did you come around our business, our family, poking your nose in? You're not some investigative reporter with any clout or class, you're just some useless bloody freelance looking for a story for a few quid! My brother is sitting in a police cell and it's all down to you!" He towered above Victoria, jabbing his finger close to her face.

"I simply told the police how Nicole looked when she arrived here. It's hardly my fault he didn't have an alibi for the time she died, is it?" Victoria tried to stop her voice quavering.

With a snarl, he turned toward the door and then spun round to face her again. "If my stupid mother hadn't been so desperate for attention in the media, to be seen as the queen bee in the company, so bloody important... If I'd had my way, I'd have told you to get lost at the outset. Turning up with that farming idiot, poking around the factory, who do you think you are for Christ's sake?"

"That farming idiot has heard far too much damned noise and bluster from you, you spoiled brat!" boomed Albert as he filled the doorway. Some of the impact of his entrance was lost as he was clutching a large blue floral duvet. As if sensing this, he flung it to one side and advanced towards John. Victoria gave a squeak of alarm – surely they weren't going to have a punch-up in her kitchen?

She jumped up, suddenly feeling very small between these two tall men. "It's OK Albert – just get out John, now!" she shouted, far more bravely than she felt. Albert was looking thunderous (and, she thought, rather dashing). John took a wide berth around the heavier man and slunk out of the kitchen door like a dog with its tail between its legs.

There was a silence and then Albert snorted, hands on hips. "Farming idiot indeed? Bloody little squirt! I was all prepared to smack him in the chops then if you hadn't piped up!"

She couldn't resist a smile; just the expression 'smacking someone in the chops' was so very Albert. She gave him a big hug. "Thank you! You were marvellous!"

"Steady on!" said Albert, patting her back distractedly. "I only raised my voice!"

Chapter 13

Albert looked at Victoria and then at the remaining chunk of the bread he'd brought round as part of the 'essential supplies'. Moving in to protect her overnight was one thing; going without decent toast at breakfast was quite another, it seemed. Victoria smiled. It was so kind of him to be protective. She could see why Aunt Edith had been so fond of him; it must have been like having a son to look after her.

"I'm still feeling rather shaken after John's visit last night," said Victoria.

"Well it's understandable – he's a pretty aggressive fellow. Never did take to him when I met him years ago, nasty little boy I reckon he was. Just the type to pull the wings off flies or trap insects in a pot of jammy water and laugh as they drown."

"I'm not sure that's proof he might grow into a murderer, though?" Victoria looked over at him and smiled as she spotted some jam on his chin, then lowered her gaze and said nothing.

"Now what's got you smirking?" he asked.

"Nothing – well, almost nothing – you've got some jam on your chin, just didn't like to say."

Albert roughly wiped at his chin with some kitchen paper that was handy and then scowled at her. "It'd take a lot more than damn jam to embarrass me, so remember that." His reaction proved that her first thought had been right and she probably shouldn't have mentioned it. Best to move on swiftly. "So who do you think might be responsible then?"

"Responsible for what?" said Albert as he looked hungrily at the end of the loaf.

"Oh Albert, do keep up – for the murders, I mean."

Albert paused, bit his lip and thought for a while. "You know I'm not sure. I feel pretty darned sure they were both murders – not just accidents as the police keep harping on about – but who?"

Victoria nodded. "William does seem an obvious possibility. I was so shocked by how Nicole described his behaviour, and he seems to fit the bill somehow."

"Mmm I'm not so sure," said Albert, "seems too easy a solution. I'm still worrying about John, nasty business that last night. He was a desperate man, I'd say. Makes me wonder if it's him." They both fell silent and Albert took the opportunity to finish off the loaf, covering the last piece with loads of butter and home-made marmalade.

Victoria mused, "I still think Mandy had a lot to gain from both deaths. She didn't want them to sell out to Berry Brothers so Henry's death was good news for her – and then she must have been mad at Nicole for sticking a spanner in the works, so to speak, financially."

"True, true… and she's no stranger to getting her own way and I doubt she would like being crossed." Albert brushed the crumbs off his chest onto the floor then looked guiltily at Victoria.

"Oh for heaven's sake don't worry; Jean will help me give the kitchen a good clean when she comes." Victoria got up and took some plates over to the sink. Turning to face Albert, she said, "You know, one thing that's worrying me in all this is how safe Grace might be. I feel sort of responsible for her in a funny kind of way. She was good friends with Aunt Edith and it seems just awful that first she loses her husband and now one of her sons may be a murderer."

Albert snorted. "She's no weakling – only a female with a lot of fight in her could have built the business and done the amount of work she did. I think she'll cope. I've always felt there's a core of steel in that woman."

"But, don't you think I ought to go over and just check she's OK? I can't go bearing gifts, as you've eaten everything!" She smiled at Albert to show she was only teasing. "But I could go and be neighbourly and see if she needs anything or just wants to talk over a coffee, or something?"

Albert looked unsure and frowned. "Well, I don't know. Grace doesn't need any help from the likes of us. What she really needs to do is to get her family round the table and sort things out, and that's not something we can help with, is it?"

"I know, but she was very kind to me that first day I moved in and all this has left me feeling rather sorry for her."

"Yes, I can see that, but you're getting very involved in all this, and I worry for your safety too. John was very unpleasant last night, and if William gets to you... Come to that, I'm not sure Mandy would be the best person to spend time with either just at the moment." He rubbed his chin. "Why not just stay home and we can do some checking on the internet? I wanted to find out more about that bee-sting allergy thing, not something I've ever taken an interest in before, not being allergic and that. I'd like to know a bit more about the facts."

"Perhaps you're right," replied Victoria. She went over to the file they were gradually building up and looked again at the printed photos of the factory and Henry that Albert had printed out for her. "But do you at least think I should show her the photo of Henry with the epipen in his pocket? Maybe she would have better luck with the police than if you or I went?"

"There you have me," said Albert. "They obviously weren't much interested in either death being a murder, guess it generates too much paperwork. Suits them nicely if they were both accidents – they can close the case and go home and put their feet up."

Victoria smiled. "If you don't mind, I think I will pop over there. My conscience will only bug me if I don't."

Albert sighed. "Well if you're going then I guess I'd better come with you, better safe than sorry." "Please don't Albert," she said, shaking her head, "I really will be alright. I think it'll be easier if there's just the two of us, a sort of 'woman to woman' chat. She might feel awkward in front of a man."

Albert screwed up his face. "Well I'm not happy, not happy at all – but if you've made your mind up, I don't reckon I can change it. Alright then, you leave me to the computer bits and just make sure you have your phone with you in case there's a problem with the car or something."

Victoria smiled. "Of course I will. Leave the dishes – I'll do those when I get back. It shouldn't take too long."

She paused before she opened the car door, and then laughed out loud. She really was so melodramatic at times. Thoroughly indoctrinated by too many crime programmes on the TV, she had actually hesitated in case the car was booby-trapped. She looked towards the farmyard and shook her head. What was she thinking? Things like that just didn't happen in pretty country areas like this – scary gangland Los Angeles this was not!

She got into the car and started the engine. Albert had assured her that it really wasn't necessary to lock it as the local crime rate was close to zero but, being a Londoner, leaving it unlocked still left her feeling unsettled. She reversed the car out of the shadow of the barn into the sunlight and, looking across, spotted something white on the passenger seat.

Her heart thumped a little faster as she slowed and reached across for the envelope, steering with one hand. The flap was only tucked in, not stuck down which seemed strange. She flipped it open and eased out the single sheet of paper.

Keep your nose out of other people's business. None of this concerns you, and you are putting yourself and others in danger she read.

Victoria felt her heartbeat increase even more. She stopped the car and read the note through again, then tucked it back in the envelope and drove on. It suddenly made it all seem real, whereas before it seemed almost as if she and Albert had been playing with a puzzle, solving a mystery game like Cluedo. She wondered whether to go straight back and show him, but it made her even more determined to go and see if Grace needed help. She also wondered about going via the police station to give them the note, but then remembered how dismissive they had been.

She decided to compromise and picked up her phone to dial Albert. She was still on the drive, so didn't feel guilty about using her phone while driving – well, not much anyway. "Albert? It's me. I know I've only just left but, I wondered, did you see anyone hanging about the farm yesterday, in the evening? After John had gone I mean?"

She swerved as she nearly went into the bank. "Whoops! No, it's OK, I'm nearly at the end of the drive now. So you didn't see anyone? Oh, it's nothing, I just, ow!" She braked hard as a fox shot out of the hedge right in front of the car. "Right, that's it – I'm hanging up! Just narrowly missed a fox! I'll catch up later after I've seen Grace." She dropped the phone onto the seat and then tossed it into her bag, tutting at herself for trying to do two things at once.

Victoria turned into the road at a leisurely pace, preoccupied with her own feelings and what she knew about all the possible suspects. Every time she came back to William. But then the memory of John's face, and his anger, crept in... Of course John could have dropped the note off when he came round last night – he certainly knew where she lived.

She would stop at the village shop and buy some chocolate. She wasn't really hungry but fear was nagging away at her stomach and hopefully a few squares would help her calm down and cope better.

She slowed the car and stopped just before the shop, smiling to herself at the splendid array of Lavender's specials outside today. There was a pretty pink wellington boot sitting in state among some bunches of ivy that must have been gathered from the garden behind the shop. A battered suitcase lay on the ground, propped open to display a collection of old magazines (well, not so much old as ex-doctor's waiting room, she guessed). And guarding the suitcase was a large but well-loved teddy bear that sported one eye and a bowtie.

Lavender's eccentricity had a wonderfully calming effect on her and she wondered if she needed the chocolate anymore. Then she remembered one of her friend's sayings: "A girl can never carry too much chocolate in her bag..." She rather doubted the truth of this statement, but it seemed apt.

Tucking the bars of chocolate into her bag as she left, she reflected on her move and how life was so vastly changed, and for the better. Dahlia, Iris and Lavender were all a bit odd but loveably so, and their huge enthusiasm for gossip and trivia made every shopping trip more fascinating than any you might have in an urban supermarket where a mere nod from a cashier was usually par for the course.

It seemed that everyone in the village had their own opinion on Nicole's accident and were convinced that she, Victoria, must have inside information as she had been the last to see Nicole alive. At least she had been spared Trudy Mudge or Jean on this visit and so didn't have to – once again – deny knowing anything that might add to their ever-growing cloud of conjecture. She hoped the police had the sense to listen to the village gossip as surely they might learn something.

She headed towards Grace's house and ate a couple of squares of chocolate on the way. They (whoever 'they' are, she thought) were quite right: there really is nothing quite like chocolate! She hoped her intention to reach out and help Grace would be taken in the spirit it was intended. She didn't pity her, but felt sorry for her and hoped she could be a bit of an Aunt Edith substitute. Victoria was quite sure her aunt would have been over with some edible offering and given Grace some comfort. So, as with many other roles in village life, she felt she had to step into Edith's shoes.

She bumped over the cattle grid that marked the entrance to Primrose Cottage and the Simmons' large family home. Poor Grace probably rattled around in it now she was on her own, and again she felt sympathy for the older woman. At one time she would have been a busy working mother, with a husband and two young boys to care for as well as a full-time job at the factory. She must have darted between the house and the office building after school to make sure the boys had some tea waiting. Now she must feel very alone and so upset by everything that had happened – and most of all, of course, by Henry's death.

Victoria parked and got out of the car. Standing in front of the house, she found she was quite apprehensive. Seeing a movement at the window, she realised she had been spotted; too late now to change her mind and drive away. She clutched the envelope containing the photos, straightened her shoulders and walked up to the front door.

The door opened before she'd even had time to knock. "Victoria – what a surprise!" Grace stood on the threshold, a fixed smile on her face. "I certainly didn't expect to see you." She sounded slightly shrill and Victoria wondered if her presence was unwelcome. Perhaps Grace had been at the sherry or something?

Her carefully prepared words deserted her and she said, "Is it OK? I mean I can go away again if you like, but I thought you might be feeling terribly down and want some company. I mean, you know, first Henry then Nicole." She knew she was gabbling like an idiot, but she was there now so had to see it through, even though Grace was not looking particularly distraught or in need of a shoulder to cry on. "And I have something to show you that I thought might be really important – to do with Henry's death," she petered out lamely.

Grace looked at her closely. "Of course dear, do come in."

Victoria followed her inside, turning left this time and into the large, farmhouse-style kitchen. Victoria thought of her own slightly ramshackle one at April Cottage and was surprised that she preferred its lived-in look. If you'd asked her a few weeks ago to choose her perfect kitchen, she'd have suggested something like Grace's, but not any more. This was so perfect it was sterile.

"Well," Grace began, "what is all this about? Have a seat while I make some tea."

Victoria found she was addressing Grace's back as the latter busied herself with kettle and cups. "I, I don't really know where to start Grace, you see, it's about Henry's death, and then Nicole's and, well, I don't think they were accidents."

Grace became instantly still. "What did you say?" She still had her back to Victoria, which made it even harder for the younger woman to go on.

"Grace, could we both sit down and talk about this? There's

something I need to show you too." She waited while Grace turned towards her, her face like a mask. Victoria felt dreadful; the poor woman was in shock. She bit her lip, feeling a fool. "Sit down – are you alright? I'm sorry, that was a bit abrupt."

Grace sat and passed her hand over her immaculate bob. "Yes, yes, I'm fine. But what… what on earth do you mean?"

Victoria swallowed and wished she'd kept her mouth shut until she'd had a cup of tea in front of her. Her mouth was dry, but the time for a cosy chat over tea and biscuits had obviously passed. "Grace, I don't really know how to say this, but I, we… I mean Albert…"

"Who?" Grace looked confused.

"Albert Moreton, Edith's neighbour, my neighbour, he and I have been, well, mulling over the evidence."

"Evidence? What are you talking about?" Grace sat forward in her chair.

Oh God, Victoria thought, I am going to make such a fool of myself, why did I start this? But she said, "Grace I'm sorry, but we think neither Henry or Nicole's deaths was an accident. We think they may have been murdered."

The silence filled the room. Grace sat completely still, unblinking and, it seemed to Victoria, not even breathing. Eventually, she blinked as if clearing her mind. "Wh-wh-what? I don't, how can you, but the police don't…" Grace gestured helplessly. "I'm sorry, this is a bit of a shock. I don't understand at all."

With a shaking hand, Victoria slid the photographs out of the envelope. She took a deep breath. "When I came to the factory the first time, I managed to see Henry just before he drove off to go to the meeting, do you remember?" Grace nodded slowly. "He said a few words to me and seemed very buoyed up and he happily posed for some photos." Grace nodded again. "Well, when I looked at the photos, and zoomed in a bit, you can see… well, look for yourself."

She pushed the photos across the table towards Grace and watched as the colour drained from the other woman's face. "You see, we think that is his epipen, there in his pocket."

Grace touched the epipen in the photo, as if it were really there in front of her.

"Is it?" asked Victoria. Grace nodded slowly again.

"So you see, we couldn't understand why, when he was stung, he wasn't able to inject himself." She waited, but Grace didn't speak; she seemed mesmerised by the photos.

Victoria ploughed on. "And when I was at the garage, Tufty said it was odd that there were no epipens in the Jaguar, as usually there were several and again you see, we thought that was odd and that someone had removed them." She shuffled in her seat uncomfortably. "Then, with Nicole, the police tried to make out that she was drunk and she fell off the steps, but she wasn't. We had a bottle of wine between us, that's all. She'd had too much to drive, but she was nowhere near falling-over drunk, it's just nonsense!"

Grace was still looking at the photo, touching Henry's face, now the epipen. Victoria bit her lip. The poor woman. She went on. "And then well, I knew that Nicole had received a text."

Grace's head shot up. "She told you that?"

"No, not exactly, she left me a note. When I got up at about seven o'clock, she'd already gone and she left a note saying she'd received a text about an hour before and had left. I, I don't know any more than that but, the thing is Grace, William had knocked her about the night before. She was bruised and had a cut. It seemed they'd had a big row and he'd pushed her. I don't think he meant to, he didn't hit her as such, but…" she stopped.

Grace was looking strained. Her eyes were darting about the room, as if she was looking for something.

"What with William not wanting the business deal to go through and Henry never getting to the meeting, well, I think Albert and I have put two and two together and…" she shrugged, "we may have made five, but I just felt you ought to know. To be honest, I even wondered if you might be in danger yourself."

Grace was staring at her hands now, spread out in front of her on the table, the fingers splayed. "Grace, are you alright?" Victoria asked, gently.

"I don't really know dear, to be honest. It's all rather a shock."

"Look, shall I make us that tea?"

"No!" Grace said quickly. "No, actually, I think I need something a little stronger." She got up and leant on the table for a moment. "Oh Victoria, you do remind me of your dear aunt," she said quietly, "such a shame." Victoria wondered why she was thinking about Aunt Edith at this moment; but then the poor woman must be distraught.

"Right, let's have some wine and think this through." Grace walked towards a door which, when opened, revealed an old-fashioned larder with shelves filled with row upon row of bottles and jars, all labelled and lined up like a shop display. The store was large and Grace disappeared from view.

From the depths of the larder, she called to Victoria. "I've just made some parsnip wine. It's usually very good, but somehow, this batch seems a bit odd. Let's have a glass and you can tell me what you think of it."

"I don't think I should Grace, I have to drive," Victoria called towards the open door. "Nonsense! It's only my home-made plonk, it's not strong at all!"

Glass clinked, a cork popped and eventually Grace emerged with a bottle in her hands. Lord, how Victoria hated homemade wine! She didn't care for parsnips much either, but this was no time to be pernickety; she'd just have to grin and bear it.

Grace fetched two glasses. Her hand shook slightly as she poured the wine, and Victoria's heart went out to her. "God, I need this!" she said raising her glass to Victoria. 'Straight down the hatch!" Victoria closed her eyes and took two huge gulps. Grace began coughing and put down her glass without drinking. She covered her mouth and coughed again. "I'm so sorry, a tickle!"

Victoria's eyes were watering. "Goodness, I'm surprised it's not very alcoholic, it tastes strong," she said, wishing she could have a glass of water to wash away the rather strange bittersweet taste. Grace was patting her chest and clearing her throat. "Oh dear me! Well, what did you think of it?"

"It's um, interesting."

"You don't like it?" She looked concerned.

"No, no, I wouldn't say that, but it's an unusual taste."

"Have another swig and I'll top you up." Victoria did as she was bidden, and emptied the glass.

"There, how was that?" Grace sat forward, looking at her keenly. Victoria swallowed and found that she felt rather strange. "Um, fine, I think."

"Well there we are then." Grace gave an exaggerated sigh. "This is all a bit of a muddle isn't it? There we are, trying to live our lives as well as we can, doing our bit, doing our best, and what's it all for? I mean, in the end, where does it get us?" She put her elbows on the table and rested her chin on her hands and looked at Victoria. "What does it all mean, Victoria? Do you often sit and think that?"

Victoria shrugged, but somehow the simple action seemed difficult. "I don't know. I mean yes, sometimes..."

"I find, since Henry died that I am doing it more and more. Thinking, going over things that I've done again and again. Was I right? Where did I go wrong? Lord, I don't know." She looked at her watch. "Well, I don't suppose it will be long now," she said, almost to herself.

Victoria found her mind wandering and managed to drag it back to the present. "What won't be long?" she asked.

"Oh, nothing you need to worry about dear. Well that's not strictly true, but it's too late to worry about it now anyway."

"Are you sure this isn't strong Grace? I feel a bit woozy."

"Do you dear? Have some more."

"No, really," Victoria put her hand over her glass. It seemed a huge effort just to move her arm. "Nonsense!" said Grace sharply. She released the glass from Victoria's hand and refilled it. "I insist."

Victoria felt trapped by the other woman's gaze. Lifting the glass to her mouth seemed incredibly difficult. She took a mouthful and this time, somehow, the wine didn't seem so unpleasant.

"Are you alright Victoria?" Grace asked quietly.

"I don't know," she said slowly. "I think probably not."

Grace sighed. "Oh my dear girl, you are so like your aunt," she shook her head, sadly. "Same inquisitive nature. Never a good thing. I told Edith: being a good listener is one thing, but knowing when to hold your tongue and keep your views to yourself is quite another. She never quite grasped that."

Victoria stared at her, and felt incapable of response.

"You've gone a funny colour Victoria. I hope you aren't going to throw up all over my kitchen floor, I've only just cleaned it." Grace got up, took down a fresh wineglass and poured herself a glass of white wine from the fridge. She sat back in her chair and crossed her legs. "I won't be drinking that muck, thank you."

She pushed the original glass away and made a face. "Don't worry, you shouldn't stop breathing – well I don't think I put too much in the wine – but you won't be able to move either." She took a big gulp of her own, unadulterated wine. "Well, you are a clever clogs, aren't you? I didn't think anyone was going to find out about the murders, I rather thought it was all sorted." She sighed. "Oh Victoria, why couldn't you mind your own business? I bet you thought you were being really helpful, a super sleuth!"

She laughed and then sprang forward in her chair, spitting out the words. "Of course it's not William, you little fool! How could that lazy, spineless, boring man ever defend anything? Other than his damned fish, what does he care about? How did I produce such a dullard?" She snorted and took another swig. "And as for John! All mouth and trousers that one! Would happily dump me and take up with that trollop Parkin."

She twisted the wineglass stem between her fingers. "He really thought I'd just lie down and let them take it all away, sink slowly into retirement tending my roses." She smashed her fist onto the table. "I should bloody cocoa!"

Inside herself, Victoria jumped violently at the noise, but externally she didn't flinch. She was screaming, shouting, desperately trying to move, but she was incapable. Was this what it was like when you had a stroke? She was terrified, but could do absolutely nothing.

"Why couldn't you plump for that Parkin woman? She could have done it! She had plenty of motives and she's so utterly, utterly common! Poor William," she laughed and shook her head, "how could you possibly think it was him? As for Nicole – please! What a waste of space that woman was. Vacuous, totally vacuous. Only interested in her looks and in money. MY money!" She banged the table again.

How can you say that about Nicole? Victoria wanted to yell at Grace – you are so wrong! She was talented and funny and still had so much to give, but she had you as a mother-in-law, and that cost her her life.

"Obviously, I had to kill her," said Grace, with a shrug. "I sent her a text and she came to the factory, meek as you like, like a lamb to the slaughter. Of course I lured her with the promise of a deal," she laughed again, throaty and unpleasant. "You see, couldn't resist the lure of money. Bloody served her right. Silly little thing, tottering along in those ridiculous heels. One firm shove and she was gone, crashed through the handrail! I almost laughed when she ended up in the vat."

She paused. "Made an awful sound though, a sort of cracking crunch. Ugh." She shuddered, and Victoria wanted to hit her. "I found her phone in her handbag, which was lucky as I didn't fancy rooting about in her pockets inside the vat, very unpleasant. And well, her phone and mine, gone for good! The local police are so lazy they won't even have bothered to check the phone records; they just want it all swept under the carpet and signed off as an accidental death."

She leaned forward and looked into Victoria's eyes. "Which it still will be once I've managed to get you safely out of the way. How are you feeling? You look awfully peaky." Pointing at Victoria's glass, she continued, "Rohypnol dear, I have it to help me sleep. Terribly effective, but a bit nasty when mixed with alcohol in large amounts. Any traces will disappear from your bloodstream in twenty-four hours, so I'll just have to think of a way of disposing of you."

Grace sat back and drank some more wine. Victoria was having trouble keeping her eyes open and her breathing regular. She was terrified that, if she fell asleep, that would be it. She'd never wake up again. Concentrate, concentrate, she told herself.

"Now as for Henry – I bet you haven't worked that one out!" cried Grace suddenly. "If I say so myself, it was a stroke of genius," she laughed again, hugging herself. "So clever! And so very satisfying!"

Victoria looked at her through drooping eyelids. I have to hear this, I have to know… she used all her willpower to concentrate on what Grace was saying.

"Bee venom dear. Do you know about that? No, probably not! My wonderful youthful looks aren't all down to my natural beauty – I have regular botox injections. A very good place in Westerley, I must give you their card." She faltered, "Oh, but then again, you won't be needing it. Well, that's something Victoria, you'll never grow old and wrinkled, that's something to be pleased about, isn't it?" She sat up and clapped her hands like an excited child.

You are completely mad, thought Victoria, as she struggled to breathe. You are as mad as a hatter, and I didn't spot it. Victoria, you are a fool.

"Anyway, where was I? Oh yes, botox. Well, you can buy bee venom on the internet. Amazing, isn't it, you can buy anything these days! Bee venom, jolly good at 'plumping' up skin, makes it look youthful, works well alongside botox you know. Anyway, I regularly buy the stuff on line. I simply helped myself to a few very fine-needled syringes from the beauty clinic and then called Henry and told him to meet me on the way to his appointment as I wanted a final chat with him. I told him maybe we could come to an agreement that would leave him free to go where he pleased with plenty of money. Silly old fool!"

She clapped her hands again in that horribly childish manner. "He believed me! I got out of the car and went across to his window and said 'Look dear, can we talk about this?' Before he could say anything I said 'Look out! There's a bee!' Of course he went mad and said 'Where, where?' Absolute panic!" She laughed and shook her head. "Stupid man! Anyway, I said 'There!' and pointed to the passenger seat – and in one rather flowing movement whipped the epipen out of his pocket and stuck the needle of my syringe into him!"

She stopped, and looked blank. "The trouble was, he turned back towards me just in the instant I stuck the needle in, which meant it went in his face, his poor face!" She suddenly put her head in her hands. "I didn't mean to, I meant to get his neck. I didn't like that, it was awful, he looked at me and he was so shocked! I keep seeing the look in his eyes. He knew what I'd done, he knew, you see." She gave a little sob. "But I don't regret it, really I don't, but I just wish he hadn't looked at me." She brushed away a tear and took a deep breath.

Victoria watched her, fascinated and terrified at the same time.

"Actually, in the long run, it was a good thing." Grace nodded, reassuring herself. "A bee sting near the mouth is much worse as it swells up so quickly. Henry would have been in such a panic, his heart would have been racing, so I told myself it only took a moment. He probably only had a few seconds to register it all. And there we were. Gone."

She took a deep breath. "And so," she looked at Victoria almost fondly, "now there's you."

Victoria felt her insides shrivel and, at the same time, an incredible lightness in her head. She sensed darkness at the edges of her field of vision and she realised she was about to pass out. Surprisingly she felt rather sanguine about the whole thing. Well, there we are then, she thought, I'm simply being put to sleep, I won't know anything about it really. She felt herself toppling forwards and, as she did so, she saw Grace leap towards her, arms outstretched, laughing.

The last thing she heard was a loud bang...

Chapter 14

Who on earth was hammering at this time in the morning?

Victoria moved her head a little and the pain flashed behind her eyes. She almost cried aloud as the thumping ache in her head hurt her eyes, her ears… all of her. Was this a migraine? She'd never had one before, but this was worse than any headache or hangover she'd ever known.

Slowly she opened one eye and quickly shut it again; the white light stung, almost as if saltwater was being poured into her eye. Slowly she opened both eyes and moaned gently with the pain. There were paving slabs above her. No, no, they were ceiling tiles. She tried to focus on the grid-like pattern but couldn't get her eyes to work properly.

"Victoria, you awake?" Turning her head very carefully she just about made out Albert, sitting in a chair not far from the bed. Her brain struggled to work out which room they were in and whose chair that was.

"Albert?"

"Don't try and talk, it must hurt."

"Where are we, what's wrong?"

Albert scooted the chair nearer the bed and the sound of the legs scraping across the flooring made her cry out loud. He sat close and took her hand. "We're in the hospital, Westerley General, you've been here all night. You had me right worried, you really

247

did. They said you'd come round, but I couldn't be sure."

"Come round, why what's happened? I can remember drinking that parsnip wine with Grace, but I didn't drink that much I'm sure."

"It's no hangover, you were drugged – and, given a bit more time, no doubt poisoned and would be laying there dead by now."

Tears slid out of Victoria's eyes and she tried hard to piece together the fragments of memory of last night's events. She could remember going to Grace's and then it got hazy… and some things she thought she remembered simply couldn't be true. She opened both eyes and looked up at Albert. "Tell me, what happened?"

"I blame myself, I really do," he said. "I was worried about you going and I should have insisted on coming with you."

"Is Grace OK? I can just remember her getting angry and shouting but I can't put all the pieces together." Victoria winced again as she tried to sit up.

"No you stay where you are," Albert leant over and plumped up the pillow a bit. "Just take it steady, you had a rough time."

"Albert you have to tell me, this is really frustrating. What happened last night?"

"Well, don't suppose you remember the fox that trotted across the drive in front of the car? You were on the phone to me at the time – yes?" Victoria nodded, and then wished she hadn't as pain shot across her forehead.

"Well when you swerved to miss the fox, you must've been in a flap because you didn't switch your phone off, must've pressed the wrong button. So you left the line open." Albert stroked her hand and then smiled. "By the way, did you know you talk to yourself in the car?"

Victoria closed her eyes and just hoped she hadn't been talking about Albert, as yes, she did have long discussions out loud and she had been pondering the whole murder thing while she was driving.

"Anyway, I was laughing at you and listening to your journey while I was searching the net for more details on the bee-sting reactions and things. Then I found a website that really had me worried."

Victoria mumbled "Uh-huh" to show she was listening, but kept her eyes closed.

"It was selling bee venom off the internet for one thing, and then I read, having injections of bee venom is meant to plump up your skin and make you look younger, bit like that bleddy botox stuff? I put two and two together and remembered that Grace had what we thought was botox and I realised we may have been following the wrong line of reasoning altogether."

Victoria's eyes popped open and she looked at Albert. "That's it, it was her all along and I walked straight in there." Albert looked a little miffed that his story was being interrupted and he let go of her hand. "If you just listen, I'll explain it all to you." Victoria smiled to herself.

"Anyway just as I was worrying that the killer might just have been Grace, I began to hear people talking on your phone, you'd obviously arrived at Grace's house. I know it's rude but no one can resist listening to other people's conversations can they, so I picked up the phone and listened. It was a bit muffled, stuck in your handbag I suppose, but I could hear right enough and within a minute or two I realised you were in danger so I grabbed the car keys and ran."

"My knight in shining armour!" said Victoria, groggily.

"Oh it gets better than that," he said with a self-satisfied smile. "I drove faster than I have ever gone before round those twists and turns, Monte Carlo rally had nothing on me!" Albert was obviously very proud of his exploits. "All the way I was listening to the conversation, switched it to speaker phone and was getting more and more worried whether I was going to get there soon enough. I heard every word Grace said, all about Henry and then Nicole and I was pretty sure you were going to be victim number three!"

"I remember trying to listen," said Victoria trying not to wince as she shifted her position.

"Well I drove down that driveway of theirs with those speed bumps like the very devil was after me, even banged me head on the roof at one point!" he laughed. "So I shoved open the back door when I got there and you were slumped forward with your head on the table and Grace was standing over you holding a cushion. I thought she'd killed you, I really did!"

He stopped and took a breath. "Then I realised she hadn't got to you yet and you must have passed out. I grabbed the cushion from her and well, I may have been a bit rough." Albert looked momentarily shamefaced. "But I had to get it away from her and her away from you! I pushed her back hard and she tripped on that fancy rug thing and stumbled into the wall, went down like a good 'un!"

Victoria couldn't help but twitch her mouth into a small smile. Albert seemed like a little boy, proud to show off about his brave adventure.

"With two comatose ladies in front of me I reckoned I better call 999 and get an ambulance and the police and what have you. The ambulance was going to be close on twenty minutes so I decided to bring you here myself and just carried you into the car and away. I guess it was a bit of a risk that Grace would come round before the police got there, but she didn't, so all's well that ends well, eh?" With the most dramatic part of the story retold Albert sat back in his chair. She thought he looked tired, poor man; it had obviously been an ordeal for him too.

"Thank you, Albert," Victoria looked seriously at him, "you

saved my life, thank you."

"Oh it was nothing," said Albert, looking bashful, "all in a day's work. I feel a bit bad about knocking out poor old Grace. Well, not knocking her out but shoving her into the wall." He tailed off and Victoria pushed herself up on one elbow. "Albert! Oh I didn't ask, is she OK, I mean did she, err is she…?"

Albert looked puzzled and then smiled. "Oh Lord yes, did you worry for a bit that your rescuer could be a murderer too?" He laughed as though the thought of him being a killer tickled him. "No, she has a nasty case of concussion and a couple of stitches in the back of her head, but nothing that won't mend in a few days. There's a police guard on her hospital room and they're waiting till she is fitter to question and formally arrest her."

"Oh goodness," said Victoria, "it all sounds so real when you say that."

"'fraid it is real, very real. Grace is a sick woman I reckon. She'd been determined enough at the beginning with how she and Henry built that business, but I think that developed into a bit of an obsession and she just couldn't control things anymore."

"But why would Grace murder Henry, the man she really loved, her one true love and all that?"

"Well," said Albert, his face turning distinctly smug again, "while you've been kipping in this cosy bed…" Victoria narrowed her eyes and glared at him.

"Well, OK, while you've been out for the count, I've been chatting to the police and Jean's friend whatshername too. Seems there are records of Grace coming into Accident and Emergency rather a lot over the years. Looks like Henry might well have been beating her and once she even had a broken arm and two ribs. So I reckon maybe her true love was even more of a bastard than we thought."

"Oh that's awful!" said Victoria

"So it seems she just stayed for the boys and the business – that was her world. Then as the boys grew up and got even more gormless than she reckoned they would, the business became the centre of her world. Bit of a tigress, protecting her family; and Grace was also always a right snob, liked to see herself as the lady of the manor and all that. So when old Henry wanted to sell up and, for all we know, nip off with a younger model and a few quid in his pocket, she wasn't having it." He paused. "Nicole, poor young maid, was just too much for her to bear. Not only would she take a large chunk of the family's money, she would damage her darling William and the business in one fell swoop."

"Poor Grace," said Victoria, quietly.

"Poor Grace? I'm not sure I'd be saying that about a lunatic who decided to drug me and was then going to smother the life out of me!"

"I still feel sorry for her though. She'll go to prison and never get to see her grandchildren grow up, or run the business, nothing that she holds dear will be hers again."

Albert looked at her. "You must be a very gentle soul to feel pity for your would-be murderer. I can't agree with you on that."

"I know, I'm being soft, but it's all been such a shock."

Albert pursed his lips. "Poor Nicole, who hadn't done anything wrong other than be pretty and marry a daft bloke for the wrong reasons, no grandchildren or life at all for her. I think that's where our sympathy should lie."

Victoria looked at her hands. "Yes, you're right."

"But I doubt they'll put Grace in prison. My guess is that she'll plead guilty and they'll say she wasn't of sound mind or some such. She'll go to some hospital or other, and have a rather pampered time of it."

Victoria nodded and then, lost for words, took Albert's hand again. He looked across at her. "I still feel bad though. I let you go alone and I shouldn't have done. I should have seen the clues earlier and just sorted it myself."

Victoria furrowed her brow and said, "Oh, that's so you Albert! The big strong hero should have solved the mystery and not bothered me, so that I could get on with growing flowers and pottering in the kitchen, eh?"

Albert looked uncomfortable. "Well, I know what I mean."

Before Victoria could placate him, a nurse came bustling in and told Albert he had to leave as the doctor was coming round and needed to check Victoria. They both tried to disagree, but the nurse expertly quashed their protests and deftly helped Albert out of the door, pointing out the waiting room.

"Now dear, you must let me give you a hand with a wash perhaps. How are you feeling? That eye will be a bit of a shiner for a while I guess." The nurse started to run water into a bowl and picked up some soap and a towel."

"Eye?" said Victoria, "What's wrong with my eye?"

"You'll soon see when you look in the mirror – here, let me help you." The nurse came over and helped Victoria come to a sitting position.

"Wow my head's just spinning, this makes a normal hangover seem child's play!"

"It is in comparison my sweet, now gently, that's it, lean on me."

With the nurse's help, Victoria slowed walked over to the hand basin and looked into the mirror. To her horror, one of her eyes was very black and that side of her face looked horribly swollen, combined with all traces of mascara having migrated from her eyelashes to her eyelids and cheeks. She looked a complete and utter wreck.

"I can't believe Albert saw me looking like this and never said a word," said Victoria.

"Ah that man's too far gone to worry about little things like black eyes and make-up dear," said the nurse nodding wisely.

"Too far gone? He's not that old!"

The nurse laughed. 'No dear, I meant too much in love to worry, not too old!"

Victoria didn't know what to say.

"Come on, let's get you tidied up. Never mind your lover boy, the whole of the Westerley police force is lined up out there to interview you once the doc has given his say so. Not often we have a string of murders here you know. Quite a kerfuffle going on with the big wigs wanting to know why nobody thought either of them was anything but an accident, quite a kerfuffle!"

Victoria allowed the nurse to get the worst off her face with warm water and gentle rubbing with a flannel. But even the slightest rub hurt as her head was so tender. She sank thankfully back into bed once she had been washed and made more presentable and awaited the doctor.

* * * * *

It was late in the afternoon before Victoria was allowed home, and never had 'home' sounded so sweet. Albert collected her in the sensible Volvo and drove all the way at about twenty miles an hour, not wanting to 'shake her up'. The police had done that job very efficiently a few hours earlier. Just how close she had come to death had been made very plain to her.

She sat in the front passenger seat, her head lolling against the headrest and watched as the steep primrose-studded banks rolled past the window. Gateways into green fields, bouncing lambs, a cow rubbing its huge rump against a gatepost in ecstasy, a startled rabbit... and she knew how good it felt to be alive.

Rohypnol had been Grace's drug of choice. She'd been prescribed it years ago to combat severe insomnia. Victoria could only wonder at what Henry had done to bring on such misery; perhaps it was Grace's own conscience that kept her awake at night. Did they even know the half of what she had done to keep her realm intact? Victoria had a vague unease that somewhere along the line her aunt's name had been brought up and that she had felt fear, but for now she couldn't find her way through the remaining fog in her brain to figure it out.

Her eyes closed and she felt Albert's hand on her arm. "Here, no nodding off! Not until we're home, anyway."

She patted his hand with her own and sat up, taking a deep breath. "I'm OK, just a bit, well, you know, foggy still."

They turned into the drive and Victoria felt a huge yearning for April Cottage, her home, complete with its impossible Rayburn, tatty bathroom and unruly garden. None of that mattered, it was home. They pulled up outside the barn and Albert leapt out, helping her from the car as if she was 100.

"I'm alright Albert, really," she smiled at him. "But thank you, it's very nice to be so..." she fought to find the right words, "so cared for."

They made their way through the barn and emerged into sunlight. There were the hens, digging in the dirt and making lovely soft cooing sounds. Victoria walked into the kitchen and was greeted with the smells of beeswax, coffee and fresh baking. She smiled. "Surely three of the most welcoming smells anywhere," she said, almost to herself.

"Oh, there you are!" said Jean emerging from the hallway, duster in hand. She gazed at Victoria closely through her thick lenses.

"Oh no, is it Tuesday? I'm sorry Jean, I forgot."

"No, no dear, don't you fret! 'tisn't my normal day, but I thought you might need a bit of extra doing." She was wringing the duster tightly in her hands. "Your poor face! Oh dear, are you sure she's alright, Albert?"

"Of course she is, she's made of stern stuff, aren't you Victoria?" said Albert with forced jollity. "Now you sit down there while Jean puts the coffee on and we can all have a piece of cake and a rest."

"Oh right ho," said Jean and busied herself with plates and mugs.

Victoria sat in what had become 'her' chair and looked around the kitchen. To her great surprise, she felt her eyes fill with tears. "Here now, none of that!" said Albert looking uncomfortable, but Victoria couldn't stop them from falling. "I'm sorry – I still seem to be a bit wobbly. It's so lovely to be home and for it all to be so, well, perfect. Thank you," she said as Jean passed her a tissue.

"I always knew that Grace was a wrong 'un!" said Jean as she sat at the table and cut the cake (a Victoria sponge, Victoria noted with pleasure). "I confess I had me doubts about that Henry, he was a right sneak and a thief, but that Grace…" She shook her head and pursed her lips. "Her had a core of steel about her."

Albert gave Jean a stern look and turned his attention to Victoria. "So how's the sponge?" She nodded, quite unable to speak, her mouth full of light sponge, raspberry jam and fresh cream. Eventually she managed, "Awful, as always!" and they grinned at each other like idiots.

"Oh my," said Jean and stirred her coffee.

Just as they finished their cake there was the sound of a car pulling up sharply in the yard. "What beggar is that rearranging all my gravel?" growled Albert.

In through the door breezed Mandy. She stopped, removed her huge sunglasses and looked at Victoria. "Christ!" she said. "Grace really did a number on you, didn't she?"

"Actually," said Victoria calmly, "I'm afraid I did it myself when I passed out. I bashed my face on her kitchen table."

"Same bloody thing! Thank God you're alright Victoria," said Mandy. She seemed to suddenly remember she was clutching a bouquet. "Oh yes, these are for you. Sorry, no idea what to get but I thought these might be a bit cheering. Crap at this sort of thing."

Jean gave a sharp intake of breath and Mandy glowered at her. "I never knew you cared, Mandy," said Victoria, but she was smiling. "Thank you, that's very kind."

"Well, you know…"

"Do you want a seat? Piece of cake?" offered Albert half-heartedly. Mandy tossed back her mane of chestnut hair and eyed him. "Thank you Albert, but no. I'll leave you to do all the hand-holding."

Did she see the very slightest hint of a blush, Victoria wondered as she looked at Albert out of the corner of her eye?

"Anyway Victoria, I'm pleased to see you're pretty much in one piece and very glad this awful saga is at an end. Needless to say, there won't be a deal of any kind going through now. I think Janner's Jams will do perfectly well on its own."

"I am sure it will," said Victoria.

"Right, best be on my way, places to go, people to see!" She turned on one very expensive heel and left the kitchen. "Trollop," said Jean under her breath and continued drinking her coffee.

Albert looked at his watch. "Ah, right, back in a tick!" he said, and disappeared in the same direction as Mandy.

"Well my dear, what a drama!" said Jean when he'd left. "Did her really have a knife?"

"No she didn't, just some awful parsnip wine, a drug and a pillow."

"Oh my, now that is odd," said Jean and frowned. "That's not what I'd heard. But that Albert, he burst in and saved the day didn't he? How romantic! Did he really bash her in the chops?" Despite everything, Victoria couldn't help laughing. "No! Wherever did you get all these ideas from, Jean? Yes, I can honestly say Albert saved my life by arriving just at the right moment, but Grace tripped and banged her head."

Jean nodded sagely. "Ah yes, that's what he's telling you dear, but I bet he wrestled with her, got her to drop the knife and then sloshed her one!"

"No, really!"

Just then Victoria's mobile started ringing. "Oh bother, where is it?" She patted her pockets frantically, looked under the table, got up, looked under the seat cushion, felt dizzy, sat down and then Jean handed her the phone from her handbag hanging on the back of the chair. She mouthed "Thank you" as she pressed the button.

"Hello?"

"Victoria, darling! How are you?"

"Oh hello Georgie, I'm fine, thank you, everything's going really well."

Jean raised her eyebrows in surprise and then sighed. She got up, picked up her cloth and went back into the hall to finish dusting the grandfather clock.

"Darling, I'm sorry I haven't called before and now of course it's Sunday, but you know how it is."

Victoria felt her stomach tighten, She was about to get the brush-off after all that work and a near-death experience – all for the sake of a damned article.

"We've had such a lot on but hey, I just wanted to say we love it! Absolutely adore it!"

Victoria couldn't seem to take it in.

"Are you there darling?"

"Yes, of course. You love it?" said Victoria weakly.

"Yes, marvellous, exactly what we wanted. In fact, we'd like a series of articles focussing on rural businesses, the good and the bad, problems with funding, location, transport, and all that lovely local colour you throw in as well, and photos. Does that sound acceptable?"

Victoria couldn't find her voice.

Georgie rushed on to fill the space. "We can negotiate the fee of course, I realise it will be quite a lot to tackle each month, but I hope that sounds OK?"

Victoria was nodding like an idiot, making her head throb again. "Absolutely Georgie, I'm sure we can come to an arrangement."

"That's cool. Oh, and another thing, we'd also like a country blog, just for the website, you know, the sort of thing us townies like!" She gave a peal of laughter. "More light-hearted, more gossipy, you're good at looking at things in a quirky way. Five hundred words every week. How does that sound?" Georgie sounded very enthusiastic.

Victoria couldn't believe her ears, but forced herself to sound casual. "That's OK, I think I can fit it in between cleaning out the hens and making jam. I've got quite a few ideas for the business features, I'll send you a list."

"Sounds great. Frankly Victoria, I have no idea how you aren't dying of boredom, it sounds so sleepy down there in the middle of nowhere. Seems to me all anyone does is make jam and gossip!"

"Well, you know," said Victoria, touching her bruised face and thinking of the turmoil since she'd arrived. "We muddle through."

"That's the ticket!" said Georgie. "Look, got to fly, meeting the picture editor in Boozy's in ten minutes. I bet you miss the old wine bar?"

"Oh yes, very much," Victoria lied, thinking fondly of the Swaddle Arms.

"Must dash! Great work Victoria, speak again soon!" and she was gone.

Victoria stared at her phone. Already her old life seemed completely alien. She couldn't begin to imagine nipping down to Boozy's, or strap-hanging in the tube or sweating away in the gym; that was another life, and it wasn't hers anymore and she was glad. She sat back and closed her eyes. She could hear Jean whistling as she worked somewhere upstairs. The grandfather clock ticked steadily and reliably in the hall and suddenly she heard footsteps approaching. She sat up quickly, surprised at how anxious she felt.

"It's alright maid, no need to look so worried!" said Albert as he sauntered through the door carrying a basket, the contents covered with a blanket.

"Sorry, I didn't realise it was you. I thought… well, never mind. Anyway, I've just had the most wonderful phone call offering me regular work at the magazine!"

His face fell. "Oh, well, that's… great."

"Yes it is, but why the long face?"

"Erm… does that mean you'll be going back to London then?" He looked utterly crestfallen.

She looked at him, this big, handsome capable man, so full of surprises and contradictions, so different from anyone she'd met before. She knew she wanted to get to know him a whole lot better.

"Albert, this is my home now. I'm not going anywhere. It's freelance work that I'll do here and send up to London. In fact, it will be all about this part of the world. I love it here, and I have no intention of leaving!"

He positively beamed and stood up straight. "Well, that's a bleddy relief maid! Otherwise, getting this little beggar will all have been in vain!"

He carefully put the basket on the table in front of her and pulled back the blanket. A small black-and-white face popped up.

"Oh!" cried Victoria "What... who, I mean..."

"This is your new best friend and bodyguard!"

The basket was now rocking madly from side to side as the puppy wagged its tail furiously, at the same time craning forward to lick Victoria's face. "Oh my goodness!" she laughed, and turned so it could lick the unbruised side. "He is gorgeous! Adorable! Come here!" She picked the wriggling scrap out of the basket and cradled him in her arms as he licked and wriggled ecstatically.

"Farmer friend of mine's collie bitch got up to no good with some stray and had a litter of eight, no bleddy use to no one really," he said, ruffling the pup's ears, "never be any good for working. But he managed to get shot of seven to people who just wanted pets and this little beggar was left. And I thought, I know a lady that could do with a faithful friend to see her through thick and thin, her partner in crime, and all that," he said, letting the pup lick his hand.

"He is absolutely adorable, but I rather hoped you were going to be that."

"Be what?"

Victoria smiled at him over the pup's head. "Be my partner in crime?"

Albert pursed his lips and scratched his chin. "Well, I've got a bleddy farm to run but, well, I could muck in every now and again, as needs must."

"Too kind," she said, adjusting her hold on the pup, to cradle it on its back and stroke the fat round pink tummy.

"Does he have a name?"

"Nope, that's down to you."

"You realise I've never owned a dog and have no idea how to train a puppy?"

"Suspected as much," he said and looked resigned.

"So I'll need lots of help and advice."

"On a daily basis I suppose."

"Indeed," said Victoria, and lifted the pup up to face her. "You dear little thing – oh!"

"Yep, and getting him house trained will be the first thing!" said Albert, laughing as Victoria squealed and held the pup at arm's length as it proceeded to pee copiously on to the floor.

"Albert, you swine!" she cried.

If you'd like to find out more about Victoria and Albert
and the residents of Swaddlecombe, go to:
www.swaddlecombe.co.uk
or follow Swaddlecombe on Facebook